MAGNUM

A Dark Knights MC/Dirty Angels MC Crossover

JEANNE ST. JAMES

Acknowledgements:

Cover Artist: Golden Czermak at FuriousFotog

Editor: Proofreading by the Page

Beta readers: Whitley Cox, Andi Babcock, Sharon Abrams & Alexandra Swab

Dark Knights MC Logo: Jennifer Edwards

Author's Note

Dear readers,

You met Magnum, the Dark Knights MC's Sgt at Arms, in my Dirty Angels MC series. And ever since he showed up in book 2 (Jag's book), he interested me (and also you readers) so I knew he needed a book of his own. Well, here it is! As I wrote his book, I fell deeply in love with him and I hope you do, too!

Please note: this book occurs about 7-8 years after the last Dirty Angels MC book (book 10, Crow's book). My timelines aren't exact, please don't hold that against me. :)

Much love, Jeanne

Chapter One

With a twist of his wrist, Magnum downed the rest of his whiskey, slapped the shot glass on the worn, scarred table in front of him, planted his boots onto the floor and sat back in *his* chair, crossing his arms over his chest.

He did this all while staring at the young blonde across his bar. That was right, *his* fucking bar.

He knew she wasn't scouting.

He knew she wasn't gathering intel.

Why she would show up at Dirty Dick's, his club's bar, he had no fucking clue.

Why she would sit down and make herself at home in the Dark Knights MC hangout, he didn't know.

While he needed to find out, he was in no rush to see what her angle was. Fuck no, he'd wait a bit and see how it all played out.

His club brothers were eyeballing her, but none had been stupid enough to approach. So far.

Why? Because they all knew who she was. And like Magnum, had no idea why she was there.

But it spooked the ones who knew who her father was. A member of an ally MC, the Dirty Angels.

1

She was young when Magnum first met her and now, even ten years later, she was still too young.

One good reason to avoid her should be her father being a member of another MC.

Add the fact that she didn't grow up in that MC. Fuck no, she grew up in a rich neighborhood, attending private schools. Attending a good college.

The problem was, she was his type. Long legs, long blonde hair, green eyes and fair skinned. Not to mention—and hard to ignore—curves in all the right places. So, he couldn't help but watch her for the past few years. Once she became legal, of course.

Because he did not fuck, or even eye-fuck, jailbait. Never had, never would.

It wasn't her youth which drew him, anyway. Once she'd matured and filled out, it was those very curves, the confidence she carried and her *capture-your-soul* green eyes she pointed at him.

But even then, he had only watched her. At poker runs, at the DAMC parties, at the Toys for Tots drives, at Ellie Walker's fundraisers for the Walker Foundation, which helped needy amputees.

He'd seen her at them all.

But he'd kept his distance. For the most part.

And for good reason.

But why had he caught her attention?

He had no fucking clue. Because they couldn't be more opposite.

Was she still too young? Fuck yeah.

Did he want her anyway? Fuck yeah.

Was it smart? Fuck no.

But his undeniable interest in Caitlin was a no-fucking-go.

Not unless he wanted to cause a war.

For almost the last decade, shit had settled, and the

Knights had made strong allies. Not only with the Angels, but also with the Blood Fury MC up north.

Between the three clubs, they ruled the western half of Pennsylvania. So currently, life was easy.

It wouldn't remain that way by Cait showing up solo at Dirty Dick's.

Dawg was protective of his daughters, whether they were five or twenty-five. Whether he claimed them at birth or at almost fifteen.

You did not fuck with a brother's daughter, whether from your own MC or another's. At least not without getting permission first.

And if you approached that brother, you'd better be damn sure you planned on taking that relationship seriously. You did not approach a brother just to ask to bang Daddy's little girl. Fuck no. Not if you wanted to keep, not only your throat intact, but your nuts securely in your sac.

So, it made him wonder why the fuck she walked into his bar and sat at one of his tables.

He waited to see if any of his brothers dared to approach, in case she was there to meet one of them.

What was fucking crazy, she didn't even scan the room. Not once. She'd walked in, sat at an empty table and, after one of his girls took her order and returned with a drink, she took a long swallow and then stared at it with her eyebrows pinned together.

This did not give him the warm fuzzies. Especially with someone as outgoing and outspoken as Cait.

He raised his hand and motioned Nina over.

Nina hurried over to him, ran her long pointy nails across the skin at the back of his neck and asked, "What do you need, Big Daddy?"

For fuck's sake, Nina had been trying to get his dick for months now. She wasn't going to do it by calling him Big Daddy. She wasn't going to do it at all. Nina wasn't his type.

His tastes ran elsewhere.

His eyes slid back to Caitlin, who'd now almost finished her drink.

He jerked his chin up toward the blonde. "Why she here?"

Nina lifted a slender shoulder. "Didn't ask. Should I have?" Her claw-like nails dug deeper into his neck.

Normally that shit would get him hard. Just not from Nina.

"Yeah, get 'er another drink and dig."

"Want me to tell her to leave?"

"I fuckin' tell you that?"

Nina made a face. "No. But whatever you need, Big Daddy..."

"Told you what I fuckin' need. When you get 'er another drink, tell Wick to get me another shot."

"I'll get that for you now."

As she spun away, Magnum reached out and snagged her wrist, jerking her to a halt. "Problem with you, Nina, is you don't fuckin' listen. Told you what to do. Now do it."

Nina's nostrils flared and her jaw got tight, but not as tight as his. Then a second later, she nodded and, *thank fuck*, kept her mouth shut.

Magnum released her and she scurried away. He watched her long enough to make sure she was doing what she was told, then his eyes sliced back to Cait.

With her gaze still directed at her glass, she was clueless two of his brothers were moving in. Like two fucking panthers stalking a doe at a watering hole.

He caught Cue's eye and cocked a pointed eyebrow at him. Cue slapped Cisco's arm and both quickly fell back.

Smart move on both their parts.

Nobody from his club was touching her. No-fucking-body.

Not even him.

Nina approached her table again and set down a fresh drink. She hovered for a few, trying to make convo with Cait.

A few seconds later, Nina's mouth became pinched and her lips flattened out before she swiped the empty glass off the table and headed back to the bar.

She was beside Magnum not a minute later, putting two more shots in front of him.

Magnum downed one, then waited. Of course Nina just fucking stood there. She was a beautiful woman but he swore she was missing shit upstairs. Another reason he wasn't into her. He might not be very educated, but he liked a woman who had more than two brain cells to rub together.

"Jesus fuck," he muttered finally and shook his head.

Nina's hands flew up and she huffed. "No fucking clue, Big Daddy, she wouldn't say much besides thank you."

Christ.

"Maybe she's waiting for someone."

Maybe.

"A date or something."

Magnum raised his eyes to hers. "When the fuck you ever seen someone in here on a fuckin' date?"

Nina shrugged. "Don't know. I don't really pay that much attention to it."

"Especially a white girl in a black biker bar?"

Nina pursed her full lips and rubbed the back of her neck. "Plenty of white girls in here. With one of the brothers."

"She with a fuckin' brother?" he just about shouted.

"Not yet."

His fingers curled into fists and he stared at them, trying not to lose his shit. "Go. Go back the fuck over there an' bring 'er here."

"But—"

"Now, Nina."

Nina huffed again and headed back over to Cait's table.

Nina said something to her and Cait's head raised, she answered, then her neck twisted toward him. Nina jerked her chin towards Magnum and the blonde stood and, without an escort, headed in his direction.

She took her time, all eyes in the bar on her, which annoyed Magnum more than it should.

Since she was taking her sweet time, so did he, running his gaze from top to toe.

Yeah, that fourteen-going-on-fifteen-year-old who Dawg discovered was his and claimed, was no longer that thin, petite blonde young girl. She'd graduated fucking high school, she'd graduated college and she was beginning to carve her way in the world. And along that way, she'd developed into a woman, attitude and all.

Made no sense why she was in Dirty Dick's. None at all. But he was about to find out.

"Hey, Mag," she said softly with a *barely-there* smile that got him smack in the middle of his gut.

Trouble, nothing but fucking trouble, he reminded himself. "Sit the fuck down."

That start of a smile slipped upside down as she plunked her drink down on the scarred and scratched table—*his* fucking table—and yanked out the chair opposite him.

Magnum waited until she settled her bones. Once she did and opened her mouth, he threw up his hand to stop her.

He shook his head, then locked his gaze with hers to make sure she was listening. "Story time. Long time ago a really fuckin' hot redhead did a stupid thing. She walked into this fuckin' bar. Didn't know she was DAMC property at the time. What she did wasn't smart, and it really pissed off her man. That man, you know as Jag, dragged her ass outta here. Ivy came in scoutin' for info. See if we were doin' a territory grab. We weren't, but it still coulda caused a shitload of problems between your father's club and mine. Luckily it didn't because we were busy dealin' with a bunch of fucksticks called the Shadow Warriors. We had a common enemy and goal. Now we don't. Wanna keep it that way, Cait. You showin' up here, especially when you stand out the way you do... Blonde, green-eyed, with great fuckin' tits and ass..." He sucked in a breath and shook his head again. "History's proven wars have been started over less."

She opened her mouth again and he cut her off, making her eyes narrow and her lips thin, but he didn't give a fuck.

"Likin' the peace right now. All I gotta do is protect my brothers from themselves, not protect them from an enemy. You fuckin' showin' up here can make us an enemy. You hookin' up with any of my brothers will start that war. Your daddy ain't gonna like you're here. Pretty sure he'd expect me to squash any shit you start with one of my brothers."

Her voice wasn't so soft this time when she announced, "I'm not here for any of your brothers."

He leaned forward, still keeping their gazes locked. "Then what the fuck you here for?"

"You."

His brow dropped low. *Bullshit.* "Why didn't you approach first thing? Why'd you sit over there if you're here for me?"

One of her long slender fingers with a light pink painted nail distracted him as she traced the word "KNIGHT-HOOD" raggedly carved into his table by someone's knife. "I was gathering my thoughts... and..." The breath hissed softly from her.

He raised his eyes back to her green ones, the color reminding him of a gemstone. "An' what?"

"And my courage."

His head snapped back. "Nobody more confident than you, Caitie."

Fuck. He didn't mean to call her that. It was just a slip of the fucking tongue. Just like what happened at Diesel's wedding. A slip of the goddamn tongue.

If she was here for that... If she was here for more...

Whatever this was, whatever she was here for, he needed to shut this down. And do it right fucking now. "Already lived half my life. You're just startin' out. You don't need the hassle that comes along with a man like me. Got your whole life ahead of you. What we did at D's weddin' was a mistake. Told you that. Thought you understood."

"I'm not here about that."

Yeah, it was over a year ago, but he still hadn't forgotten it. Still hadn't rid himself of the memory of how sweet she tasted on his tongue. It was the one and only time he did something more than watch her.

He did something he shouldn't have. And he was lucky he hadn't been caught. Once he realized what a stupid fuck he was being, he got away from her and stayed away.

He didn't need that temptation.

But here she was.

Her lips twisted. "I mean, you're hot and all that. But you're not irresistible."

He cocked a brow, pursed his lips and sat back in his chair. "I'm pretty fuckin' irresistible."

"Mmm." She tilted her head and made a show of studying him. "Jury's out on that. Irritable, more like it."

He surged forward, slammed his palms on the table and growled, "Didn't..." He flared his nostrils and sucked air deep. She played him. *Jesus fuck.* "Woman, spill it or get the fuck out of my bar."

She glanced around. "This is *your* bar, Magnum, or the Knights' bar?"

"The Knights', which means it's mine. Talk, Cait."

The flame in her eyes suddenly extinguished.

As much as he didn't want to see her in Dirty Dick's, he also didn't like seeing that light dim.

His chest tightened as she leaned back in her chair and closed her eyes, her fingernail now nervously picking at the carved letters and making little shavings. If she didn't stop, she'd shred her nails and they weren't very long as it was.

Something was up and he didn't like it. He didn't like it one fucking bit. "Cait!" he barked, because he couldn't take much more of her hesitating.

Her eyes slowly opened, and they looked troubled. That did not help his damn soaring blood pressure at all.

"I need your help."

Those four words made his heart seize, then begin to pound as loud as a bass drum in his ears. Why the fuck was she coming to him? What the fuck was going on?

Keep your shit together, brother. Keep it the fuck together. "Don't need my fuckin' help, Cait. Got a whole club at your back. And it's not mine. Like I said, don't need a fuckin' war."

Goddamn it. He didn't need anything to cause tension between the Knights and the Angels. No fucking way.

"I can't go to anyone in the club with this. It'll create more of a... a mess than it already is."

Goddamn it. "The Shadows."

"They work for Diesel who won't keep shit from Dad."

Goddamn it. "The pigs."

She sighed. "Axel. He'll tell Bella and Bella will tell D or Dawg."

Jesus fuck. She was probably right, Axhole would run to his wife like the pussy-whipped pig he was. "Yep, screwed no matter who you go to."

"Except you."

He could debate that, too. Because there was nothing more he wanted to do than pound her like a nail into the wall.

He downed his remaining shot, slammed his hand on the table, making his empty shot glasses jump, as well as her Jack and Coke—or whatever the fuck she was drinking, or actually not drinking—spill over the rim. "Nina!" he bellowed and lifted two fingers. "Now!"

Not even a minute later, Nina rushed over with two more shots and slid them both in front of him. She gave Cait a frown, who gave her an answering shrug and then scurried away.

The woman was at least smart enough to know to stay away from him when he was not in a good mood. And right now, he was on the wrong side of a good anything.

He downed one double shot, then the next, and waited for the warmth to hit his gut and his pulse to stop raging. But it ended up being more of a searing burn which turned his stomach. "So far, you haven't told me shit. And not sure I wanna hear it if you can't tell anyone in your club. You belong to them, Caitie. You're Angels' property. I can't step in and interfere."

"I'm not property of the club."

Her cheeks were now flushed, and her eyes held a hard glitter. She was getting pissed. Good. Because so was he.

"Babe, you became property of the DAMC the second your daddy's swimmer hit your momma's egg."

Fuck yeah, she was getting pissed.

"I didn't know my father until I was almost fifteen!" she shouted.

"Don't fuckin' matter."

She shot to her feet. "Fine! If you don't want to help me, I'll go elsewhere."

Oh, *now* she was getting an attitude. *Fuck that.*

He reached out, grabbed her wrist and jerked her back into her seat. "Sit the fuck down and fuckin' spill it, Cait. Least tell me what the fuck's goin' on that's got you all fucked up."

"You have to promise not to tell anyone."

He almost rolled his fucking eyes. And it took a lot for him to do that. "Not promisin' shit."

"Then, fuck you." She tried to surge to her feet again, but he still held her wrist. That outburst had him tightening his grip to keep her in her seat.

"Woman, you walk into this fuckin' bar, try to get me involved in shit and now you're gettin' an attitude with me? That shit ain't gonna fly."

When she squeezed her eyes shut and her wrist trembled within his fingers, he knew that very fucking second he was not letting her leave without knowing what the fuck was going on. Even if he couldn't help her, he wanted to know.

He *needed* to know. Because now his thoughts were spinning, and his gut was a raging fire.

"Cait, you're killin' me here." He had done his best to soften his tone, even though he was ready to flip the fuck out. "Cait!" he barked so loudly, she jumped and opened her eyes.

What could be so bad, she was afraid to say it?

What happened to her unwavering confidence? What the fuck happened to *her*?

He rose from his seat, not releasing her wrist. He was not risking her running out of that bar and him being left in the dark. Because he could not chase her down if she did that. Especially if she ran back to Angels' territory and back to Dawg's house in the DAMC compound.

That would raise way too many red flags. And he hated the color red.

No, he was getting to the bottom of whatever the fuck was going on and he was doing that right now.

Chapter Two

Cait's heart became a deafening beat in her ears as Magnum pulled her out of her seat and began to drag her from the back corner where he "ruled" the Knights' hangout with a meaty fist. He slammed the double swinging doors to the rear of the bar so hard with his palm, if someone had been standing on the other side, that person would've been knocked out. He continued through the kitchen where several heads popped up, eyes went wide, and mouths dropped open.

She understood their reaction. She was having it, too.

She had no idea where he was taking her, but he was on a mission. His long, thick legs propelled him like an out of control locomotive past the kitchen staff as he dragged her along, with her attempting to keep up.

She had long legs for a woman, but not as long as his. It also didn't help she was wearing heeled ankle boots with her jeans. They weren't crazy high like stilettos but enough of a heel that she would've stumbled a couple times if he wasn't like a Belgian draft horse pulling a loaded cart.

Her being the cart.

She was surprised he hadn't simply tossed her over his

shoulder so he could hoof it to wherever they were going even faster. Though, for a big, bulky man, he moved pretty damn quickly.

Suddenly, they were at a rear door with an emergency exit bar, which he slammed, then they were outside in the dark of the mid-September night.

He did not hesitate, he did not pause, he kept barreling along.

"Hey," she said, getting a little worried as they got farther away from the rear of Dirty Dick's.

Did she trust him? Yes, definitely. But he was still freaking her out.

"Hey!" she tried again, louder this time.

Nothing. He had a mission and he was on it.

Which she realized was him heading toward what looked like a garage behind the bar. Was that the Knights' church? Was that where the members met?

Stopping in front of a solid metal door, he jerked a ring of keys out of his front pocket, inserted one into the deadbolt and twisted it. She was surprised when the key didn't snap in half.

"Are you kidnapping me?" she asked halfheartedly as he shoved the door open and pushed her inside. "Magnum!" she snapped when he didn't answer.

He slammed the door shut behind them, and she heard the twist of the lock before the lights came on, blinding her for a second.

She blinked.

Whatever this was, it was not what she was expecting.

A garage, yes. A storage building, yes. But what she found was neither of those things.

It could be said the inside did not match the outside. Not even close.

While anyone would think this was just a plain building that stored vehicles or someone's stuff, it was anything but.

He finally released her wrist and moved past her deeper into his...

House? Apartment?

The interior had a totally open floor plan similar to a loft apartment where the lower level consisted of the main living space, with stairs along one wall to an open loft above. She could barely see the edge of a large bed and a couple dressers up there, but from where she stood that was all she could see.

"This is," she whispered, "unexpected."

"You showin' the fuck up at my bar was unexpected, too." He jabbed a large finger at a high quality, dark brown leather sectional and barked, "Sit."

She turned around in place and took it all in. It was really freaking nice. Like he'd brought in some sort of interior designer and just let whoever it was loose to do his or her thing.

"Brooke or Kelsea?" Those were the only two designers she knew, and it would make sense if he'd used them since they were two people he could trust to be in his personal and private domain.

He only grunted as he moved into the nice sized, open concept, *modern* kitchen, jerked open the stainless-steel fridge door and pulled out a beer.

He didn't ask her if she wanted one, nope. After guzzling the whole beer down, he slammed the empty bottle on the counter, then grabbed a second one, ripping off the cap before directing his sights on her and moving back to where she now sat.

In the hot seat.

He took a long pull from the second beer, offered the bottle to her but she shook her head.

Her stomach was already in knots. Beer would not help. *Hell,* the first Jack and Coke she downed in Dirty Dick's hadn't even taken the edge off her nerves and that had been strong.

She blew out a breath.

"Talk," he barked as he stood over her. "Say whatever shit you need to say. No matter how bad it is. No one's gonna overhear it in here."

She was really rethinking about coming to him for help. But she'd wracked her brain on where she could go, on who she could trust, to help handle her issue.

When she said she couldn't go to anyone in the DAMC, she wasn't lying. The situation was a touchy and embarrassing one, and either her father, the club enforcer, Diesel, or Diesel's former Special Ops crew, the Shadows, would take that situation and, instead of handling it smoothly and efficiently, it would be a major explosion with casualties left in their path.

But with Magnum, while his club was an ally to the Angels, he wasn't tied to them. In truth, he had no obligation to tell them anything. Or reveal what she was about to tell him.

At least, she hoped so.

Yes, he was afraid of causing issues between the clubs but as long as neither of them said a word about it to anyone, just kept it between the two of them, then no one would ever know.

No harm, no foul, right?

Enough harm and a major foul had been already done. Damage control was now needed.

She looked up at the one person who might be able to handle it. "Are you just going to stand over me?"

"Yeah."

Her lips flattened out. "Can you not?"

"Cait."

"What?"

"Got five seconds before I lose my fuckin' shit."

She closed her eyes, twisted her fingers together in her lap and whispered, "Okay." She kept her eyes shut as she began and hoped she didn't regret it. "I think you know my stepdad got me my job—"

Magnum's loud grunt told her exactly how he felt about Paul. Not that the men ever met each other before and most likely never would since they ran in totally different circles.

A nervous giggle almost slipped out from her as she pictured Magnum and her rich stepfather sitting down together, having a beer and shooting the shit.

The two men couldn't be more opposite.

Even so, she was sure Magnum knew of him and about him and the whole situation between her mother, stepfather —who she had been told was her father for almost fifteen years—and her biological father, Dawg.

She shook those thoughts loose and continued, opening her eyes and directing her gaze to the huge man hovering over her and wearing a major scowl.

She had kissed those broad, powerful lips once... About a year ago...

She mentally shook herself again. That was not why she was here. "So..."

"Woman!" he bellowed so loudly, she swore the windows in the place shook.

She sucked in a breath, braced herself and continued, "Anyway, Gallo Marketing Agency is one of the top marketing firms on the east coast. It's small but powerful, it's tight knit and Henry Gallo—he prefers Hank—"

Magnum growled.

She ignored that because for him to understand the situation, he needed to know the background. "Hank only hires the best and brightest to protect the firm's reputation and to land and keep big name clients, which he does. He's got a lot of clout in the industry."

"Should I give a fuck about all this?"

"Do you want me to tell you or not?" she bit out. She already felt like a tight wire about to snap. He didn't need to make it worse.

"At this rate, gonna be dead from old age before you fuckin' finish."

"You want to know why I can't go anywhere else and I'm going to tell you. Just let me..."

"Talk," he barked.

She should just say screw it and leave. Find another way. Just like any hard-headed biker, he was impossible to deal with. She had found that out only too well in the past ten years being around them.

"Cait!"

She sucked in another deep breath before she did just that. "Hank likes to think of his employees as family. A close-knit group. And for the most part, it is."

"Cait, fuck me," he groaned, scrubbing a big paw over his bald head and down his smoothly shaven face.

"Give me a chance!" she snapped. "Christ, Magnum, stop being a dick. You either want to hear this or you want me to go. Which is it?"

His black eyebrows pinned together. "Talk."

She pulled a long breath in through her nose. "Anyway, it's hard to get in there but it's a great firm to launch your career if you can get your foot in the door. Paul pulled strings with Hank to get me hired after I graduated from U of P. I mean, without him, I wouldn't even have had a chance. Not even close. But I was offered an entry level position there as a Social Media Specialist. This was a golden opportunity to prove myself and move up the ladder, eventually get promoted to a manager, even earn my masters with them paying the tuition for me. I'm telling you, it's a golden egg. And I *love* my job. I'm learning so much, getting experience under my belt, making connections, building my resume. Maybe enough to start my own firm down the road."

"Didn't know any of this shit," he said at a more reasonable volume and with a lot less obvious irritation.

She lifted her face to him. "Of course not. We don't talk. And that one time—"

He cut her off. "Not hashin' that shit again. Keep goin' since my hair's turnin' white faster than you're talkin'."

Since he had no hair, he had to be making a joke. Sort of.

But she felt more like puking than laughing right now. The more background she told him, the longer she could put off getting to the issue that kept her from sleeping.

"I just need you to understand how important this job is to me, how important it is for my future. This is what I got my degree in, this is what I've been working toward, so I can't just walk away. No," she said firmly and shook her head, "I *refuse* to walk away. And I *refuse* to be chased away, too."

She caught the flare of his wide nostrils and his dark brown eyes got sharp and intense again. The man was handsome, especially when you were on the receiving end of one of his rare smiles, but he was also scary as hell. He was like a clone of Diesel, the Dirty Angels' Sergeant at Arms. He was almost as big and just as frightening when he was pissed, but with just a lot darker skin tone.

If either of those men directed their ire at you, you'd shit your pants. Or at least have a tightly puckered anus. Their fists were like sledgehammers, their tempers short and their unbridled strength could be deadly.

Both were also much smarter than most people realized. Their looks, the way they talked and the fact they were bikers deceived how intelligent they both were. Not necessarily book smart, but street smart, for sure.

She recognized it, though. Another reason she'd been

attracted to him for the last few years, even though acting on that attraction wasn't smart when it came down to who they both were.

She knew it. He knew it. And it was the reason that one moment they had—that slip—was chalked up as a huge mistake.

But she'd never forget that moment, that sliver of time, when they both forgot who they were, what they were and where they were. A door slamming in the distance at the DAMC clubhouse had knocked them both quickly and abruptly back into reality.

"My boss doesn't know who my real father is. Who my extended family are. Hank and the rest, they only know my mother and stepfather. They believe Paul is my biological father, not Dawg. And, of course, Mom and Paul don't tell people otherwise."

Magnum made a sharp noise at the back of his throat. "You embarrassed?"

"Paul and my mother are, but me? No, not embarrassed." Her eyebrows pinned together as she searched for how she felt. "More like a fear of being judged, or my dad, Emma, my sisters... all being judged harshly for something others don't quite understand. A lifestyle that's not easily accepted because of preconceived notions, I guess. I love my father. I love my family. I've come to love everyone in the club. The sisterhood, the brotherhood, all the kids... I guess I want to protect them?"

"No, that ain't it, Cait. You're afraid that judgement will affect your job and your future."

She was afraid of that, too. "I've been there less than a year, so I'm easily disposable. Most marketing majors would kill for the position I'm in. The job market in general is tough after graduation, especially for someone without experience."

"Makin' excuses."

"They're valid ones."

He only grunted.

"Now you're judging me."

"Waitin' to hear why the fuck you're here, Cait. Why the fuck you searched me out to get your ass outta whatever jam you got yourself into."

"I need this to be handled delicately because if it's not, it could screw up my career. I could very well be blackballed from the industry."

"Jesus fuck, Caitie, you kill someone?"

If only. "No. No, but I... made a major mistake. Put myself in a situation I shouldn't have. And now it's haunting me."

"An' you need to kill that ghost."

"No, not kill. If I wanted that, I'd go to my father, Diesel or Mercy and my problem would be solved. I just need to remove the power that ghost has over me right now. At least until I can make a name for myself in marketing or maybe find a job at a different firm."

"The DAMC's got plenty of businesses for you to work at. Don't need to work there."

She wasn't surprised by his answer. "This is what I want to do, it's my passion. I'm not going to settle on something I don't want because I'm..."

Dawg would love for her to work within the cocoon of one of the DAMC businesses. Her mother? She would be livid and think it was a waste of her education.

"Even if the club offered to set up my own business, I don't have a reputation yet to make it successful. Plus, the club will want a percentage as they do with all the businesses. I'm not club property, they shouldn't get a cut of anything I do."

"Babe, tellin' you, you're club property. Might wanna deny it, but the rest of us know it. Might not have those colors inked into your skin, but it's stamped all the fuck over you. You reek of Dirty Angels." She opened her mouth, but he stopped her with a large palm and a sharp tilt of his bald head. "Need to rewind. You ain't gonna settle on doin' somethin' you don't wanna do 'cause of what?"

Once she answered that, there was no going back. Magnum wouldn't let her slide. Her fingernails dug into her thighs and her knee began to bounce, which he noticed, and his scowl got even deeper and darker.

"Christ," he muttered.

"I'm not going to be forced into changing my career path because of being blackmailed." She wasn't even sure if it *was* blackmail.

His massive body jerked and he bellowed, "What the fuck for?" so loudly she cringed.

She dropped her gaze to her lap and rubbed a hand over her forehead. Bile was rising up her throat. "There's a video..."

She didn't have to look to see he went wired, because she felt it in the air, shimmering around them both. Every one of her nerves began to tingle from it and not in a good way.

Not like when they had kissed. *That* had stolen her breath. This was just making her sick to her stomach.

She finally lifted her face and dared to peek at him.

When she did, he repeated in a soft, but dangerous sounding growl, "You took a video."

"Not me."

"Of what?" That question held such a deadly undertone, a shiver sliced through her.

Shit. Shit. Shit.

She didn't want to tell him. Not him. She didn't want to tell anyone. But she had no choice because the evidence was in living color. And she had no idea what that person was going to do with it.

"Of what, Cait?" he once again yelled so loudly her ears rang. "Better be of you committin' some fuckin' crime, like murder, an' not what I'm thinkin' it is. It fuckin' better be. Just sayin'... *Fuck*."

Cait tried to force down the lump in her throat by swallowing, but it wasn't going anywhere. She reached out and grabbed the bottle he held in a death grip within his fingers. After a slight struggle, he let it go and she let the beer slide down her throat, hoping that wedge would loosen.

It didn't.

But at least he wasn't holding it anymore, which lessened the chance he'd throw it against a wall with what was coming next. "I didn't know."

She said it so softly, he barked, "What?"

She set her jaw and tried to meet his blazing eyes. "I didn't know." Heat flicked up her throat and into her cheeks.

This was not a good idea, coming to him. This was a mistake. This would be just as bad as telling her father and could turn into a total and complete disaster. For her, for him, for everyone involved.

She began to get to her feet, but he stopped her with a loud, "Don't you fuckin' move."

She plopped back down. He stood between her and the door, and he wouldn't just let her walk away. Not now that she'd dropped that bombshell.

"Didn't know you were bein' recorded," he prodded.

"No. I didn't know what happened until I saw it."

"What the fuck do you mean?"

"I don't remember anything that happened that night," she whispered. *God*, she was stupid, stupid, stupid.

Magnum let out a noise that instantly made every inch of her skin break out in goosebumps. Because she had her eyes focused on his boots, she knew the exact moment he stepped back and turned to give her his back.

She lifted her gaze to stare at his insanely broad back and the colors he displayed on it. He abruptly spun on her, making her start. "Who the fuck was it? Gonna fuckin' kill 'im." She opened her mouth, but he cut her off. "Need a fuckin' name. Fucker's gonna die."

Her heart leapt in her chest. "No! That's the exact reason I'm coming to you. I need help but that's not the help I need."

His eyes went wide, then narrowed quickly. "Better start explainin' then, 'cause the little you just fuckin' told me means a bullet between the eyes."

"He—"

"Who the fuck is *he*?" he bellowed, fury lining his face.

"Let me... Mag, this is hard. Fuck... *Please*."

His body stiff, Magnum shut his eyes and his fingers curled tightly into fists against his outer thighs. After a few seconds, he opened his eyes and pinned them on her. She could see his struggle not to go ape shit. The exact fear she had if she had told anyone in the Angels.

"Okay," he forced out. "Okay. Okay... Gonna... just... just... Fuck. Just say it. Gonna stand here an' listen. Gonna just listen..." He wasn't talking to her, he was talking to himself.

She removed the fingers she had nervously pressed to her mouth. "I'm going to tell you and will just keep talking, even if you interrupt me. Because I'm telling you this once and once only. I just can't..." She sucked in a shaky breath. "I just can't. So, yes, just listen."

He gave her a sharp nod and said nothing. Though, that effort made him look like a freshly shaken two-liter bottle of pop. She needed to hurry before that cap exploded and shot across the room.

She spoke quickly. "My boss, Hank, has three children. All adults, who all work at the firm." *Deep breath*. "Because he wants us all to be a close-knit 'family' he invites us to after work activities, like dinners, drinks, bowling, whatever. Even retreats up at a place in Lake George. While it's by invitation, it's strongly encouraged we go. Which means, if you want to make a name in this business, if you want to be considered for a promotion within the agency, then you become a team player. Part of that includes attending these social gatherings. He's very generous and a great man from what I've learned about him in the last ten months." *Deep breath.* "Like I said, his kids all work there and hold high positions, of course. One of them being his youngest son."

Magnum's jaw was working, and Cait could practically hear his teeth grinding. The veins on his forearms protruded like underground mole tunnels as he continued to press his fists against his thighs. The corded muscles in his neck were visibly strained and looked ready to detonate. His full lips were pinned together so hard, his mouth had become only a thin slit.

She pushed on anyway, though she worried he would just implode. "One of the senior marketing managers nailed a huge client. I mean *huge.* So, Hank invited all of us, even us entry level employees, to not only celebrate but to show us where we could be in a few years if we worked just as hard. Was it motivating? Yes. Of course, I went after work like I normally did and I... I need to circle back for a second..." *Just breathe. Breathe.* "Hank's youngest son, Nate, has been... Had been..."

Again, she heard a noise at the back of his throat, not loud this time, but enough to catch her attention. Enough to worry her.

"Nate was really nice at first. Said all the right things. Compliments, both personal and business-related. Told me I was great at my job, an asset to the company. I liked the attention, until he began to ask me out."

Another noise. Possibly a gurgle.

She ignored it and powered on. "At first I considered it. He was smart and nice... But sometimes you just get that feeling something is off. And something was off with him, and not just in the way he pursued me. He became pushier, not physically, but by insisting we go out together, insisting he could help me get ahead in my career. A promotion, a raise, things like that."

Magnum took a step toward her but managed to say nothing. It was probably killing him to remain silent, as much it was killing her to get out what needed said.

"I said no. He asked so many times it was to the point of harassment. And normally an employee could go to HR about it, but he was... *is* head of Human Resources. The director, in fact. And Hank thinks the sun rises and sets on his kids, especially Nate... So, I kept carefully saying no. Told him I wasn't interested. I even told him I had a boyfriend. None of that discouraged him."

She steepled her hands together, pressed them over her mouth and nose and simply breathed. *In. Out.* Deep, slow breaths to soothe her rattled nerves.

When Magnum took another step forward, almost close enough to where his jeans touched hers, she realized she needed to hurry up and finish.

She dropped her hands. "When we were around other people, like that night a couple weeks ago at the private club Hank belonged to, he was like everyone else. Friendly, happy, chatty. Treated me like anyone else at the firm. But I screwed up that night. I did something I never should've done because I was surrounded by people I thought I could trust." She glanced up at him and whispered, "Unfortunately, I was wrong."

His nostrils flared wide and right before her eyes his body seemed to expand, to swell larger than life with barely contained rage.

Coming to the man before her wasn't a good choice. It wasn't. Just like leaving her drink unattended while she used the bathroom. She should've known better. She should have known not to trust any man around her drink, even her boss's son. She had been among peers, among the firm's "family," who she should be able to trust.

She had been so wrong.

So fucking wrong.

Her voice shook as she whispered, "I didn't know what happened. I wasn't feeling well after only having one drink. Nate assured everyone he'd get me home safely. And they looked at him like he was such a fucking hero. A goddamn hero." Her dry throat convulsed. "The next morning..." *Breathe.* "The next morning I woke up in a motel room, my head pounding, sick to my stomach and no memory of what happened. But I knew." She squeezed her eyes shut, reliving that dread, that panic. "I knew, I knew, I knew."

Even with a fuzzy head, she'd never forget the sick feeling waking up naked in a motel room. Her purse sat nearby untouched with her car keys in it. Her clothes were found neatly folded on a chair. A "note" had even been left behind. A large heart had been drawn on a piece of the motel's stationary with the lipstick she carried in her purse. It also included two words: "Thank you."

Like she had been a willing participant in whatever had gone down.

She began to question herself. Had she wanted whatever happened? Had she been willing? Had she said yes?

Had Nate taken her home like he said he would, and she'd gone back out and hooked up with someone else?

She couldn't remember anything other than leaving the private club. Nothing. It was all a blank.

"I didn't know what to do, so I sort of panicked. I scrubbed myself down in the shower, gathered my things and got a car service home. I was scared to accuse someone of doing something I had no recollection of happening." Whoever it was had apparently worn a condom but had taken it with him.

When Magnum's deep, rage-filled voice filled the space,

she jumped almost as if she had forgotten he was there for a moment. "Want details. His fuckin' name, where to find him. What he drives. Where he fuckin' eats. Fucker's gonna get what's comin' to 'im."

And there was one of the issues. "I don't know for sure it was him. If it wasn't for the video sent to me at work a few days ago..." Her brain hit auto-play and she began to see it all over again, like it had hundreds of times. Over and over in her head. Each time it didn't get any easier. "Even with that, I still can't prove it was him. I don't have any proof. There's a video, yes, but not of the man's face. Just... Just everything else. Nate doesn't act any differently. When I asked him what happened after we left the club, he said he took me home, helped me into my apartment, then he went home. He acts surprised I don't remember anything. He still asks me out and I tell him no. Nothing else has changed. I even called the motel to ask who rented the room and they wouldn't tell me, saying they couldn't give out that information.

"So, I can't accuse my boss's son of drugging me and.... and worse... and it be false, because it was someone else. I'll lose my job and my career will be screwed. I'll be considered an HR nightmare and no one in the industry will want to hire me.

"I can't throw everything away, Magnum, I can't. I want to forget about it, but I can't do that, either. Whoever it is has that video and I don't know what he's going to do with it. My only guess is for blackmail, but I don't know why or even what I have that someone would want to blackmail me for. None of it makes sense."

She lifted her gaze and found his normally dark face even darker. She didn't even think that was possible. Now she knew it was. And it was not knowledge she ever wanted to have.

She opened her mouth to voice her concern and shut it

when he simply shook his head. After a very loud explosion of breath, he growled, "Wanna get this straight. Some fuckin' fucknut spiked your goddamn drink at a work function, took your ass to a motel, *raped* you," his voice was getting louder and tighter as he talked, "recorded it, left you there passed out, then sent you a video. And you won't go to Dawg, Diesel or Mercy for this 'cause you're afraid that fucker's gonna die? Are you fuckin' kiddin' me?"

"I—"

"Expected me to handle this better?" He was now shouting loud enough to make her wince. His barely restrained anger was beginning to bubble over. "Expect me not to kill that motherfucker? 'Cause if that's what you fuckin' expected, you're dead fuckin' wrong. If you didn't want this Nate motherfucker to die, then you never shoulda come to me, Cait. Never. 'Cause to think that..." His whole body surged forward even though his feet didn't move. "That... Christ! Motherfucker! Goddamn... *Fuck!*" he exploded with his face twisted into a mask of fury.

Then he turned on his boot heel, stomped out the door and slammed it shut so hard the wall shook.

She heard a loud, hair-raising roar outside which shot a shiver down her spine.

She froze, not sure what to do. Not sure if he'd only gone outside to blow off some steam.

Her heart raced and so did her thoughts. He never agreed to help. And now she feared he'd go to Diesel. Or worse, confront Nate, assuming he was the one in the video.

She had no proof it was him. Suspicions, yes. Proof, no.

Was Magnum going to do exactly what she didn't want? *Fuck!*

She needed his help but not like that. Had she ripped herself open for nothing?

Should she stay? Should she go?

She had no idea what to do, with not only her current

situation but also the one she came to him about. Things were now more fucked up than ever and could even get worse. Once again, it was all her fault.

She waited ten more minutes, her nerves a tangled mess, her stomach in tight knots, and when she realized he wasn't coming back, she had no choice but to leave.

So, she did.

Chapter Three

MAGNUM STRADDLED HIS SLED, his eyes glued to the low-rise building made up entirely of what looked like reflective glass. His sled was quiet, his brain was not.

He hadn't fucking slept the last couple nights. No matter what he did... No matter how much he drank, how much he toked, nothing... *fucking nothing* could erase the imagery of what happened to Cait.

Not one goddamn thing.

And he hadn't even seen the video yet.

He would. Because before he took care of whoever did this to her, took advantage of her, he needed to know everything.

In truth, he didn't want to see it, knew it would not only haunt him, but spin him out of control. More than simply hearing her words summarizing what happened had. He knew once he saw it, once he knew for sure who it was, nothing, *nothing* would stop him from wiping that mother-fucker from the face of the Earth.

He hated he knew. He was also relieved he knew.

He hated she came to him. He was also relieved she came to him.

With the conflict raging inside him, he understood why she didn't go to Dawg. And going to Diesel or Mercy would have been the same as going directly to her father. Because there was no damn way either of those men were keeping that foul shit from Dawg.

And he knew why.

Because as a father himself, if he found out what happened to Caitie happened to his own daughter...

Jesus fuck.

The Earth would burn. And he'd be the one holding the match.

But he had to remind himself that while this Gallo fucker seemed like the obvious person, he needed to be sure.

And once he was...

He was finding himself a pack of fucking matches.

She wanted to keep her job. It was important to her, a part of her future. He heard it, he got that, too. But he also couldn't forget the look on her face when she spilled what happened.

But after what happened, if it was this Nate, the son of the CEO? Cait not only deserved to keep her job, she deserved to own that whole fucking building.

However, he didn't want her to get fucked after already being...

Being...

He sucked in a sharp breath through his nose, pressed his palms over his eyes and tried to clear the rage from his brain so he could think clearly.

If he was smart, he'd go to Diesel. Doing shit behind the man's back wouldn't keep the fucking peace. Knowing and not saying anything, not giving them a chance to take care of the problem, was a deep, maybe unforgivable, betrayal.

Not giving them the info so they could step in and protect what belonged to them, protect their club property...

He hissed from the sharp burn in his chest.

Him considering doing this on his own was dangerous. The day he knew the last Shadow Warrior no longer existed, he breathed a fuck of a lot easier.

He did not need to get his brothers into another war. Especially over a female.

But this wasn't any female and he would do his fucking best to prevent a war. Because he also wasn't sure he could just walk away and let someone else handle it. Now he had a deep-seated need to exact revenge on whoever drugged her and... and, *fuck*, did what they did.

Yeah, Cait was Angels' property, but if it was up to him, she would be Knights' property instead.

She would belong to him.

She would be under his protection and it would be on him to handle this problem.

But she didn't and she wasn't. Even so, here he sat, letting the shit she told him eat him from the inside out. It made his gut burn, his blood boil and the urge to snuff the fucker pulled at him.

Normally, he handled shit neat and efficiently within his club. If someone needed to be put in his place, he put the asshole in his place. If someone became a cancer within the club, he extracted them like a surgeon's blade. If outsiders, like the Warriors, caused trouble, he dealt with it swiftly and permanently.

His prez gave him free rein to handle shit the way it needed to be handled.

But Caitie's situation was different. Him getting involved would piss off his prez, if he knew.

It might even get his colors stripped.

It might even get him killed. By the Angels or by his own brothers.

Touching this situation was like handling dynamite. One wrong move could cause a devastating explosion, change the rest of his goddamn life. And he had a good one.

At almost forty-one, he liked where he was currently sitting. He had only one fucking regret and that was losing his kids. He couldn't do shit about it, so he had to accept it. But other than that, life was pretty fucking good.

He wanted for nothing, except maybe a warm body and an even warmer pussy in his bed every night. But that was a want and not a need.

Just like Cait.

He wanted her but could live without her. He had for the past almost seven years. But after last year, after that slip, it became more difficult. Every tall, curvy blonde he saw, he thought it was her.

Every blonde he fucked, he closed his eyes and imagined it was her. Every time he fisted it, he did it thinking about her.

It was the safest way to have what he wanted without causing major issues. But it was getting to the point of obsession and he avoided heading over to the Angels' church in case she was there. As long as he didn't see his temptation, he could avoid it.

But no matter what he did, he couldn't avoid her when his eyes were closed late at night in bed, whether there was another woman under him or not. If Dawg knew what Magnum was doing to thoughts of his daughter...

Best not find out.

So yeah, he shouldn't touch her and probably shouldn't help her, either.

The first part would be difficult, the second... impossible. There was no fucking way anybody else was handling this but him. No way someone else would get the pleasure of making whoever it was who recorded Cait, whoever made her a victim, pay.

The tables were going to turn and whoever it was would regret that decision for life, no matter how long or short that life was.

His spine snapped straight, and his fingers curled into fists as he spotted H. Nathan Gallo, Jr. take long strides to his parking spot, one reserved for the Director of Human Resources. Even though the lily-white motherfucker with his gelled hair had his nose glued to his cell phone, Magnum recognized him from the pictures he'd pulled up online. First from the Gallo Marketing Agency's website, then from his social media accounts. Magnum also had snapped a picture of his car and license plate when he'd first pulled into the lot. Hard to remain anonymous when you posted all kinds of stupid shit online and parked in the same spot every day that practically had your name on it.

The only thing he hadn't gotten yet was a home address. Or his routine. But then, that was why Magnum was here. To track his fucking ass. To see what this fucker was like, whether he was capable of drugging and sexually assaulting women or if he just had an unhealthy interest in Caitie.

Even if it was just an interest, the man needed to learn that the word no from a woman meant just that but with a goddamn capital N. So, yeah, even if this Nate mother-fucking Gallo was only being "helpful" by taking Cait home, Magnum was still going to make sure that interest was squashed.

Magnum hit the starter on his sled as soon as Gallo backed his Jaguar F-Type out of the space.

He would've thought a man with some scratch, driving a sweet ride, would be able to get pussy without drugging them first.

But maybe he was wrong. Or the man was just fucked in the head and was a menace to women at large. Maybe Cait wasn't the first one he'd done it to.

If that was true, she'd be the last. Guaranteed.

Because drivers of a cage like that Jaguar tended to drive fast and reckless. And sometimes driving like that could be fatal.

———

For the last three fucking days, he'd followed that squirrely motherfucker. From work, to the gym or a sports bar, then home. He lived in one of those *expensive-as-fuck* condos behind a guarded gate. Though, the gate and the guard were more of a joke than anything.

He hadn't heard from Cait, but then he hadn't expected her to reach out to him again after he stormed out of his house to avoid trashing the whole place the other night.

He was itching to tell her that he had this covered, but he still wasn't sure if it was a good idea to get involved. No, he was fucking sure. It wasn't.

But, fuck him, he couldn't let it go. And he'd fucking tried.

So here he was again, stalking that motherfucker outside of Cait's work, waiting to see what the fucker's pattern would be today.

Unlike Diesel's Shadows, Magnum had no military training, so he wasn't stealth like them. Because of that, he once again parked his sled behind a large vehicle and hoped like fuck someone inside didn't notice him from one of those big-ass windows and call the fucking pigs.

Because a black fucking biker hanging out in the Gallo Marketing Agency's parking lot on a blacked-out, customized sled stood the fuck out. In fact, in the time he'd spent in the lot for the last three days, he'd hardly seen any people of any shade except the light variety go in or out.

It shouldn't surprise him, but it did.

As soon as he'd slide his Harley between two vehicles, he would slip off his cut and stash it in one of his saddlebags but keep his black leather skullcap and dark sunglasses on.

He also parked away from Cait's cage, a newer Camry Dawg had bought her when she graduated college. The man had been proud of his daughter and wanted everyone to know it. No doubt existed in anyone's mind that Dawg loved his girls and would do anything for them, including die.

So, yeah, the more he thought about it, Cait hadn't gone to her father because he'd end up in prison after killing whoever did that to her. He was the kind of man who'd lose his shit, walk point blank into the Gallo building and toss that fucker out one of those plate-glass windows from the top floor. That was, after he cut off the asshole's dick.

Cait would lose her job, Dawg would catch a murder charge and his younger daughters would grow up without their father.

Cait being Cait was looking out for them.

Thinking about her must have conjured her up, because, once she stepped out of the shadows of the front overhang, the sun hitting her blonde hair caught his attention.

His heart pounded as he watched her head in the direction of her car. Not only was she so goddamn smoking hot, she was wearing a tight black skirt that stopped right above her knees, high heels that were all business—but still sexy as hell—that showed off her long calves, and a short-sleeve fitted blouse in a green he was sure set off her eyes. He was also sure it set off her tits.

She had what looked like a jacket that matched her skirt thrown over one arm and a purse in the same hand as she began to hoof it more quickly.

He knew why.

That Gallo fucker was on her tail, hurrying to catch up. From where Magnum sat on his sled, he could barely hear it, but the man was calling Cait's name.

"Caitie! Hold up."

Oh no. Fuck no.

Magnum dismounted from his bike, removed his skull cap and threw it on the seat, then took a direct and determined path between the rows of vehicles to Cait's cage, where she was scrambling to get her keys out of her purse.

He would have to teach her to never leave a building without those fucking keys in her hand.

As Magnum moved toward them, Gallo now blocked Cait's driver's door by standing between her car and the one parked next to it. He wasn't touching her, *thank fuck,* but he kept glancing up toward the office building as if worried someone might see him.

The fucker was smart. He made it look like they were doing nothing but having friendly conversation. But from what Magnum could see, Cait was jumpy as hell.

"I have to go, Nate," she was saying as Magnum got within earshot.

"Just a drink, Caitie. One harmless drink."

One drink wasn't so damn harmless last time.

"I can't. I told you I have a boyfriend."

"Just as friends, Caitie. Co-workers. We can discuss those strategies on how to impress my father. Nothing more."

Nothing more.

Except him drugging her and then sticking his dick in her once she was knocked the fuck out.

Fucking motherfucker.

"I can't, Nate. I haven't drunk anything since the celebration party for Laura."

Magnum knew that was a lie since she drank at Dirty Dick's the night she came to find him.

"Then don't drink, come with me to dinner. My treat."

"My boyfr—"

Gallo flapped an impatient hand around. "You've never brought a boyfriend to any of the get-togethers, Caitie. I'm thinking he doesn't exist."

"Oh, he exists," Magnum growled as he moved directly behind Gallo.

Cait's eyes widened as soon as she saw him, but she quickly schooled the surprise and confusion from her face.

"Hey, baby," he purred to her. "You ready to go?"

Gallo's head twisted and once he got an eyeful of Magnum, his eyes widened, and his body jerked. But, like Cait, he quickly hid his expression. "Oh, I didn't know you were seeing anyone, Caitie."

Lying motherfucker. "Just heard her tell you she was." Magnum's lip curled as he fought the sneer. He failed. "Name's Caitlin, not Caitie."

Fuck this guy for using Magnum's nickname for her.

Gallo's eyebrows knitted together as he sized up Magnum and held out his hand. "Nathan Gallo."

Magnum stared at the hand he could easily break. White, soft, weak. Probably never did a day of manual labor in his life. Setting his jaw, he grabbed it, grumbled, "Malcolm Moore," and just about crushed it to the point where Gallo winced and struggled to tug his hand free.

Magnum reluctantly released it just before hearing the satisfying crack of bones.

Gallo's cheeks were now flush, and he grabbed his injured hand with the other one, trying his best not to reveal his weakness. "Oh, well then... I guess he would be your plus one for the annual retreat at Lake George next week," he said to Cait, then turned to Magnum, like he cared about whatever this asshole was spewing. "It's a week-long conference, but it's very casual. We do team exercises, have motivational speakers, spa time. Sports. Games. Boating. Fishing. Whatever you're into."

Magnum interrupted him. "I'm into Cait."

Gallo's eyes slid to her. "I... uh... I can see why, she's a beau—"

Magnum released a low growl.

"Yes... Well, anyway. You should come!" Gallo said with a forced enthusiasm.

"I don't think—" Cait began.

He shoved past Gallo and dropped an arm around her, pulling her into his side. "Sounds like a fu— *fun* time," Magnum forced out. "Cait already invited me and I look forward to it." He dropped his head and kissed her gaping mouth. "Right, baby?" he whispered against her lips.

"I—" Cait started.

Magnum straightened and focused on the fucknut staring at them. "Now, we gotta fu— *go*." He squeezed her shoulders.

Goddamn, not letting "fuck" fly was going to be hard. And if he had to do it for a week? He just might explode.

But there was no fucking way she was going on this "retreat" run by the Gallos alone.

No. Fucking. Way.

He held out his hand. "Baby, keys."

"I can drive..." she murmured, once again confused.

He cocked a brow in her direction. "Since when do I ever let you drive?" He shook his open palm. "Keys."

With a frown, she dropped her keys into his hand, and he gave her a soft smile for the asshole's benefit. "Get in the cage... *car*, baby." He jerked his chin, indicating she should get in on the passenger side.

She opened her mouth but quickly shut it when he gave her a look and she moved around the back of the sedan. He kept his eyes focused on Gallo as she got into the passenger seat and shut the Camry's door.

"Now," Magnum said in a low voice. "We got things to do. Was there somethin' important you needed to tell Cait? That why you chased her down out here? Was it somethin' to do with work?"

From the neckline of Gallo's dress shirt to the top of his cheeks turned a brighter shade of pussy and he cleared his throat. "Yes, I just wanted to discuss some work strategies with her."

"Then you do it before four o'clock when she walks out that fu—" his jaw shifted, "*front* door." He took a step closer to Gallo, making the man tip his head up farther. "A man doesn't appreciate another man askin' his girl out for drinks to discuss work when you have eight hours, five days a fu—*week* to do so." He leaned in. "Get me?"

"Malcolm... May I call you Malcolm?"

Fuck no. "No."

"Uh... Okay, Mr. Moore, then. We're one big family here at the Gallo Marketing Agency. We encourage our employees to socialize outside of work. That's one reason we have these get-togethers and retreats. And it's another reason our agency is so successful."

His agency. More like his daddy's agency. "Let's get one thing clear right now, Gallo—"

"You can call me Nate—"

"My wo—" Magnum sucked in a breath and his head twitched, "*girlfriend* does not do drinks or anythin' else with another man unless I'm there. Ai—" He sighed. "Not gonna point this out again."

Gallo's brown eyes landed on her cage and Magnum wasn't sure if, from where they stood, the man could see Cait inside. Even so...

"Need to hear that you get me, Gallo."

Gallo's mouth opened and closed a couple times before he said, "I can see one might take my invitation in the wrong light."

No fucking wrong light about it. It was exactly what Magnum saw. A man sniffing after Caitie. Whether he was the one in the video or not, Gallo hadn't hidden his interest.

So, it was up to Magnum to crush that interest with his boot like a roach scurrying across the floor. "You get me, Gallo?"

"I understand your concern. But in truth, it was meant

to be a harmless invitation. We're friends besides being co-workers."

Bullshit. "I ask Cait that, that what she's gonna say?"

Gallo's mouth tightened around the edges. "I would hope so."

"Gonna ask her then," Magnum crossed his arms over his chest, "but not while you're standin' here." He gave Gallo a pointed look. One he was pretty fucking sure wasn't hard to read.

"Oh, yes... Okay. Well, then. I look forward to seeing you in Lake George next week, Mr. Moore, and getting to know you much better. Welcome to the Gallo family."

That motherfucker was crazy. Especially when he stuck out his hand again. This time Magnum didn't take it. He let it hang until Gallo curled his fingers into his palm and then strode quickly toward his Jaguar which wasn't parked anywhere near Cait's Toyota since the fucker had front row parking. Unlike Cait.

Magnum ripped open the driver's door and tried to squeeze in. "Jesus fuck!" he growled and leaned in, plugged the key into the ignition to move the power seat as far back as possible. He lost his patience as he waited for the thing to whir back slowly. When it didn't go any farther—he made sure of it several times—he folded himself into the driver's seat and started the engine.

"Where are we going?" Cait asked, her green eyes wide.

He reversed out of the spot, pointed the cage toward where his sled was parked, slammed it into drive and headed to the rear of the treed lot. He found another spot out of Gallo's view, in case the fucker was being nosy. After putting the Toyota in park, he locked the doors and twisted his head to stare at Cait staring at him from the passenger seat.

Unfortunately, his attention was pulled elsewhere. Her skirt had slid up to mid-bare-thigh and he could see the top curves of her fucking tits way too easily in that blouse. He needed to focus somewhere else. He wouldn't lie, it was a struggle. "Told 'im you got a boyfriend."

"Yes, I told you that the other night."

"Got one I don't know about?"

"Uh... no?"

"Sounds like you ain't sure. You sure?" Before she could answer, he continued, "Coulda got Coop or Rooster or any of the prospects to pretend to be your boyfriend at those fuckin' 'family get-togethers' to get him off your scent. You told Dawg you had someone sniffin' 'round you, he would've insisted someone be with you durin' those things."

"Jesus, Magnum—or should I call you *Malcolm?*—I'm not having a prospect or anyone from DAMC with me during a work function."

He didn't give a fuck what she called him. It was the other part that needed his attention. "Why not?"

"Because..." Her mouth hung open as she stared straight out of the windshield. "Because they wouldn't fit in with that crowd."

"And you don't want 'em knowin' your pop's DAMC."

She shook her head. "No."

"Yes."

Cait made a face, then sighed. "Okay, yes. Like I told you, they think Paul is my father. It's better they think that way."

Because life was so much fucking better when your daddy was rich and had pull versus when your real daddy was full of tats, wore club colors, rode a badass sled, used to manage a strip club where he met her stepmother, Emma, had a long, scruffy beard and took no shit unless it came from his wife or daughters.

Yeah, life was so much easier when it was clean and neat. And fit society's standards.

Dawg, Magnum and the rest of them did not.

"Fuckin' Caitie," he grumbled, his jaw tight.

Cait flung her hand toward the building they currently couldn't see and then dug her fingers into her hair, yanking it back from her face. "I'm just starting out, Magnum... Christ! I have a long way to go to make decent money and to make a name in this industry. Why the hell would I do anything to handicap that?"

"An' your pop bein' a biker's a handicap." He didn't even bother to make it a question because he knew it was the fucking truth. This was exactly why that goddamn kiss had been a mistake. The one where he wanted to pin her against the wall and fuck her long and hard until she screamed his name, until he staked his claim.

And if she hadn't taken a breath when she did, hadn't broken that fucking kiss when they heard that door slam, he might have done just that and in the end would have been the worst mistake she ever made. Or maybe the second worst after leaving her drink unattended, thinking she could trust the people surrounding her.

Just like she thought she could trust him. Trust him with her secret. Trust him to do the right thing. Trust him to help her and then they both go on their merry fucking way afterward.

"Jesus fuck," he bit off.

She twisted her head toward him and when her eyes hit his, it got him.

It fucking got him.

Right in the chest. Causing an ache so painful he struggled to take his next breath.

"I don't have a problem with my father being a biker, you fucking know that." Her voice was thicker than normal. "I love him. I love my sisters and Emma, too. I also love everyone in the club. Everyone shouts about how they're family. And it's true. Could I have gone to anyone in the club and asked for help? Yes, I could have. But I also know... I don't want to be responsible for..."

She dropped her head and stared at her lap. Her body expanded as she inhaled a ragged breath. And when she turned back to him, those green eyes of hers were shiny and that got him right in the chest, too, pulling him deeper than he already was. A puddle so fucking deep if he ever escaped, he'd never be able to completely scrape off the mud.

Her lower lip trembled, her voice was now thin and on the verge of breaking. "I should've never asked you to help me. It was wrong. But I didn't know what to do."

Fuck. She was showing an emotion he'd never seen from her before.

She got her steel balls from her father, but right now, she was as vulnerable as her youngest sister, Emmalee.

"Caitie," he whispered, that uncomfortable ache swelling to the point he thought it would split open his chest.

"No." She shook her head. "I'm sorry I ever asked you. Sorry I put you in this situation. Just forget about it. I'll handle it."

She unlocked the doors and before she could open hers, he hit the locks again. "Don't you get out of this cage 'til we're done."

Her bottom lip trembled again as she tried to keep her shit together. Seeing her upset guaranteed one thing.

If it was Gallo on that video, he was going to die.

"I came to you by mistake because I panicked and didn't know what to do or how to handle it. I know now that I need to do this on my own."

I came to you by mistake...

"How? How the fuck you gonna handle this?"

Her eyes hit his, and they were no longer teeming with tears, they were hard and focused. "How the fuck are *you* going to handle this?"

He would tell her the truth. A truth that would probably make her father's head explode. A father who managed a fucking gun shop full of weapons and ammo. But he told her anyway. "As if you were Knights' property, Cait."

She stared at him for the longest time, their breathing the only sound heard. Finally, she whispered, "But I'm not."

No, she wasn't. Not now. Maybe not ever.

"I never should've gotten you involved."

"Too fuckin' late."

He caught the twinge of relief that crossed her face. It was there and gone quicker than shit.

"So, now what?"

"Gonna tuck my fuckin' balls between my legs and go to some goddamn retreat at a fuckin' lake I never heard of. Try to keep my goddamn temper and not murder that motherfucker durin' a goddamn motivational speech."

She pressed her lips together *hard* and it took her a while to be able to say, "You don't have to go."

She was dead wrong about that. "The fuck I don't. The fuck if you're goin' somewhere where that motherfucker is for a week without protection."

"I can take Coop, like you said."

Coop would probably fit in better if he shaved that out of control shit off his face and cut his hair, or at least brushed it. He was white, still on the early side of thirty, and if he hid his tats and wore the right clothes, he'd be a more believable boyfriend than Magnum.

But that wasn't ever going to happen. Not on Magnum's watch. And the fuck if Coop was staying in her room at some resort in another state.

"How the fuck you explainin' that to Dawg? Coop disappearin' would raise questions."

Her lips twisted. "Good point."

"Got 'em sometimes."

Her mouth twitched slightly, which made his do the same.

He was glad the threat of tears was long gone because

her being upset made him mental. It shouldn't but it was now a proven fact it did.

He reached out, slid his fingers into the long hair alongside her ear and pulled her toward him. Before he thought twice about it, he pressed his forehead to hers and just breathed for a few heartbeats. "Baby?"

"Yeah?"

She did not fight him calling her that. And that mud at the bottom of that puddle suddenly became bottomless. Muck he might never fucking escape.

"Know all this sucks. Sorry this shit ever fuckin' happened to you. Know you feel you're stuck between a rock an' a hard place. But I'm gonna find a way to move that rock, yeah?"

"I think I'm expecting too much from you and I should've gone to the police."

"Then the shit you were tryin' to avoid woulda happened. I get there are times we gotta avoid goin' at things directly and take the long way around to get where we're goin'. And that's the path we're takin'."

"We?"

"Yeah. I'm all in, Caitie. Gonna find out who the motherfucker is who did that to you and gonna take care of it."

Going to take care of *him*, whoever the fuck he was.

Her fingers spread along his jaw, the tips pressing hard into his cheek. "I don't want you going to jail for me."

"Ain't goin' to jail."

"You promise?" Their faces were so close, her breath whispered over his lips.

He couldn't promise that but he'd do his best not to land in the joint.

But if he had to, he'd do time for her. To get her justice. He'd done time in the past, and, yeah, it fucking sucked. Even so, he'd do it again, if needed. It just needed to be worth it.

"Would you care?" he asked in a whisper.

"You know I would," she whispered back.

"How do I know that, baby?"

She placed a hand firmly against his chest and spread her fingers over his heart. "You know."

You know.

This was dangerous.

You know.

With their foreheads still pressed together and their lips so fucking close...

Her scent...

That fucking skirt that hugged the flare of her hips and thighs.

Her tits. Her smooth, ivory skin that needed his mark.

That silky green fabric like shiny Christmas wrapping paper he wanted to tear off his present...

He wanted to touch her, but he also kept thinking about how someone recently touched her without her wanting it. Shit he'd never do with her because he'd want her to want it just as much as him.

Like that kiss at D's wedding a little over a year ago.

It wasn't a simple kiss. It was like they were trying to absorb each other. Neither wanting it to end until...

He shouldn't even be letting his thoughts go there.

Because it was dangerous.

Not for her.

For him.

Not only because he'd get his dick severed off and shoved down his throat before dying a slow torturous death, but because he had a feeling once he had a real taste of her —more than a kiss—he'd be done. And giving her up would just about be impossible.

But he'd have no choice. She'd want things he couldn't give her.

He'd lived a life, hers was only beginning.

There were things a woman in her twenties would want, if not now, eventually.

This was a good reminder of her age. And his, too.

He was close to the same age as her father. His oldest kid was just a year younger than her.

Christ. "How old are you now?"

"You know exactly how old I am. You've watched me for years. I've watched you, too."

I've watched you, too.

He knew that. He'd felt her eyes on him. In the beginning, he tried to ignore it. Just a teen with a crush, maybe. As she got older, he chalked it up to it turning to lust.

Or maybe wanting someone who was forbidden. A taboo idea to get her blood rushing.

But then there was the kiss...

That fucking kiss...

Something so goddamn simple. Something he'd done a million damn times.

Why had it been any different?

Why had it been so fucking hard to push her away? To gather his shit, to recognize at the time it was a mistake.

Something they both needed to forget.

But he wasn't the only one who hadn't forgotten.

"Magnum." His name on her breath stoked the fire in his gut.

"Just as much a biker as your father. You don't want 'em knowin' Dawg's a biker for whatever reason." He knew the reason. "I'm no different, Caitie. Not gonna change for no one."

He wasn't changing for anyone. That's why he lost his ol' lady a few years back. She kept demanding something he wasn't willing to give her.

She'd finally had enough and split.

The same would happen with Cait.

She had one toe dipped in the life and another whole

foot planted outside of it. If it wasn't for her DNA, she never would've gotten involved with the MC life in the first place.

But DAMC blood ran through her veins, so she was pulled into it—even against her mother and stepfather's wishes. Even with her parents fighting hard against it, and even though she wasn't born into it, the club embraced Cait as soon as Dawg discovered he had a daughter, even almost fifteen years after she took her first breath.

Cait never shied away from it and embraced it as much as she could while managing to hold on to both worlds.

Again—age difference aside—those two worlds were why his thoughts were dangerous. Why what he wanted to do with her in the Camry was fucking stupid.

"Magnum," she breathed.

He squeezed his eyes shut, his fingers fisting tightly in her hair.

She was the daughter of an ally.

A fucking daughter of an ally.

One his club couldn't lose.

They might forgive him for protecting their property but not for stealing it.

He uncurled his fingers and sat back, opening his eyes, seeing the reality of his current situation. Her cheeks a dark pink, her eyes holding a fire that could scald him.

And the outline of her goddamn nipples against that smooth fabric.

His fingers itched to touch them. Even if it was only a light brush to test how hard those tips were. To see how he affected her. To let her know she affected him the same way. He turned away from her and curled them around the steering wheel instead.

He needed to get the fuck out of her cage, and he needed to do it now. "When's the retreat?"

A burn started deep in his gut with the thought of being

with Cait somewhere outside of DAMC and DKMC territory. While he was capable of protecting her himself, she didn't belong to him.

"We leave Sunday, since it's about an eight-hour drive without stopping."

Fuck. That was only a few days away. He gritted his teeth at the thought of what he was getting into. "When's it over?"

"I think Saturday after breakfast, but a lot of people are staying until Sunday morning as a mini get-away with their significant others, since children aren't allowed during this trip."

Significant others. "Means we're sharin' a room."

Since he wasn't looking at her—no, he was fucking staring straight out of the windshield still trying to avoid temptation—he heard her reaction to his words rather than saw it.

"I... It's..."

"Gonna hafta work," he finished the sentence for her. He ground his molars together, already not looking forward to making it actually fucking work. It might be the second hardest thing he had to do in his life.

The first one was the day he finally gave up the fight for his kids. When he had no choice but to walk away or face more jail time by breaking the Protection from Abuse order.

That day fucking killed him.

That day was the darkest day in his goddamn life.

He wouldn't go through that shit again. He would not have his own blood ripped from him, taken against his will, and then poisoned against him with lies.

Never fucking again.

Cait squeezing his thigh had him shoving the door open and scrambling out of the cage, almost cracking his head on the door jamb.

Once he was out of the vehicle and sucking in air that

did not smell of Cait, he leaned into the open doorway. "Sunday. Dirty Dick's. Takin' your cage."

She pinned her lips together and reached for the passenger door handle.

"And Caitie..."

She glanced back at him.

"I'm drivin'."

Chapter Four

With his fingers fisted in Cait's hair, the pull against her scalp sent a shiver through her, making her already aching nipples pebble even harder.

His lips claimed hers, his tongue took control. She couldn't get enough of his deep grunts with each even deeper thrust. Her fingers dug into his ass as the muscles bunched and flexed, his knees buried in her bed as he drove fast and hard. Filling her, stretching her.

She lifted her hips with each thrust as much as she could with him pinning her to the bed, a crushing weight she welcomed.

This was what she wanted. Him to claim her. The same as she wanted that day in a hidden corner of the commercial kitchen that divided the DAMC's church and The Iron Horse Roadhouse. That moment they both allowed themselves a taste of what they both desired but avoided.

This morning they weren't avoiding it. They were letting it consume them.

Each powerful drive brought them closer to the point of no return.

With one broad hand planted in the mattress by her

head, the other cupped her breast and squeezed so hard, she whimpered into his mouth.

That's it. That's what I want. Give me more of that.

Each forceful pound drove the air from her lungs and into his mouth. And not once since he slid his cock into her had he broken that kiss.

His size made her feel tiny but not helpless. Everything he did to her made her feel worshipped. Every part of her he touched became marked.

She squeezed around him tightly and threw her head back, finally freeing their mouths so she could gasp for air.

And then it happened.

Her climax burst from her center, making every nerve crackle, every muscle ripple. Then with a last low, long grunt, he exploded, filling her, marking her as his inside as well.

Erasing anybody else's touch who came before him.

Because now there was no one else.

No one else existed before him. No one else would exist after him.

"Baby," she heard soft and low in her ear.

"Yeah?" she said on a breath, her muscles still twitching around him. The satisfaction settling deep within her bones making her smile softly.

She didn't want him to move. She didn't want him to leave her. She didn't want to lose his heavy weight. He felt good right where he was. Perfect even. Deep within her as if they were one.

Connected like that, they were.

His deep, soothing, familiar voice moved through her. "Need to wake up."

Her eyes popped open and she immediately squeezed them shut again. "Shit," she breathed as reality smacked her in the forehead and burrowed into her chest.

Her own fingers filled her, not Magnum. Her own

thumb pressed against her swollen, sensitive clit. Her own hand possessed her breast.

She had caused her own explosive orgasm, not him.

But if he was as good as she imagined him to be...

Damn, that was such a realistic wet dream, or whatever it was. They were leaving for Lake George this morning and tonight they would share a room. If this dream returned?

So what if it did? And he was close by. If she had the opportunity to turn her fantasy into reality, would she ignore it? Would he?

She thought he was going to kiss her in the car the other day. It had been so close to happening she had practically tasted it.

He hadn't and he just about jumped out of his skin when she touched his thigh afterward. She never saw the man move so fast.

To escape her. To give them space.

He had wanted her. That kiss in the club kitchen... She had no doubt to how much he had wanted her that day. His cock had been hot, hard and long as it pressed heavy and thick against her stomach.

Maybe things had changed for him. Maybe they changed after she told him what happened to her.

Maybe.

But Magnum didn't seem to be that sort of man.

Things probably should've changed for her after what happened, after what she saw on that video. But she had watched and wanted Magnum for so long...

She still did.

So, fuck that guy. The asshole in the video who stole from her. Who stole her choice to say no.

She would not let him steal anything else. Like her desire for Magnum.

She would not let that man break her.

Not now. Not ever.

She slipped her hand from her panties and turned her head to glance at the clock.

She needed to get her ass in gear. All the employees were meeting in the parking lot at work to carpool and caravan up to Lake George. Except for Hank Gallo, of course, who was taking a private helicopter north. He would arrive Monday morning before the retreat's kickoff breakfast where he was the keynote speaker.

When Nate, Drew and their sister Natalie arrived? Cait didn't know. And when it came to Nate, she didn't care.

What she did care about was, she needed to shower and had two stops to make before joining that caravan of co-workers heading to the Adirondacks.

The first one to get really, really strong coffee.

The second was Dirty Dick's to pick up her roommate for the week.

She had no idea how him coming along would help with finding out who was in the video or how to get rid of it. Or even if that was his motive for going.

But she guessed she'd find out soon enough.

———

WITH HIS HEAD and face now shaved smooth, the hot water sluiced off Magnum's scrubbed-clean body, his cock hard and throbbing as his fingers circled and squeezed the root, making the veins in both his forearm and erection stand out. His balls hung heavy in the steamy heat and blood filled his dick, making it an even deeper dark purple, the color of eggplant, the head a lighter pink-tinged brown. The shower washed away the precum as fast as it beaded at the very tip as he squirted more soap along his length and began to stroke.

His head dropped forward and his lips parted as his heart and lungs began to pump as fast as his hand. He imagined Caitie being this tight, this hot, this slick when he plunged inside her.

He closed his eyes, water dripping off his eyelashes and onto his cheeks, as he pictured her beneath him. Her flushed ivory skin showing every mark he gave her to claim her. As his. As Dark Knights' property.

Her nipples were swollen and peaked, now a darker pink and shiny from his lips, his teeth and his tongue. Her mouth opened, the noises coming from her making him lose his goddamn mind.

Her body arced off the bed, those diamond hard tips brushing against his chest as she tried to get closer, begging for more. He gave her everything she wanted, everything he had and he got the same in return.

Slick. Hot. Wanting. Welcoming.

Squeezing him. Taking him as deep as she could.

He dropped his head a little more and captured her bottom lip within his teeth, biting softly enough for her to want it, hard enough for her to feel it.

The flush that began at her chest traveled up her throat and into her cheeks making it almost impossible for him to hold back. His brain told him to slow down, his balls screamed at him to let go.

He squirted more liquid soap into his right palm and switched the position of his grip, so his thumb was closest to his body instead of his little finger. He dropped the body wash to the shower floor, slammed his left palm against the stall wall, leaned into it for support and...

His hips pumped, his ass clenched, his thigh and ab muscles tensed, his neck strained and bowed as he imagined slamming relentlessly into her soft, pink, *wet-as-fuck* pussy, not giving her even a second to take a breath, just forcing the air out of her with each thrust. Her nails ripped down the skin of his back to his ass and his name came out in broken syllables as she encouraged him to take her *there*.

With one last powerful thrust, she fell, he fell. And he came deep inside her, filling her, knowing with satisfaction she was now his.

And nothing and no one would change that.

———

Magnum released a low growl. Every-fucking-one in the caravan was driving like they were eighty years old, senile and had cataracts. For the most part, while on his sled, he didn't mind cruising at a decent clip. In a cage, all fucking bets were off. Especially when he pulled his '69 Camaro SS 427 out of storage and beat that bitch like it was a naughty girl begging for a spanking.

But they weren't in his big block muscle car. Fuck no. They were in Cait's Toyota Camry, doing the fucking speed limit in a line of just as boring, fuel efficient vehicles.

The large coffee Cait had shown up with when she arrived at Dirty Dick's had been so damn strong, he was now wired and itching to do something, anything, other than drive that wimpy 2.5L four-cylinder. Dawg should've at least sprang for the 3.5L so the damn vehicle could get out of its own way.

He didn't know if he could take eight-plus hours of this. And it didn't help that they stopped on the hour, every hour, for a goddamn piss break.

Right now he was pretending the steering wheel was the neck of the driver in the lead vehicle and that driver was into autoerotic asphyxiation.

"I'm not sure what you aim to accomplish by coming along on this retreat."

His eyes slid to her. The day was already hot as fuck for the last week in September, so Cait had shown up wearing khaki shorts that showed off her long fucking bare legs. Legs that called to him to touch to see if her skin was as soft and smooth as they looked. If she was his woman, he'd be driving with one hand on the wheel and the other on one of her thighs. But she wasn't, so instead the sight tortured the fuck out of him.

She was too goddamn close but also too far away due to various reasons that he needed to keep front and center in his brain.

Her blonde hair was loose and natural, not stiff and styled. Her face clean of any makeup and, for once, he'd noticed how blonde her eyelashes were. She must normally use that black shit on them. The shit that smudged and gave women raccoon eyes when they teared up from taking his cock all the way to the back of their throat.

He cleared his own throat and shifted in the seat that was not built for a man of his size.

There was a reason his road name was Magnum.

He was not small.

Anywhere.

Some big men had tiny dicks. He was not one of them. The universe had blessed him with being proportionate *everywhere*. Made it hard to find boots and gloves that fit well, but he managed.

But he wasn't sure if he could manage driving Cait's cage for another six or more hours. Thank fuck it wasn't a Yaris. He'd be crippled for life if he could even wedge his ass in there.

"Magnum."

"Yeah," he grunted, now trying to keep his eyes on the minivan with the stick figure family on the back window in front of him. Dad, mom, three kids in various sizes, a baby in diapers, four cats, a goldfish bowl, a turtle, and one dog. Poor dog. Probably tried to escape that madhouse whenever it could.

"I asked you a question."

"Wasn't a question."

Silence. A few seconds later, a long sigh filled the interior. "Do I need to form it as a question?"

"If you need a fuckin' answer."

"Somebody's grumpy."

He hadn't been sleeping well ever since Cait showed up at Dirty Dick's and fucked up his brain with her problem. He had a hard time turning that shit off. He imagined she did, too. "That a question?"

"It's a fact. No answer needed."

He grunted again.

"Okay, Mr. Grumpypants, I'll preface any question with the warning 'question' and then proceed to ask it. Fair?" From the corner of his eye, he saw her lift her hand in his direction. "Question: Is that fair?"

He grunted again.

"Besides English, I understand biker grunt-grunt, so I take that as a clear yes."

He pressed his lips together to smother his grin.

He really wanted to jerk the cage off the road, pull her into his lap and kiss the fuck out of her until her lips were swollen, her eyes were heated and her pussy dripping wet. But then he'd want to rip off her shorts and have her ride his cock until they both came.

Unfortunately, there wasn't enough room between him and the steering wheel to do that. Plus, the pigs frowned upon sex in a cage on the berm of the highway. And anyway, today was not a day where he wanted to be pepper sprayed, dragged over pavement and loose stone to an awaiting cruiser, only to be hog-tied due to his "threatening size and dangerous demeanor," and secured in the back while they checked the "white girl" to make sure she wasn't an unwilling participant.

Yeah, that.

Then twenty minutes later he'd be released with a fake apology, a firm warning, given a bottle of water to clean out his eyes—when he knew from experience water only made it worse—and told to move it along even though he couldn't see shit.

His jaw shifted as he ground his teeth.

That was one of the few times he'd let a woman drive while he was in a cage. Normally if a woman didn't like his rule? Then she could hoof it.

A lot of women came into Dirty Dick's thinking nabbing a biker within her claws would be exciting. Or something to check off her bucket list. In fact, he'd found with a lot of bitches of the pale variety, a black biker checked two off the list.

After getting what she came for from one or more of his brothers, if they didn't understand the life, if they didn't understand their place within the life, they did not stick around.

He'd seen a few power walk out of the bar, never to be seen again. They probably pointed their BMW's back to their middle to upper class neighborhoods, took a scalding hot shower, and then decided to burn their bucket list.

The woman in the seat next to him would, most likely, drive one of those expensive Beamers one day, the difference being she wasn't afraid to get her hands dirty with the likes of him.

However, she knew she'd need to keep those lives separate, like she did now by pretending her stepdaddy was her real daddy. Rich, white and well connected. As opposite as can be to Magnum, who—besides his SS 427 and his custom Harley, which had both set him back a whack—only lived a basic life, which consisted of protecting the club and his brothers, overseeing the bar, and making sure he had a roof over his head.

He didn't need much more than that.

Maybe warm pussy not of the imaginary kind.

He pursed his lips. No maybe about it.

However, as much as he wanted Caitie to fill that spot, she couldn't. Her stepdaddy would not be the only daddy unhappy about Magnum doing his daughter. Paul was actually the least of his worries.

"Magnum," he heard groaned from the seat next to him. It wasn't the kind of groan he wanted coming from Cait's lips.

He grunted again.

"Asked you a question."

"You *preface* it with 'question?'"

"Yes!"

"Hit me with it again." He wasn't going to admit he hadn't been paying attention because that usually pissed off women.

It was one thing to piss off a woman and be able to walk away from them while they were bitching. It was another when you were stuck in a cage with them and had nowhere to escape.

And, even worse, a long fucking ride ahead of them.

He'd rather get kicked in the nuts.

Because most women, once pissed, sank her teeth into whatever got her panties stuck in her crack and didn't let it go for days. He'd learned that lesson the hard way, just like the one about sex in a fucking cage on the side of the highway.

He was a fast learner.

But then being tased, pepper-sprayed or getting your balls punted into next week would teach you right quick.

Cait's muttered, "Holy shit," sank into his caffeine-wired brain. Now he was the one who needed to piss.

He glanced at the clock. He expected everyone's turn signals to start synchronize blinking in approximately five minutes. Then the long line of vehicles would turn into a gas station or truck stop and a similar long line would form outside the his and hers shitters.

"Next stop I'm pissin' in the bushes and continuin' north without 'em."

"But—"

"Seriously, baby, can't take much more of this shit. Don't mind a formation durin' a club run, but this mommy mobile shit's gonna kill me. Want me to die before we even get there?"

"Sounds a bit dramatic."

"Ain't dramatic if it's true. Vehicle's got GPS. Can find our own way. This don't gotta be the re-creation of a wagon train followin' the fuckin' Oregon Trail."

A giggle slipped from her lips and he smiled at the windshield at the sound of it.

"Question: What do you know about the Oregon Trail?"

"All I gotta know is it sucked. Like this does. So, we pull in, I piss, you make your excuses and we split. Got it?"

"Got it. I'm tired of staring at Laura's stick figure family anyway."

No shit, she wasn't the only one.

Then he did a thing, which afterward he realized he shouldn't have done. He reached out, put his hand on her knee and curled his fingers around the warm, smooth skin. Her hand didn't push his away, it settled over top of his instead, her fingers taking up the empty space between his. Her hand was small enough to let their fingers fit together like a perfect puzzle.

He wondered if she noticed the same.

He let himself have that moment and a few more.

"Question: Why are you coming with me, Mag? What do you expect to get out of this?"

If he wasn't careful, a whole lot of hurt.

If he was, some answers.

"Biggest reason, makin' sure no one fucks with you, Caitie. 'Til we know who it is, he's a big fuckin' unknown.

That leaves you vulnerable. Gonna be with the same group of people you were with that night, yeah?"

"Yeah," she whispered, her fingers squeezing his.

He turned his hand over and intertwined their fingers. "No one's gonna fuck with you this week, baby. No one. Got your back." And while he was watching her back, he was going to be paying attention and watch that Nate fucker closely. Seeing how others interacted with her, too, on the slim chance it wasn't him.

But that fucker not only showed an interest, he'd had the opportunity to take the advantage.

And that shit boiled Magnum's blood.

He wasn't sure if his hands would be dirty at the end of the week, but if they were, a thirty-two-mile-long lake with some areas being one hundred and ninety-six feet deep and including over a hundred and fifty islands, would be the perfect place for a rapist to disappear. He'd done some research and saved a map of the lake to his phone. He'd also picked what might be a good spot, if needed. He wasn't sure how he'd get to that location, but he'd figure it out if he had to.

Wouldn't be the first time he'd made something or someone disappear.

He did what he had to do to protect himself, his club and his brothers. He just was careful about doing it and never talked about it, either. Assholes who bragged about shit they did, ended up regretting those loose lips down the road.

But he was hoping one particular asshole would run his fucking mouth. Magnum would just need the opportunity and to come up with a way to get Gallo talking.

Right now, he had no fucking clue how he would do that.

But he would.

For Caitie.

The right blinker of the minivan in front of him began to flash. With that, he reluctantly peeled his fingers from Cait's and followed the long line of vehicles into the rest stop.

If this is what it was like to be an average working sheep, working a nine-to-five, doing your best to blend in with society, working long hours hoping you didn't die before you got a chance to retire, blindly following a well-beaten path, he was sure fucking glad he lived the life he had.

Wasn't perfect. Never would be perfect.

But it was his.

Chapter Five

THE SPRAWLING Black Mountain Resort was tucked along the shoreline of a huge cove on the east side of Lake George. It was, for the most part, quiet, and definitely beautiful. The foliage hadn't started changing yet, but being north of Pennsylvania, it would start soon. Cait was sure it would be a stunning display of color.

Another stunning display of color was Magnum as he stood on the balcony of their room, staring out over the lake. The setting sun beyond him gave his dark skin a glow. From where she stood inside, his back blocked most of the view of the lake since it was just that broad, but it did give her a great view of him.

It was weird seeing him without his cut and he probably felt naked without it.

When she'd picked him up early that morning at Dirty Dick's he'd been wearing a long-sleeved Henley. As soon as they had checked in, had their bags delivered to the room, and grabbed a quick bite to eat in the café, he was jonesing to change out of that shirt because he was "sweatin' his goddamn balls off." The unseasonably warm day was a good reason why she was wearing shorts. But now that the sun was beginning to set, the temp was quickly dropping.

He'd pulled on an old, worn T-shirt that hugged his bulk —she assumed in case any of her co-workers saw him— before stepping out onto the private balcony. That tee covered the club colors tattooed onto his back and the random tats on his chest and stomach, as well as some of the tats on his upper arms. He most likely suffered through wearing the Henley to cover all of those and during this week would probably continue to wear shirts that would cover him to his wrists.

She knew why he would do so and appreciated the effort, even though she hadn't asked it of him.

It was hard not to stare at him a little while ago as he walked around their room without a shirt to cool off. His torso was thick and broad, his nipples almost black. He had a little bit of hair on his chest, which was connected to a dark line that ran from the small center patch down his belly, past his navel and disappeared into his jeans.

Studying that narrow trail, she had licked her lips, tempted to follow it with her mouth. Or at least her fingers.

He'd done his best to ignore her as he assessed the room situation.

The room situation.

The room reminded her of one in a bed and breakfast, where there was a separate bedroom large enough for a single king bed, a decent sized bathroom that included a single-person Jacuzzi tub and a small sitting area with a large screen TV, a desk and a couch. What would normally be considered cozy almost felt too confined with a man as large as Magnum in it.

His presence alone was overwhelming.

Because of that, she wasn't sure how this *room situation* would shake out. He'd thrown his bag at the end of the couch after pulling out the T-shirt, then he ripped off his

Henley and did a quick tour of the room bare-chested while Cait had done a quick tour of his half-naked body.

She took a deep breath and walked through the wide-open sliders and settled into one of the dark green Adirondack chairs to his right that faced the serene lake.

"Daddy Gallo pays for all this shit?"

His voice was low but rough and it did all kinds of naughty things to her. But then, those things would also occur just by his presence alone.

He'd always fascinated her, and he'd caught her attention the first time she'd seen him, even though she knew he was off-limits. One reason being she was only fifteen at the time. Her teenage girl dreams had become very interesting after that.

"From what I heard, he knows the owners and rents the whole resort for a week every year. He probably gets a great deal since it's after most of the summer tourists and fair-weather fans head back home but before the leaf peepers show up."

He turned his head from where he stood at the balcony railing.

The man had a strong, beautiful profile, but when he looked directly at her, as if he *saw* her, it always made her heart skip a beat.

"Leaf peepers?"

"People who come up for the changing leaves." She gripped the chair's armrests as his gaze ran over her, not missing anything. She did her best to keep her breathing steady, though her nipples decided to be traitors. And since his gaze hesitated there longer than anywhere else, she figured he noticed, too.

"They also change in PA," he finally mumbled, sounding distracted.

"Later than here. Plus, look at that view. Imagine it with the mountains and shoreline full of fire."

"Full of fire," he murmured, now staring at her lips.

"The colorful leaves," she clarified, her heart thumping heavily in her chest.

"Knew what you meant, Caitie."

Her nails dug into the painted wood armrests. "I wish you wouldn't call me that," she said softly.

He lifted one brow. "Why?"

"It makes me feel like I'm twelve."

A muscle jumped in his cheek. "Hardly twelve. That's for fuckin' sure." With one hand still holding onto the balcony railing he turned toward her, the disappearing sun now hitting his features. "Caitie'll be mine."

Well, that didn't help slow her racing pulse. "The name or me?"

His brow furrowed and he turned back to face the lake.

"Since you've been standing out here for a while now, I assume you've thought about the *room situation*." She air-quoted the last two words even though he was no longer facing her.

He grunted what Cait recognized as a "yeah" in Neanderthal speak.

She wasn't kidding when she told him earlier she was fluent in grunt-grunt. Bikers learned to grunt before they learned to talk or walk. All the DAMC boys were already doing it since they parroted their fathers.

She assumed any sons born to the Knights were the same way.

An intense and sudden heat swirled through her as she stared at Magnum and imagined him holding a newborn to his bare chest.

Holy shit, where did that come from?

A bead of sweat popped out on her forehead as her ovaries went into overdrive. Squeezing her thighs together, she shifted in the chair, ripped her gaze from him and directed it toward a tiny island in the middle of the wide cove.

Her heart was now not only racing, her breathing had shallowed, and an invisible hand squeezed her throat.

"Caitie."

His gruff voice shot a shiver down her back and her nipples instantly tightened and ached.

Holy shit, this *room situation* was going to be a disaster.

She wanted him so badly she could taste it. He didn't hide the fact he wanted her, too. But he was so right. If they gave in to their desires, a war between the clubs could break out, destroying the hard-earned and welcomed peace currently occurring.

She would not be the cause of it.

"Caitie."

Her gaze sliced from the island so small it only consisted of a few boulders, rocks and maybe a dozen trees, to the man she needed to keep at arm's length. His arm, not hers, since his was longer.

"Malcolm," she said in response.

His big body rocked on his boot heels and both hands tightened on the metal railing.

"I need to get used to calling you that, right?" she explained, sounding way more breathless than she should. "For this week?"

Even sitting to his side, she could see his eyes shut, remain that way for a few breaths before he reopened them. "Right," he grunted. When he turned, crossed his arms over his chest—clearly closing himself off from her—and leaned back against the railing, she worried if it would hold his weight.

"Please don't lean against that."

"It's good."

"No, we don't know that. Just... don't." If that railing gave way...

He frowned, his eyebrows pulling together, and he settled with a soft grunt into the other Adirondack chair which actually flexed under his big bulk.

At least if that collapsed, he wouldn't have far to fall. Unlike the balcony railing since they were on the third—and top—floor of one of the many buildings scattered along the property.

One corner of his beautiful lips pulled up as he planted his boots wide, giving his massive thighs some space. "Worried about me." It wasn't a question.

"These buildings aren't new, Mag— Malcolm. We don't know when those railings were last replaced."

"Worried about me," he repeated, satisfaction coloring his words.

Whatever. "It would suck trying to explain to Dad why your brains got splattered against the concrete at a resort I just so happened to be at."

The other corner of his lips pulled up, creating a smile. "Worried about me."

Instead of rolling her eyes, which she was about to do, she wanted to roll around in his rich, sexy laughter and cover herself with that carefree sound like a dog rolling in a scent. It had come from deep within his belly.

She wasn't sure if she ever heard him laugh before.

His dark eyes had a glint to them that made her breath catch. Maybe that spark was just from the waning light.

"What did you want?" she asked.

That light in his eyes dimmed, his smile fell, and his laughter became a memory.

Damn. She had made him happy then took it away in a flash. She wanted to see more of the first and a lot less of the second.

"That's a loaded fuckin' question."

Yes, it was.

"Need to tell you somethin' before you go signin' us up

for any kinda activities or whatever the fuck's goin' on this week."

"Like the karaoke we're going to sing? I'm already picking out some great songs for us to duet together. I'm leaning toward Captain and Tennille's *Muskrat Love*. Though it's not technically a duet since the Captain never spoke, we can easily make it one." She smothered a giggle-snort at his expression.

"Don't even know what the fuck that is."

"Trust me, it's a classic."

"Yeah, okay, ain't singin' shit. You wanna sing, I'll watch you sing. But just remember, I won't be the only one watchin' you."

Her lips flattened out. "Thanks for the reminder."

One of his shoulders lifted and fell heavily. "Need to stay vigilant, Cait. Some asshole drugged you and..." He opened his mouth and nothing but air came out. His face turned to stone. "And... taped that shit. Sent it to you for some unknown reason. 'Til we know why, know who—besides bein' a sick fuck—you need to be wary. Here to help you with that but can't do certain shit."

Her eyes hit his and held. "Like what?" What couldn't this man do?

"Can't swim."

They were staying at a huge lake for the next five-plus days and he couldn't swim? She forced her dropped jaw to close, since he probably wouldn't appreciate that reaction. All the activities, other than the speakers, would be based around the lake.

Shit.

Maybe she should have brought Coop. She turned her head and glanced through the open sliding glass doors into the room.

Nope. That wouldn't have worked, either. Coop was

easy-going but he'd also expressed some interest when no one was looking. And up here, no one would be looking.

"Any water shit's a big no fuckin' go. No swimmin', no water skiin', no tubin', no flyin' in the air attached like a kite to the back of one of those boats. Fuck it, no boats at all. Land, I'm good. Water's a no-go."

"Oh, we're definitely going on a boat. There's a sunset dinner cruise I'm told we shouldn't miss." She had taken a quick peek at the week's agenda that had been emailed out last Friday. She'd been looking forward to a lot of the activities because she loved the water. She had grown up with a large pool in her backyard and spent all summer in it when she wasn't at summer camp, which also had a lake and a pool. She was usually the first one in and the last one out.

"Gonna miss it."

Oh no. "I can go on my own."

His head spun toward her. "Let's get this shit straight right fuckin' now. Ain't goin' nowhere on your own, Cait. Gonna be your fuckin' shadow this week. Nobody's touchin' you, no-fuckin-body's spikin' your shit..." He stared over the lake again, his jaw clenching and unclenching. After a few moments, he asked tightly, "How big's the fuckin' boat?"

"Big. It's a large steamboat. Bigger than a restaurant."

"Won't tip, right?"

"With you standing at the railing? It could."

He tilted his head toward her again and gave her a look. "Think you're funny."

She shrugged and smirked. "I don't *think*, I *know* I'm funny."

His eyes became two dark flames. "Caitie."

She ignored the way her name on his lips in that baritone voice made butterflies spread their wings in her belly. She needed to keep them both on track. And that track shouldn't be headed toward the king-sized bed not far from the balcony they were sitting on. No matter how badly both of them wanted it.

"Does it bother you that you can't swim?" He didn't seem embarrassed at all about it.

He probably gave zero fucks on what people thought of him. Her gaze swept down his tattooed arms. Though, he had covered his tats to hide them from her co-workers. But he did that for her, not for himself. His dark skin tone and his size made him stand out enough with the crowd she worked with.

Now that she thought about it, the workforce at the Gallo agency wasn't very diverse.

Huh.

His answer pulled her out of her wandering thoughts. "Nope. Just stay out of water and I'm good."

"But what if you fall in?"

"Either drown or learn to swim real fuckin' quick. But since I'd probably drop to the bottom like a concrete block, doubt I'd have time to learn."

That thought scared her. "Maybe you should wear a life vest any time you're near the water."

One eyebrow cocked. "Think they got one my size?"

"No, but I bet they have some boat bumpers down at the dock. We can tie some of those around your waist." The picture of him having large bumpers strapped to his middle made a giggle escape her before she could smother it.

"Don't know what the fuck a boat bumper is and sounds like I don't wanna know."

"Come here," she encouraged, getting to her feet and going to the railing.

The chair creaked—probably in relief—as he pushed to his feet and moved to her.

His body heat hit her back as he stepped even closer behind her.

She leaned over the balcony to where she could just see

the resort's dock and she pointed. Her words got caught in her throat as his big hands spanned her waist, holding her securely.

Maybe now it was he who was worried about her falling to her death if the balcony railing gave way.

She cleared her throat, heat sweeping up her neck and making her cheeks warm. "See those blue things along the dock and tied to that boat? White ones, too?"

The grunt he released in answer moved her hair enough to tickle her ear.

She pressed her hands over his as she straightened. When she turned to face him, he didn't back away, nor did he release her waist. "Did you see them?"

His eyes weren't looking at the dock or any bumpers. They were focused on her.

"Malcolm..."

He slowly closed his eyes at his real name and then reopened them just as slowly. His wide nostrils flared even more, then she noticed exactly when his dark eyes turned from heated to troubled.

"Saw 'em, baby."

She didn't know what she liked more. The fact he wanted to be the only one to call her Caitie? Or when he called her baby.

Both were dangerous.

Especially when he stood so close while touching her. She pressed one hand to his stomach and followed its rise and fall as they did nothing but stand there and breathe.

The squeal of the sliders opening in the room next door snapped them both out of whatever trance they had fallen into. He twisted, taking her with him, then used his hands on her waist to push her inside, following closely behind.

When she turned back toward him, he gently pushed her away with a hand to her belly, giving them space and shaking his head. "Worried about me dyin' 'cause of that railin'. That would be instant. Touchin' you would cause me to die, too. But not instant. Fuck no. It'd be slow and torturous by Mercy's hand. And I'd rather go fuckin' walk into that lake without wearing those fuckin' boat bumpers than have him play his sick fuckin' games with me."

"You don't think—"

"Don't wanna know, Caitie. Seen some of the shit he's done. Don't wanna be on the receivin' end of that."

She didn't want him to be, either.

He moved farther into the room, staring at the couch. "This room situation... Gonna take the couch, you get the bed. Keep the bedroom door closed when you're in there. The bathroom door closed when you're in there. Wear no less than what you're wearin' now when we're in here." He pointed one thick finger to the floor at his feet.

"Shouldn't matter what I wear," she murmured.

He spun on her. "Cait, normally would say you're fuckin' right. Now, I'm not. Hangin' by a fuckin' thread here. Problem is, I make a move, you ain't sayin' no. You want it as much as me. Ain't smart, so I need to resist makin' that move. You walkin' around the room in some silky fuckin' nightie or whatever, ain't gonna help me resist. You like my touch, I like touchin' you. That's a problem."

It was only a problem because he was making it a problem.

No.

No, he was right. He knew the tension and the issues it would cause. They both did.

And honestly, it pissed her off that she couldn't have what she wanted. Instead, who she didn't want forced himself on her.

Life was so damn unfair sometimes.

She wanted the man who stood before her. The biker who talked roughly, cursed a lot, was covered in tattoos, smoked pot, sometimes drank too much, and could be violent when required since that was his job. He was no-nonsense, said only what he meant, took no shit and would be fiercely loyal.

Everyone else expected her to be interested in a man like Nate Gallo. A seemingly polite man who wore expensive suits and watches, worked out in a gym— though, not enough to actually become as strong or big as Magnum— held a "respectable job" in his father's agency, had a lot of family money due to that agency and got "respect"— whether real or fake—from his peers. He also knew how to play society's game.

Magnum didn't give a shit about society or games.

Nate Gallo was considered "put together." Unlike what the world saw in Magnum. A rough and tough *grab-the-world-by-the-balls-and-squeeze-them*, tattooed "thug."

He knew her past, where she came from, who she grew up with. He also knew her family, at least on the DAMC side, and heard about her family on her mother's side.

She knew nothing about him. Where he came from, how he was raised, who raised him, or why he was who he was.

What little she knew about him had come from the DAMC sisterhood, some by eavesdropping on her father's conversations with his club brothers, and the rest from watching the man every chance she had gotten. Which wasn't often, but if she heard the Knights would be at a DAMC function, she made sure to be there.

Now she had him all to herself, away from the DAMC, away from his club, too, they could simply be Cait and Malcolm.

The only problem was, when they went back home, they'd go back to being Dawg's daughter and Magnum, the Dark Knights' Sergeant at Arms.

And if something happened between the two of them

while they were here, would they be able to forget it ever happened once they drove away?

Even if Magnum could, she wasn't sure she could. And that made the whole thing even more frustrating.

Even if she said, "Hey, Mag, how about you bang my brains out this week and once I drop you back off at Dirty Dick's, we'll pretend nothing ever happened?" she didn't think he'd agree.

She also knew the age difference between them bothered him. He'd mentioned it after the kiss they shared at Diesel's wedding. He'd mentioned it again the other day.

Did it bother her? She didn't care what his age was. No one else should care, either, since they were both consenting adults. And it wasn't like she was barely eighteen and he was sixty. She had recently turned twenty-five and he was knocking on forty-one's back door.

And, anyway, they weren't talking marriage or having babies, or even doing anything more than hooking up and having fun, right?

She closed her eyes and once again pictured Magnum with an infant cradled against his chest. He'd probably fiercely protect his children.

"Caitie, tell me you heard me."

Her eyes popped open. "I heard you. I'll ask around for a prairie dress, knee high socks and a bonnet." What was supposed to be funny, fell painfully flat. "I understand your worry about my father, but do you think he'd have a hard time with us if I wasn't sixteen years younger than you?"

His expression turned grim. "Don't know. Probably the biggest reason but not the only one."

She considered the other possibilities. "My dad wouldn't care you're black."

Magnum tilted his head, his brown eyes searching. "You sure?"

She would be extremely disappointed in her father if he

did. She really doubted that would be a problem since she'd never seen any signs of Dawg being a racist. The DAMC wasn't even all white since Crow was Native American. They were more diverse than the Knights who only had black members.

Now, the Knights' ol' ladies were a different story. From what Cait had seen, they were all colors of the rainbow. They liked a variety of women.

"My dad also wouldn't care you're a biker."

One thick brow rose. "Again, you sure?"

"He's one." That would be hypocritical if he did.

"Yeah, Caitie, he's one. Don't mean he don't want better for his daughters."

She had no doubt Dawg wanted that. For all three of them. But still... "Do you think someone like Nate Gallo is better than someone like you?"

He grunted. "Need to ask that?"

"I don't want to be with someone who would judge my own father or my family. And when I say family, I mean the club."

"But you're afraid of the people you work with judgin'."

"I'm not the one who introduced you as Malcolm. I'm not the one who told you to wear a long-sleeve shirt in sweltering weather."

"No, but you don't want 'em knowin' who your pop is. You said it, Cait. Heard it. Think they'd be any less judgmental if they knew your 'boyfriend' was a biker? That we can hide. Can't hide the fact I got dark brown skin."

"And that shouldn't matter."

"Right. Shouldn't. Remains to be seen. Hadn't had much interaction with any of 'em yet. Did notice Gallo don't hire folks much different from himself."

She couldn't argue now that she'd noticed it, too.

"This world... this small world you work in is just a small piece of a bigger one, Caitie. That's a fact. 'Cause of who you are and what you look like, you have no fuckin' clue. You're in a bubble."

"I'm not in a bubble!"

"You're in a goddamn bubble. You didn't put yourself there, but the world did."

"Then I need to pop that bubble."

"Not with me you don't."

She took a step back as he ripped his T-shirt over his head, threw it on the couch, grabbed her wrist and tugged her into the bedroom. He didn't stop until they were standing in front of a full-length mirror. He pulled her in front of him, facing the mirror, and held onto her shoulders, forcing her to look at the two of them together.

The physical difference between them was startling.

"Look," he grumbled. "We're so goddamn different. Yeah, it's our age. Yeah, it's our skin. But look beyond that."

"You said I was property of the DAMC."

"You are."

"Then there's no difference."

"You denied it."

She couldn't argue that, either.

"You got a whole goddamn life ahead of you, Cait. A good career. Eventually a family, kids. You can have it all. With me? What you fuckin' see in that mirror's all you'd fuckin' get."

"There's nothing wrong with that."

His fingertips pressed harder into her shoulders. "Lotta folk wouldn't agree with you. Includin' Dawg. For him, the sun rises and sets on you. You were my daughter, I'd want better for you, too."

"But—"

"But nothin'. He's a good fuckin' man, Cait. He's gonna want to make sure you're on the right path. He's the kind of man who's gonna want grandbabies. He's the kind of man who'll wanna make sure you're financially secure. He's gonna wanna man who can give you the fuckin' world because *he* wants you to have the world, somethin' he didn't have himself 'til Emma. 'Til you. 'Til Lily and Emmalee. You are his fuckin' world. You're his baby girl no matter how fuckin' old you get. You get that?"

Yes, she got it. She really did. It was one reason she never wanted anyone judging him. He might be a rough-looking biker on the outside, but on the inside, her father had a heart of gold. She saw it the first time she met him almost eleven years ago in that diner for their first supervised visitation.

Her mother had been forced by the courts to tell Cait who her real father was and to admit Paul was her stepfather. She remembered the fear, the betrayal and the shock of finding out the truth. Her mother never said anything nice about Dawg. Not one fucking thing, which made her even more scared about meeting him.

The judge had left it up to Cait whether Dawg was awarded regular visitation—at first supervised, then eventually unsupervised—after that initial meeting because her mother and stepfather kept fighting it. And they had the money to do so. Unlike Dawg.

But that day... That day she met him, he didn't hide anything. He wore his cut proudly and he told her about his life and asked about hers up to that very moment. He had been completely honest with her. That day changed her life completely.

When she had decided she wanted a relationship with her biological father, it was because she could see past the exterior the world saw and saw what really counted. The same way she saw Magnum.

Her father opened her eyes in a lot of ways. She had been sheltered somewhat and Dawg's life was completely different. So different.

She ended up immersed in that life. So, when Magnum

said their lives were completely different, that wasn't quite true.

"I wasn't born into it, but I spent the last almost eleven years around an MC. You know I moved in with Dad and Emma as soon as I graduated high school. My mother did nothing but tear my father down, while Dawg said nothing bad about her. Not once. And I'm sure he had plenty of things to say."

"So, there you go, your mother tears Dawg down when him bein' your father ain't a choice. I'm a choice, Caitie. Wanna alienate her by bein' with someone whose lifestyle she hates?"

"She apparently didn't hate it when she got pregnant with me." Which Cait brought up endless times.

"Biggest mistake of her life," he echoed her mother's response.

"Yes, that's what she says."

"But she got you out of it."

She said that, too. "She also almost lost me because of it. If I hadn't moved out of her house and in with Dawg..." She shook her head. "Our relationship might have been irrevocably broken."

"Another good reason why us doin' anything together is a bad fuckin' idea. Not just Dawg but your mother, too. Really wanna lose her?"

"She'd never know."

His head jerked back, and their gazes locked in the mirror. "Whataya mean?"

"She hasn't met everyone I've..."

"Everyone you've what?"

"Dated," she ended weakly. She not only felt the heat of her blush but saw it in the mirror.

"Dated," he muttered under his breath. "Yep, not a fuckin' discussion we're gonna have."

"I wasn't a virgin before..." *Before.*

"Yep, not a fuckin' discussion we're gonna have."

"I'm one hundred percent sure you're not one, either."

He released her and took long strides out of the bedroom. "Not a fuckin' discussion we're gonna have," he yelled over his shoulder and slammed the door shut behind him.

Chapter Six

CAIT QUIETLY OPENED the bedroom door and stopped dead.

Magnum was sprawled out on his stomach, the sheet under him in a bunched ball, the sheet that was supposed to be covering him... wasn't.

Not quite anyway.

It draped over him from mid-thigh to barely the top curve of his ass cheeks. And, *hell*, his ass had the perfect curves.

He was worried about her walking around in a half-undressed state and here he was sleeping naked.

And with Magnum, that was a whole lot of naked.

He was way too big for the couch. His head was practically hanging off one armrest with his face turned away from her and his feet dangled in the air over the other one.

One dark, tattooed arm trailed on the tiled floor.

During the night she had heard a thump and a loud curse. When she rushed out to check, she found him on the floor, very naked then, too. But the sheet must have wrapped around his middle as he rolled off the couch. So, she hadn't seen much more than what she was seeing now.

She had offered to call the front desk to get him a foldaway. But he refused, wanting to make sure there was no question to the rest of the guests whether he was her boyfriend or not. So, after going back and forth about it until he got extremely pissed off, she shrugged, went back to the king-sized bed with expensive high-count cotton sheets, surrounded by thick pillows, while he wedged himself back on the couch.

He was only in Lake George because of her, which meant he shouldn't be the one suffering. Tonight she would insist he take the bed. And if he insisted she not share it with him, even platonically, she'd take the couch.

She moved closer and watched his back rise and fall slowly as he slept. It was getting closer to the time when she had to go to the kick-off breakfast where Hank was the keynote speaker. It would look bad if she missed it.

She could go without Magnum, but after their conversation yesterday, she was pretty damn sure he'd be pissed if she snuck out and let him sleep.

She squatted next to the couch and whispered, "Hey."

Nothing.

"Malcolm."

Still nothing.

She reached out, hesitated for only a second, then lightly trailed her fingers down his spine. The black ink in his skin didn't stand out as much as it would with someone lighter, but it was still discernible. Her fingers slipped back up his spine, then brushed over the top rocker that read, "DARK KNIGHTS" then the bottom one that read "PENNSYLVANIA."

The center emblem consisted of a sword jammed into the top of a skull that had wings. The bottom ribbon included the words: *Ride Free.*

Ride free.

She doubted Magnum completely rode "free."

Her fingertips skimmed back up, over his shoulder and

down the arm that had dropped onto the floor. It had quite a few tattoos. All in nothing but black ink. But one caught her eye. Or two, actually. From a distance, they had blended in with the rest. Now close up, they were easy to pick out. They consisted of two lines each with three block letters and then numbers, all written vertically and side by side down his right bicep.

She assumed they were initials. ABM with a date and MAM with a date a year later than the first one.

Did he have kids? Adult kids?

If so, no one ever mentioned them. Not even Magnum. And if it was true, the oldest was only a year younger than her.

Yikes. She was sure that could be a little weird. For both of them. Maybe that was what made their age difference more of a problem for him. Maybe his kids wouldn't approve.

She wondered what they looked like, who their mother was, where they were, or why he never talked about them.

She hadn't known Dawg existed for almost her first fifteen years. Maybe it was the same for his kids.

Shit, she hoped not.

His large hand curled around her ankle and slid up her calf, then her thigh, until his fingers slipped under the bottom of the above-the-knee skirt she had decided to wear for day one of the retreat. Professional but still comfortable.

His fingers skimmed the bottom lace of her panties at her thigh, then stilled. Without looking at her, his rougher than normal voice said, "Got five seconds to walk away, Caitie."

"What if I don't want to walk away?"

"Need to walk away."

His large hand seared her skin, but it remained planted on the back of her thigh.

"Need to walk away," he said again. "For me."

For me.

He was here at this retreat for her, to help her. She needed to do what he asked. It was only fair.

But it was unfair, too.

He was right. She needed to walk away. They needed to get down to the breakfast before it started. She needed to make a good impression with Hank and the upper management. Show she was a team player.

If she didn't walk away now, if she pushed him, they wouldn't be going to breakfast, they wouldn't be going anywhere except for that king bed where she tossed and turned all night.

And then they'd be tossing and turning but not because of sleep.

Her pussy clenched and heat flooded her belly.

"Let go, so I can walk away," she whispered.

"Not holdin' you there, baby."

"Yes, you are." He wasn't holding her there with his strength but by his touch alone.

He held more power than he knew.

It took a few moments for him to drop his hand, to let her go, which made her wonder if he'd also struggled with his decision.

Even so, he was stronger than her.

She needed to give him space, but she needed it, too. "I'll go down, sit by the pool and wait while you get ready. We have about fifteen minutes until I need to be in the restaurant. If you want to be there with me, then you need to hurry."

His face still turned away from her, a grunt was his only answer.

With a nod he didn't see, she moved toward the door.

As she opened it, she heard, "Pool. That's it. No food, no drink, nothin' 'til I'm with you."

With another nod she wasn't sure he saw, since she kept

her back to him, she continued over the threshold and shut the door behind her with trembling fingers.

Walking down the hallway, she forced herself to breathe.

———

MAGNUM HALF-JOGGED down the steps from the third story of the building, where their room was, all the way to the ground level. She had told him fifteen minutes. He'd done what he needed to do in ten.

It had helped that he'd shaved his head and face last night during his cold as fuck shower. The one where he still managed to jerk off and blow a huge load down the drain, despite his skin turning numb.

He was tempted to relieve the hard-on she had given him when she was touching him this morning the same way. But that would've made him late.

As he came around the corner, he spotted Cait immediately, her blonde hair hard to ignore since it was glowing in the *way-too-fucking-early* morning light. She was curled up in a lounge chair by the pool, but she wasn't alone.

A man in a dark suit was sitting sideways on a lounge chair he had pulled close to hers. He had both feet planted on the concrete, his hands laced together and hanging between his bent knees as he concentrated on Cait.

Oh. Fuck. No.

The man had dark hair similar to that Gallo fucker, but it wasn't him. As Magnum picked up his pace, he noticed the expensive gold watch on one wrist and a big gold ring on his right hand, but no wedding band.

He needed to keep his shit together. It wouldn't help Cait if he snapped and growled at everyone who sniffed around her. They could just be talking business.

As he stepped behind Cait's chair, the man's head swung toward him and his eyes widened, but he quickly hid his surprise. The suit planted his hands on his knees and sat straight with a stiff spine as Magnum forced his own to relax, curled a hand around the front of Cait's throat and leaned over, kissing the top of her head. "Hey, baby," he purred.

She twisted in her seat so she could see him and plastered on a big smile. "Hey... *Hey!* I was wondering where you were." She glanced at the suit. "Drew Gallo, this is..." Her blonde eyebrows drew together. After a second they relaxed and she finished with, "Malcolm Moore. My... boyfriend."

This Gallo, who looked older than the one he met the other day, the one who had chased down Cait, rose to his feet and extended a hand.

Magnum's jaw shifted but he accepted it since he needed to play the game. And that was all it was. A game to keep Cait safe. To find out who violated her.

That last thought made a vein in his temple pound. "Take it you're one of Gallo's sons?"

Drew Gallo's bright white smile widened. "Yes, Hank is my father."

"Speaking of Hank, we need to go before he starts talking," Cait said, unfolding her legs from under her. Magnum did not miss when Gallo's eyes fell on those legs since her dark blue skirt slid higher up her bare thighs.

Magnum moved between them, blocking the view, and held out his hand to assist her.

"Thanks," she whispered, accepting it.

"Anything for you, baby," he whispered back, but loud enough so Gallo heard him, and pulled her directly into his arms. He pressed a kiss to her mouth but before she could open her lips to kiss him back, he pulled away.

Gallo clapped his hands. "Well, we need to get moving if we don't want to miss Dad's opening speech. It's always inspiring, Cait. I'm so glad you're joining us this year. At the end of this week, you'll be looking forward to the next one, I promise."

A corner of Magnum's upper lip curled but he did his best to smooth it out.

Gallo turned to him with a smile. One that did not reach his dark eyes. "And I'm so glad you've joined us, Malcolm. I had no idea Cait was seeing someone."

Magnum grunted and snagged Cait's hand, intertwining their fingers as Gallo led the way toward the center building where the resort's main restaurant was.

Gallo kept talking while walking. "How long have you two been seeing each other?"

"Eight years," Magnum said before Cait could answer. Her fingers twitched in his.

Gallo's stride stuttered. "Oh... I..." He turned his head to glance at Cait, a frown crossing his face. "I thought you only recently turned twenty-five?"

"Ye—"

"She did, Drew. Got a fu— *problem* with me bein' her one *and only*?" Magnum hoped the man picked up on his *not-so-subtle* meaning. If he had them believing Cait had never been with anyone other than him, the only other person who could dispute that fact was the person who had videoed her. Whoever did that deed would think Magnum wasn't aware of the video or didn't know Cait had been with someone other than Magnum, even if she hadn't been willing.

He ground his back molars. Every time he thought of it, he wanted to smash shit. And he hadn't even seen the video, yet.

He'd been putting it off. But soon he'd have no choice.

Fuck.

"Uh... No. Not at all."

Right. "Soon as I saw her, knew she had to be mine."

"That's very... romantic."

Magnum gave him a wink. "Sure fu— *was*."

Gallo's mouth opened, closed, then he frowned. "Funny, during all those years Paul never mentioned you."

"There a reason he should?" Magnum asked as they entered the main building. He held the door open for Cait and escorted her through, not unaware of the bugged-out eyes she was giving him. Or the color in her cheeks because he was making it known that Magnum had taken her and her virginity at a young age.

Drew Gallo shook his head. "No, I guess not since we're not that close. I only see him occasionally at the club. But Dad plays golf with him regularly."

Most likely a country club with a limited membership just as diverse as their agency.

And Magnum didn't give a fuck who Hank Gallo played golf with. But it made sense on how Cait got her job, if it was true that jobs were hard to come by at the Gallo agency.

Gallo waved a hand at the entrance to the restaurant, indicating that Cait and Magnum should enter first. Magnum didn't like having the man behind him where he couldn't see him. But he spread his hand along the small of Cait's back, right above her ass and propelled her into the room.

"Are there assigned seats?" Cait asked Gallo.

"No. Feel free to sit wherever you'd like. It's like that all week, Cait. Very casual and laid-back. A working vacation, if you will." As his gaze wandered down Cait, Magnum's spine turned into a steel rod. "And though you look beautiful this morning, you don't need to dress up. Casual wear is fine." Once he was done thoroughly eye-fucking Cait, he turned to Magnum, his mouth curled in a fucking smirk that needed launched by his fist into next year. "Same for you. Though, it looks like you received the memo, Malcolm."

Magnum grunted at the slight snub. He had on black jeans, boots, his belt—which he'd removed his DKMC buckle—and wore a black collared, long-sleeved shirt he had found at the very back of his closet at home. He'd probably worn it to court, a funeral or something similar and luckily still fit in it. Barely.

As long as the buttons didn't pop or the seams didn't rip, he'd be good.

"In a suit," Magnum grumbled.

"I'm sorry?"

"Wearin' a suit."

"Ah, yes. Only because I'm officially opening the retreat and introducing my father as this morning's keynote speaker. After this, you'll see me in nothing but khakis and comfortable polo shirts, I promise."

Magnum couldn't wait.

As he glanced around the crowded restaurant, he noticed Nate Gallo waving in their direction.

The man was fucking kidding, right?

"Ah, look. My brother is trying to catch your attention, Cait." Under his breath he said, "No surprise."

Magnum cocked a brow at that.

Nate Gallo stood up and waved in their direction again.

"Wants you," Magnum told Drew.

"Oh, no. He doesn't." The man sighed and said to them, "See you two around. Don't forget about the couples massages this afternoon. Hopefully you grabbed a slot, Cait."

Couples massages.

Now that sounded like fucking fun.

Him massaging Cait. Her massaging him.

"I haven't, but I will," Cait answered as Gallo walked away.

The younger one rushed up. "I saved you a couple seats at the front. The first breakfast of the week is always packed because everyone wants to hear Dad. But after that, some of the meals and sessions thin out."

"Probably helps people are fu—" Magnum grimaced and cleared his throat, "hungry."

Nate answered, "That, too. But there are a couple other places to eat at the resort. Plus, some people drive into the town of Lake George or over to Vermont to explore. Or they even borrow one of the boats to putt around the lake on their own."

He and Caitie wouldn't be doing that, boat bumpers or not.

The only exploration he wanted to do was...

A bad idea.

A very bad fucking idea.

He needed that tattooed onto his balls, his dick, his hand and his forehead.

"Come sit. Dad should be out in a couple minutes."

Magnum leaned over and said into her ear, "Don't gotta sit with that fucker if you're uncomfortable, Caitie. Just say the word."

She glanced around at all the tables. "The rest of the tables are full."

"We can leave. Grab food somewhere else."

"I can't miss this," she whispered.

"Yeah, baby, you can." He blew out a breath. "Tellin' you, might throat punch 'im if he sniffs you right in front of me."

She impatiently tugged on his hand and they followed Gallo to the front near the podium set up on a low makeshift stage.

Nate pulled out the chair next to him, offering it to Cait.

Fucker had a goddamn set of balls on him.

Magnum released her hand and jerked the chair out two down from Gallo, settled her in it and then sat between the two, making the man's smile falter.

If Gallo didn't like it, tough shit.

As soon as they took their seats, and before Cait could

introduce him to the others at the large round table, Drew Gallo and a man who was obviously the senior Gallo stepped onto the stage.

Magnum needed food, he needed coffee and he didn't need a whole bunch of yapping.

But that's what he got.

An enthusiastic speech on loyalty and teamwork, working hard and... *whatever*, making him thankful he never had to live this life.

He preferred the wind on his bald head and a powerful engine between his thighs.

A warm, curvy woman on his dick.

Sweet pussy on his tongue.

Fuck, he was hungry.

Luckily, the *rah-rah* cheerleading speech only lasted about fifteen minutes. And then the old man disappeared, and a swarm of servers appeared with plates, silver carafes of coffee and more.

Thank fuck.

After draping her cloth napkin over her lap, effectively cutting off the little he could see of the ivory thighs he wanted to bite because he was that fucking hungry, she reached over, plucked his off the plate, shook it out and placed it over his lap.

Only problem was, when she did it, her knuckles brushed against his dick.

Whether by accident or on purpose, he didn't know. More importantly, his dick didn't care. It liked it and wanted more.

Magnum reminded it silently it wasn't getting any more and it needed to take what it just got and be happy.

It wasn't and neither was he.

Suddenly a man appeared behind him and Cait. "Eggs Benedict or stuffed French Toast for you, sir?"

Magnum twisted his head and looked up at the waiter

who had two different types of dishes in his hand as he paused behind his chair with an arched brow. "Both. And a whole sh— *container* of that coffee. The sh— *stuff* with the caffeine."

The waiter's mouth gaped, then closed quickly before saying, "Very good, sir," and placing both plates in front of him.

He stared at the food, then at Cait, who now had Eggs Benedict in front of her. "That it?"

Her plump, kissable, fuckable lips twitched. He'd be taking a cold shower tonight again and hopefully not clogging the damn drain with his load.

"You need more than two breakfasts?"

"Need to keep my strength up."

"There's the café," she suggested.

When Cait picked up her fork and knife, Magnum stopped her with a grunt, then he swapped out their plates. Once he was done with that, he also swapped out their water and their coffee that another server had poured her when he was distracted by the waiter with his food.

Unfortunately, he liked his black and she like sweetened brown milk, which in his book, was not fucking coffee.

But unless he was the one who handed her the food, he was not taking any risks. His only worry was if the man who drugged her, decided to drug him, too, to disable him.

Fuck.

He was not good at this shit. He wasn't good at thinking of all the backdoor ways a fucker could hurt him or Cait. He was used to facing threats head on.

Which again made him wish she could've went to one of Diesel's Shadows with this. Those fuckers were good with stealthy shit. They had the training, the experience and the tools.

They knew how to jump out of planes, trains and automobiles without stumbling, slice a fucker's neck, dispose of the body and then be playing fucking poker fifteen minutes later with a cigar and a beer.

He was just a goddamn biker who knew the ins and outs of a Harley, running a bar and beating the life out of someone with his fists.

They got through their meal without either of them passing out from laced food, so that was a good sign. He'd also sucked down a whole carafe of coffee. After the sleep—or little sleep—he had last night, he wasn't even sure that was enough.

He also had no idea what the plan was after breakfast. If he had to suffer through more of those fucking speeches, he needed something stronger than coffee. Like a whole bottle of something. Or some good quality bud.

Right now, he had neither. But luckily, he had tucked a couple blunts in his bag.

His belly somewhat full, he sat back in the chair, and wrapped a possessive hand around the back of Caitie's neck.

She gave him a soft smile at the gesture, which made him rethink it but he knew everyone around the table was watching the two of them carefully. As Cait had introduced him while they ate, he could see they had a hard time believing Magnum was Cait's boyfriend.

Because of that, he'd made sure to be extra sweet to her and call her "baby" enough times so those sitting with them got the picture.

"So, what do you do, Malcolm?" Nate Gallo asked next to him as one of the waiters rushed in to remove his now empty plates.

"Whataya mean?"

"For a living. Your career."

Cait leaned forward and toward them, which meant into him. He wondered if she was aware her tits were pressing against his arm as she did so. "He owns a bar."

"Oh! How fun. What's the name of it?"

Magnum pressed his lips together and waited for Cait to answer, "Dirty Dick's."

Which she did not do.

"Dapper Dan's."

Dapper fuckin' Dan's. Jesus fuckin' Christ.

"Never heard of it," Nate said.

No shit. Because it didn't exist. "Yeah, well, ai— *it's* not a country club."

"It keeps him very busy," Cait added. "That's why you all haven't met him before. It's hard for him to get away."

"Well, we're glad you can join us," said a redhead across the table with a genuine smile. The first one he'd seen so far that morning. The rest were too busy calculating their age difference in their head and also trying to figure out why the fuck Cait was with him. He was tempted to tell them it was because of his monster cock.

That genuine smile might fall flat or get even larger, depending on what the redhead was into.

"Appreciate that," Magnum mumbled instead. Again, trying to play a game he wasn't sure he knew the rules to or was good at.

He once again wished to fuck that she had a Shadow she could've went to, one she trusted to deal with this whole situation without it all blowing to hell. He was starting to worry he'd fuck this whole damn thing up.

He was out of his element at this resort, with these people. *Way* out of his comfort zone.

"How did you two meet?" asked the redhead's man, who did not wear a genuine smile.

Magnum scratched his chin and pursed his lips. He had no clue how to answer that and hadn't been prepared for that question. Which he should've been. If he knew what the fuck he was doing.

Luckily, a quick-thinking Caitie stepped in again. "At a

fundraiser for the Walker Foundation. Have you ever heard of it?"

Only problem was, he'd told Drew Gallo they'd hooked up eight years ago. The Foundation wasn't even around eight years ago.

But he sat back, his fingers massaging the back of her neck, as she explained everything about Ellie Walker's foundation which she ran for amputees who needed financial assistance with getting prostheses.

The enthusiasm with which she talked about it almost gave him a genuine smile of his own. All of the DAMC sisterhood and the Shadows' women were very dedicated to that cause.

Magnum had helped the Shadows and Angels do a bunch of fundraisers for it, including poker runs, bikini contests and wet T-shirt contests at both Dirty Dick's and The Iron Horse Roadhouse. Any way they could get not only bikers but the public to part with their scratch, they'd done it.

But that wasn't where he first saw Cait.

Could be she was right, though. Maybe one of those fundraisers was where he first *noticed* Cait had grown up. Became a woman hard to ignore.

He didn't remember the first moment she caught his attention, he just knew she did. And from then on out, he couldn't miss her. When he heard her voice, when he heard her laugh, when he saw her smile, when her green eyes turned his way. When she noticed him noticing her, which made her expression soften and her lips curve upward.

And not for one second had she been shy about that attention. Fuck no. She'd catch him staring at her while she was talking to someone, laughing at a joke, or just walking past him and she wouldn't look away. In fact, she'd catch his gaze and hold it. Almost challenging him to make a move.

Yeah, she was fucking dangerous.

Being here, sitting next to her, staying in her fucking room, was goddamn dangerous as fuck.

His name on her lips drew him out of his thoughts. He stared at the mouth he wanted to claim right there at that table, then he lifted his gaze. He didn't know if it was just her, or because he couldn't have her, that made him lose his fucking brain cells. "What?"

"Nate asked you a question," she murmured, lifting a brow and her chin in the fucker's direction.

He turned to the bastard on his right, hating every second of this motherfucking game he was forced to play. "What?"

"Do you golf?'

"Not my thing."

"What's your thing?"

His nostrils flared and he looked Nate Gallo directly in the eyes and reminded the asshole, "Caitie's my thing."

She squeezed his upper thigh under the table. Her fingers were way too close to his dick. He dropped his right hand to hers, interlaced them, and pulled them to his mouth, brushing his lips across her knuckles before pinning them to the table where everyone could see them clasped. And he didn't let go to either the back of her neck or her hand. If that wasn't a clear message, then nothing would be.

He also had another message he needed to deliver to the man sitting next to him. "Gotta thank you for gettin' her home when she wasn't feelin' well the other week."

"I'm glad I could help. I was deeply concerned when she suddenly became ill. And since we're one big family at Gallo, that means family takes care of family."

His fingers twitched, digging into Caitie's neck and hand as the anger began to swallow him whole.

He'd been good until now. He'd been fucking civil; he'd kept his temper. But, *for fuck's sake*, he didn't know if he could do this. If he could handle this.

All he wanted to do was murder the fucker sitting next to him. He wanted to shove his fist down his throat and yank his dick back up through his mouth. The dick he touched Caitie with.

He wanted to smash the man's fingers with his boot, the ones curled around a coffee cup, the ones that touched Caitie, until they were unrecognizable.

And he wanted to rip his mouth off his face. The mouth that...

He sucked in a deep breath and slowly released it.

"Malcolm..." Caitie was wincing and shaking their tightly clenched hands. "Malcolm... I need to get some air."

He peeled his gaze from the man who "helped" Caitie and forced it on her. "Yeah. Air."

"Will we see you two later?" Gallo asked as Magnum surged to his feet and helped Caitie up, not letting her go. If he kept his hands busy, then he might not murder the man in front of all of her co-workers.

He needed to get a plan together. But he also needed to see that fucking video.

And that was the last thing he wanted to do.

Chapter Seven

He had snored through most of their hour-long couples massage. Before they had both stripped down—her donning a robe and him having to wrap a sheet around his nether region since he didn't fit in any of the spa's robes, nor did he want to—he had made it quite clear to the women massaging them, if they promised to keep the tattoo on his back a secret, they'd get a big fat tip.

Cait wanted a big fat tip, too. Just not one consisting of money. The whole time her masseuse was working on her, she wished it was his fingers instead. Though, she was sure any massage he gave her would not last a whole hour. She doubted it would last a whole five minutes.

When the ladies finally left the room, they whispered to her that they could take their time getting up, to make sure they drank plenty of water, and recommended they come back before the end of the week since Magnum's muscles were full of knots.

How he slept through his masseuse working those deep knots, she didn't know. But he did since he was that exhausted.

"It's natural for some men to have a physical response to

massage," Magnum's masseuse also whispered to her in sort of an awe-like semi-apology before leaving the room, which pulled her from her euphoric state and had her turning her head to glance at him.

And, yep, he was on his back, his mouth slightly open as he snored lightly and the sheet covering his cock was in full-on pitched tent mode. Like circus big-top, not a pup tent.

She had to smother a giggle so she wouldn't wake him, and let him sleep until the sheet lowered to a respectable level.

If the ten minutes it took was any indication, the man had some staying power. Either that or he was having a really good dream.

It was obvious when he awoke, because he jackknifed up to a seated position, almost losing that sheet, and yelled, "What the fuck?" in a confused manner. Once he realized where he was and where she was—dressed and sitting in a chair, waiting—he relaxed.

"Don't lemme do that again."

Her lips quirked. "What? The hard-on part or the sleeping part?"

His hand instantly grabbed at his junk, confused. "I got hard?"

"The poor woman ran out of the room screaming about Godzilla."

He snorted. "Sounds about right."

Cait had rolled her eyes.

She was surprised he hadn't fallen back asleep during a *way-too-long* "working dinner" where two guest speakers, who were top marketing experts in the industry, droned on. He'd yawned about a dozen times and couldn't sit still, but his eyes remained open. Barely.

That night's group activity was a version of *The Dating Game*, and there was no way they were showing up for that.

She could just see them being wrangled into playing and not getting one answer right, which would be a bit suspicious since Magnum told Drew that they were together for *eight years*!

Eight!

Which, in theory, meant Magnum had started "dating" her when she had been underage. She had no idea why he said that other than to imply he'd taken her virginity. But he could have at least come up with an answer that would have inferred she had been at least eighteen.

There were still eighteen-year-old virgins in the world, weren't there?

She had lost hers at seventeen, but the boy had been the same age, not thirty-three which could've meant jail time. And her father finding out her first time was in the back seat of a BMW, especially if the teenager she was with had been twice his age, could've meant death by rusty butter knife castration. And she wasn't sure their forty-five seconds of fumbling was worth dying for.

No matter what, Magnum had said it, Drew had heard it and that horse had already escaped the barn.

At dinner, she had made sure to find a seat far away from any of the Gallos because she had been worried during breakfast when Magnum had gone wired as he and Nate mentioned that night.

That night.

She blew out a breath and stared at the lake from the Adirondack chair where she had planted herself on the balcony after they'd returned from dinner. It was now dark and the moon was reflecting off the still water. Fireflies also decorated the night like flashing lights, while frogs and crickets singing their melodies could be heard in the distance.

Cait let the peacefulness seep into her bones, since she knew that wasn't going to last long. On their way back up to their room, Magnum announced he wanted to see the video tonight.

That request had turned her stomach into a knotted mess, made her want to expel her dinner, and any benefit she'd received from her earlier massage was completely lost.

He was currently on the phone, pacing inside the room. She guessed talking club business since as soon as she stepped out onto the balcony with the huge rum and Coke she had made with the items in the minibar, he'd shut the sliders behind her to make those calls. To prepare herself for him seeing the video, she'd used one splash of pop and every miniature bottle of Captain Morgan she could find. She had hissed at the first sip, but forced it down, letting the alcohol help ease her anxiety.

If the booze and the serene view wasn't going to help, nothing would.

Not showing him the video could also help and she was starting to question whether he needed to see it.

Fuck. She didn't want *anyone* to see it.

It was proof she had done a dumb thing. Proof she had put herself in that situation by being careless.

A lesson she'd never forget.

The only silver lining—if she considered it one—was she didn't remember it at all. She only knew the truth of what happened because of the video.

Not living the experience in real time could be considered a blessing but also a curse, since she hadn't been awake to try to fight off whoever it was, try to protect herself and do her best to prevent herself becoming that victim.

Even though the man wore a condom, most likely to prevent leaving DNA evidence behind, she got a STD test the next day, just to be safe. She was just grateful she had been on the Pill.

For the past few weeks, she'd tried to ignore the implications that someone had violated her and taken away her power of choice, along with damaging her trust in men. Now any drink made by anyone but her or her immediate family would be suspect.

She never thought something like that would happen to her. She'd heard plenty of stories and warnings about the date rape drug and thought she was vigilant enough.

But she had been so, so fucking wrong.

One mistake had changed her outlook.

She couldn't trust all men, but she had no doubt she could trust the one behind her in their room. That was why she went to him.

But it wasn't the only reason.

She sipped her strong drink and shuddered at the burn it created in her stomach, but was thankful how it was dulling the sharp edges of her nerves.

The slight squeal of the slider opening had her gripping her glass harder and she braced it on the wide armrest so it wouldn't slip from her fingers and shatter on the concrete floor.

"It on your phone?" his deep, but unusually tight voice came from behind her.

She didn't turn to look at him when she answered, "Yes." She continued to stare at the moon's reflection on the water as, from the corner of her eye, she saw him swipe her cell phone from the little square table next to her.

She waited because she knew what was coming next.

"Passcode."

She robotically repeated the four-digit number so he could unlock the phone. Before he asked, she said, "In my Gmail app. I forwarded it to my personal email and deleted it from my Outlook account at work."

She heard a slight grunt, then the glass door slide closed behind her. She was glad he was going to watch it without her.

She had only watched it once. When she'd received it in her work email, unaware of what it was.

Once had been enough.

Once had been enough to burn it permanently to memory.

Yes, she didn't remember what happened, but she also would never forget it, either.

It was weird. Watching it had been like watching it happen to someone else. Like a stranger in a movie or a documentary. But not her.

Never her.

Besides taking advantage of her unconscious state, whoever the man was had been strangely, and disturbingly, gentle. She had not woken bleeding, broken or bruised.

Only confused.

And, besides the video, if she hadn't been left totally naked and didn't recognize the normal signs of having sex, she might not have known it had happened at all.

But, unfortunately, or fortunately—she wasn't sure how she should feel about it—there *was* video proof and Magnum was about to witness it.

Maybe she should have left the room first. But now she was imprisoned on the balcony with nowhere to go and no way to escape. Being on the top floor of a three-story building didn't leave many options.

The video was about fifteen minutes long. Fifteen minutes longer than she wished it was. However, it didn't take Magnum fifteen minutes to react.

It took less than five.

She tried to remember what happened around that five-minute mark, if it was any different from the rest. But she'd been in shock when she watched it and one minute had blurred into the next.

What sucked the most was that the man she wanted, the man who wanted her, the man she would *choose* to have sex with, would see her completely naked for the first time with another man and one not of her choice.

She wondered if he'd ever be able to get past that.

She wondered if he'd ever look at her the same again.

Hearing his bellowed curse, things being overturned and tossed in the room, the shatter of something fragile, then a deafening roar that turned into a hair-raising howl that tore through her, made her lungs seize, her heart stop and her stomach hollow out.

She remained frozen in her seat, her gaze locked on that lake, her mind locked in that room behind her, as the slamming of the door was hard enough to shake the sliding glass doors behind her.

Her heart began to thump in her chest, her neck, her temples and her ears as she worried what he would do, where he would go. Afraid he would seek Nate out and destroy him.

But she couldn't move. Every muscle and joint in her body had locked.

Then she heard it.

A phone ringing. Not her cell phone. The landline in the room. Abruptly it stopped. Then rang again. Somehow that unstuck her. Got her pushing herself to her feet, got her moving, going inside, not seeing the damage but focusing on only that ringing object.

She only answered it because she worried about him, his reaction and what he might do.

And maybe the call was about him.

With trembling fingers, she lifted the handset and put it to her ear. "Yes," she forced out, her greeting wooden and hollow, unrecognizable even to herself.

"Ma'am, is everything okay in your room?" A woman's voice. Troubled. Full of concern. Whether real or not, Cait didn't know or care.

"Yes... I'm... I'm sorry... my boyfriend is... upset. He just got some bad news. Someone close to him..." her throat convulsed, "died."

"I'm sorry to hear that. We had a couple calls about the... noise." She didn't believe Cait. She was only patronizing her. "Please let us know if you need us to call someone."

Someone. Like who? The police?

To help contain a man who just lost his mind? To deal with a man who was so full of fury he had to escape?

He could end up executed. By men who were sent to "help." By men who had no idea why he was out of control. Why he was uncontrollable.

Why he was feeling nothing but rage.

"No need. He'll be... fine. I'm sorry if he disturbed anyone. Even though he knew it was coming, the loss was... harder than expected."

"Well... The front desk is open all night, if you need any assistance..." She hesitated and when Cait didn't respond, she finished with, "Have a good night."

"You, too," she murmured and hung up the phone, staring at it for a few hammering heartbeats.

She let her gaze wander as she turned slowly in a circle. The desk was overturned, the lamp broken on the floor, the chair on its side across the room. The large framed picture that had been hanging over the desk was now hanging lopsided, the glass shattered.

Her phone was on the carpet amidst the slivers of glass. The screen was dark but not cracked, luckily. She carefully plucked it from the shards and went back to the phone, picking up the handset and pressing "0" for the front desk.

When the lady answered again, Cait apologized once more and asked for someone to come clean up the glass. She also told her that she'd pay for the damage. She once again confirmed that police were not needed to "assess the situation."

She uprighted the desk and retrieved the chair while she waited.

After a while, someone showed up and cleaned up the mess.

She tipped them well, apologized again several times, assured them everything would be okay, then locked the door after they left.

She glanced at the clock.

He'd been gone over two hours and not a word.

She'd kept an ear open for sirens. She kept the other open for his key card sliding into the electronic lock.

She heard neither.

Eventually she got ready for bed, though sleep would be impossible until she knew he was alright. Instead, she sat against the headboard, her knees pulled tightly into her chest, her arms wrapped around her shins and her cheek pressed to one knee.

And she waited.

She had no idea what time it was when he finally returned.

But when he did, he did not sleep on the couch. He walked through the open bedroom door and, in the dark, removed everything except his boxer briefs, then climbed into bed with her.

Without a word, he unfolded her stiff limbs, stretched out beside her, and pulled her against him, her back pinned to his massive chest. His heavy arm draped over her waist. His thick thigh over hers. His face buried in her hair.

And he simply breathed.

Which helped her breathe.

Eventually, she placed her hand on his, which was spread wide over her belly, letting her fingers fall between his larger ones. Where they fit perfectly like a puzzle.

She closed her eyes.

And they both just breathed.

Magnum inhaled the scent of her hair, the scent of her skin, the scent of *her*. Even with her eyes closed and her breathing steady, he wasn't sure if she'd slept at all. He hoped she did, because he did not.

He only got through a few minutes of that video. He needed to watch the whole fucking thing to look for any clues, but he couldn't do it.

What he had saw, though not violent, still shattered his mind and his heart, making him explode.

He was tempted to forward the video to Mercy, hoping the Shadow could help identify the bastard. But it clearly showed Cait's face... and the rest of her, too. So, he couldn't. Wouldn't. That meant he was on his own to take care of this problem.

He needed to forward the email to himself and delete it from her phone.

He had lost it when she had told him what happened, but seeing it...

Seeing it...

Fuck.

If she hadn't said she'd been drugged and he hadn't recognized how lax and unresponsive her body was, it could have been any couple making a goddamn sex video.

But he knew it wasn't.

He needed to figure out a way to find out who it was. Because whoever it was would fucking die. What they did to her revoked their right to breathe.

And he would be the one to make sure that happened.

But he needed to be sure. He wouldn't take the risk of going to prison by taking out the wrong man and letting the right one still walk the fucking Earth. To be a risk to Caitie, to be a risk to any other woman.

During the night, he had rolled onto his back, taking her

with him. And she'd curled around him, her arm hooked over his gut, her cheek on his chest, her breath sweeping over his bare skin.

And he held her there, kept her connected. In a silent way, assuring her he'd help protect her.

Because, *for fuck's sake*, if he said it out loud, she'd probably deny she needed protection. She only wanted help to deal with the man in that video, but that was all she wanted. In truth, she was strong like her father.

She went to work every day with this person, and most likely was now on a retreat with him.

She was not cowering in fear, she was not curling up into a fucking ball in a corner, she wasn't burying her head in the goddamn sand.

She wanted this guy, along with the video, dealt with because she worried he'd used it to blackmail her for some reason. But she needed it done carefully.

He got that.

He would do that.

And he would get satisfaction out of doing it for her.

She trusted him to handle it.

She also trusted him not to hurt her. And by claiming her, which was what every cell in his body screamed for, he might hurt her.

Not directly, but by causing issues with her family and among the two clubs.

Maybe it would be a bump in the road that would eventually smooth the fuck out, but it could also cause a complete derailing.

While he didn't want to create enemies out of allies, he also didn't want to alienate her from the people who loved her.

It would not make sense for her to give up many for one.

He could lay there with her in his arms, wishing, even pretending, things were different.

But they fucking weren't.

He'd already lived a life of hurt and disappointment. Of being cut out of the lives of the ones he loved the most. He didn't want the same for her.

He wanted so much better for her. And while he could give her a lot, he couldn't give her everything.

So, it was best to offer nothing except for his help in this fucked up situation.

He just needed to hold himself to that. To not let himself take what he wanted.

But it was hard and so the fuck was he.

Having her plastered to him, her warm, soft skin, her long hair sweeping over his chest, she fit against him perfectly.

She was not petite. She became tall and curvy as she matured. She was in no way fat, but she wasn't skinny, either.

She was fucking perfect.

Her cheek slid along his skin, until her face was tipped up, until her green eyes hit his, which tightened his chest. "You sleep at all?"

"Yeah," he lied. "You?"

"Yes," she returned the lie.

She tipped her head back down and he knew exactly what she was looking at. His cock was hard and throbbing under the sheet. There was no way to hide it so he didn't bother.

It happened every morning, so it also wasn't surprising. But he doubted that was the only reason.

Even after seeing that fucking video, for him, nothing had changed. If anything, it had made what he felt for her stronger. But it didn't matter what he felt about her, or how she felt about him.

Nope.

Fuck.

He needed to get out of that bed, out from beneath her, because she was way too tempting.

Way too fucking tempting.

And if he even made the slightest move... Or if she encouraged him in any way right now...

If she knew how weak he was at that very moment...

The wall he was trying to keep between them would come crashing down.

But, *fuck him*, he didn't want to move.

She felt so goddamn good in his arms.

She belonged there.

She owned that spot.

In truth, she could easily own him.

"Need a fuckin' shower," he grumbled, carefully extracting himself from her.

"Save some hot water for me."

"Not gonna be a problem." He was once again going to be taking a cold one.

He kept his eyes off the bed and focused on the door. Because if he saw her right now, laying in that bed, her eyes soft, her blonde hair a cloud around her beautiful face, he might not walk out that door.

And if he didn't walk out that door, he was done.

Chapter Eight

HE HAD FALLEN ASLEEP AGAIN. Not during a massage but by the heated pool earlier while Cait swam and socialized.

It proved he sucked as a bodyguard. He was pretty fucking sure none of the Shadows would fall asleep while watching one of their assignments.

Guess he wouldn't be handing his resume to Diesel any time soon.

And he hoped the DAMC enforcer wouldn't be handing him his ass soon, either.

But Cait and a bunch of the other women from the agency had decided to spend the afternoon at the pool since the warm weather was still holding. And the pool water, even if it hadn't been heated, was much warmer than the lake.

That was what they said and he'd take their word for it.

He had found a shaded spot where he could see the whole pool clearly since he was wearing another long-sleeved button down shirt. He would die if he sat out in the sun. And he also didn't want his bald noggin to burn and refused to use Cait's floral smelling sunscreen. Smelling like a daisy wasn't on the day's to-do list.

Now, he was where he didn't want to be.

On a fucking boat.

Didn't fucking matter it was a big boat.

It was still a boat.

If Caitie wanted to take the sunset dinner cruise, he was going on the fucking sunset dinner cruise. He would just have to make an effort not to fall over the side into the dark, deep and cold water.

Because drowning would fucking suck.

And right now, he wasn't so thrilled everyone had gathered on the top deck of the steamboat to watch the sunset. He was assured once that was over, they'd head down to eat dinner and then dance.

Fuckin' great.

Not only was he surrounded by water, he was unable to escape the bullshit after-dinner activities like he could back on land.

Because he was sure as fuck not dancing.

He was not.

Fuck no.

He double checked that Caitie was still occupied at the front of the boat with the other women, taking pictures on her phone of the sun that set every fucking day. Why was it more special now that they were on a fucking boat?

It wasn't. It was the same damn fiery ball that disappeared every evening.

He headed down to use the head, and on his way back up to his spot where he could keep an eye on her, he got cornered by none other than Drew Gallo. This time not in a suit, but in pressed khaki pants, a pink polo shirt and that expensive as fuck watch, which probably cost more than Magnum's custom sled.

Hell, it probably cost more than his house.

"How are things going, Malcolm?"

"Perfectly fu—*peachy*, Gallo."

"Please, call me Drew."

Magnum grunted.

"I heard there was a little disturbance in your room last night."

How about that. "Saw a roach and was tryin' to kill it."

Magnum did not get the reaction he hoped.

"Cait said your relative died."

Fuck. He and Cait didn't discuss a story. He didn't even think anyone would have the balls big enough to bring it up. He should've known one or more of the Gallos would. "Yeah, that, too."

"I'm sorry to hear that. Were you close?"

"Missed the roach by a hair."

"I meant close to the relative that passed away."

"Yeah." He had no idea who in his "family" died. Something Cait maybe should've mentioned to him.

"The front desk said there was some damage to the room."

Fuck. "Yeah. Gonna take care of that."

Gallo nodded, his dark hair not even shifting, he had so much shit in it. "Good. Good." He hesitated and Magnum braced. "We were a little concerned about Cait."

If the man only knew how fucking ironic that last statement was. "Don't be."

Gallo turned toward the front of the boat and his eyebrows lifted. "My brother has an unhealthy interest in Cait."

The sudden change in topic caught him off guard.

Magnum's gaze slid from Gallo to where Cait was. And of course, Nate Gallo was sniffing around. Again. Yeah, the Gallos had some fucking balls. Probably because of money, not real courage. "Can see that."

His urge to rush to Cait pulled at him, but he also wanted to hear what the Gallo standing next to him had to say about that "unhealthy" interest. Maybe he had some important info. And Magnum had advised Cait before stepping on the floating deathtrap not to accept food or drink from anyone but him.

But he kept a close eye on the younger Gallo's hands, in case he pulled something out of his pocket to spike the bottomless glass of wine Cait had been sipping at along with the rest of the ladies.

"Made it pretty clear Cait's mine." Gallo gave him a wide-eyed look, so he added, "That she's my wo— *girlfriend*."

"Yes, well... I don't think we were aware Cait was seeing anyone until yesterday. But, I've talked to Nate about it a few times since Cait joined our agency and reminded him he's head of the HR department, and showing such interest doesn't look good."

"That right?"

Gallo's lips flattened out. "But he gets away with more than most since he's my father's favorite."

Now *that* was very fucking interesting. "Over his oldest son?"

His eyes narrowed. "Yes, funny how that works, right? I'm the eldest. I started working for the agency first, during summers, on college break, then full-time once I graduated from college. I know the ins and outs of the agency as well as my father and could easily step into his shoes at any time. And while all three of us were told we had to earn it, my brother is somehow working his way to the executive floor a lot quicker than me and with a lot less blood, sweat and tears."

Magnum doubted any Gallo had ever worked hard enough to shed blood, sweat and tears. But, even so, somebody was jealous. Which meant tension between them. And that might mean Magnum could draw out further information from him about the night Nate Gallo took Cait "home."

"It a race?"

Gallo didn't say anything for the longest time. He finally sighed. "No. I guess not. We're all working together to keep the agency successful and to build it even bigger."

Bullshit.

Gallo patted him on the back. "Good talking with you, Malcolm. If you change your mind about golf, let me know. I've got a tee time tomorrow at ten, I'd love for you to join me."

More bullshit.

Even if it wasn't, he wasn't going to be chasing little white balls in the grass. He wasn't going to be chasing any balls at all. Except the ones attached to the man in the video.

Those he would crush.

Three hours later, after it had gotten dark, they'd eaten, and the dancing started, Magnum was sitting in his chair, his gut full after eating two main dishes and three desserts, his legs extended and spread wide. With his arms folded over his chest, he kept an eye on Cait as all the wine she drank, and was still drinking, had loosened her up enough to join some of the women on the dance floor.

While he was making sure she was safe, he also couldn't pull his eyes from her, even if there was no threat. She was wearing a loose dark pink skirt that swirled up and showed off her long, perfect fucking legs every time she spun. Along with a lace top that showed just enough tits but not too much. She was smiling, laughing and having a great fucking time.

And he felt like a father sitting there making sure boys didn't touch his baby girl. He was pretty fucking sure his face showed the same.

When the fast music slowed, the women dispersed, but before Caitie could make her way back to their table, she was cut off by a Gallo Magnum wasn't expecting. Senior.

Cait didn't look at all bothered by Hank Gallo asking her to dance and actually flashed him a genuine smile.

But Magnum still didn't fucking like it.

He didn't like any of those fucking Gallos touching her. But Senior, keeping a respectable distance between them, swept her expertly around the dance floor making her smile widen.

And if she was happy, so was Magnum.

Sort of.

What he didn't like was Gallo Sr. leaning in and talking into Cait's ear. Her smile faltered and she quickly nodded.

Before Magnum could get to his feet to find out what the fuck that was all about, the song ended and both of them headed in his direction, Senior escorting Cait with a hand on her elbow. The fact that he didn't release it until they stopped directly in front of him didn't make him a whole bunch of happy, either.

Magnum took his time rising to his feet, but when he did, he noticed he was quite a few inches taller than the older man.

"Malcolm, this is my boss, Hank Gallo."

Her boss offered his hand and Magnum took it reluctantly. He didn't normally do handshakes. He did hand clasps and shoulder bumps with his brothers and others. Not that fake shit.

"Hank, this is my boyfriend, Malcolm Moore."

"Pleasure to meet you, Malcolm. We're so glad you could join Cait on our little retreat."

He doubted it was a pleasure. It was just more fake polite bullshit.

"Paul never mentioned Cait was seeing anyone."

"Didn't know that was somethin' her boss needed to be aware of."

Cait moved to his side and Magnum draped an arm

around her shoulders while she squeezed his waist in a silent message.

"Oh, it's not. But Paul and I golf together regularly and speak often of our families. He's very proud of his little girl."

Was the fucker hinting at their age difference? "Not so little." And, *for fuck's sake*, she wasn't Paul's little girl.

Another squeeze at his waist.

"No. You're right. She's all grown up now. And after graduating at the top of her class at U of P, I'm lucky to have her on board."

Magnum's eyes flipped from the old man down to Cait, who was avoiding his gaze. She graduated at the top of her class and still needed her stepdad's influence to get her a job with his agency? Or was that what her mother and stepfather wanted her to believe?

"Yeah, me and her father are real fu— *proud* of her." Her real father.

Hank Gallo inhaled loudly and said, "Well, I'll let you two go dance. Cait's such a great dancer and it would be a shame if you didn't share a dance or two with her. We'll be heading back to the dock in the next hour or so. I hope you're enjoying the retreat."

"Been a blast, Hank."

He smiled. "Good." He squeezed her shoulder. "Take care of her."

Magnum bit back his response which would have been, "She doesn't need taken care of, she's a fuckin' strong goddamn woman who can take care of herself. Wouldn't need to be here at all if it wasn't for your fucknut of a son who drugged and raped her."

No, he didn't fucking say it. Instead he kept his teeth clenched and only nodded.

With a last warm smile to Cait, Senior wandered away to another table.

"Dance with me?" Cait asked softly.

"Can't dance, baby," he mumbled.

"It's a slow song. You only need to shuffle your feet."

He stared down into her green eyes. *Fuck.* "You don't shuffle your feet."

She had some hot as fuck moves, which made it way too easy for him to keep his eyes on her. Him dancing with her by him only shuffling his feet would do her a disservice.

"Dance with me." This time a demand but in a husky voice that made his blood surge.

"Caitie..."

She ducked from under his arm, grabbed his hand and tugged. If he dug in his heels, she would never be able to move him. But it was Caitie and he wasn't digging in his heels. With a glance to the dance floor, he noticed couples moving around, holding each other close.

He could do that. He could hold her close like last night in bed. He could shuffle his feet.

If that's what she wanted...

If it made her happy...

"No bitchin' if I break your toes." He reluctantly followed her to the center of the floor.

"Just don't step on them."

Right, that fucking simple.

She stopped, turned and stepped into him, snaking her arms around his waist and pressing her cheek to his chest.

All the tension he hadn't realized he'd been holding onto disappeared with her in his arms.

Then she moved.

And she moved some more.

"Move your feet," came muffled from his shirt when he stood like a statue in the middle of the dance floor.

Carefully and slowly, he moved his feet since he was afraid he *would* break her damn toes.

He shuffled in a circle, her softness pressed against him.

He also got a good whiff of her floral scent. Whether it was her hair or her skin, he didn't know. But he was starting to recognize it as Cait.

He pressed his jaw against her temple and pulled her even closer until there wasn't even enough space to slide a piece of paper between them.

And he was okay with that... until he wasn't.

Holding her that close, having her move against him... Her hips swaying gently, her tits pressed into his chest. Her hair tickling his nose. Her hands barely above his ass. The fingertips of his brushing the top curves of hers, too...

He wanted to slide his hands down, to cup her ass cheeks, to pull up her skirt, to tear her panties to the side and fuck her with her legs circling his waist.

But they were on a boat, with her co-workers, on the middle of a dance floor.

Unfortunately, his cock didn't care.

And Caitie didn't help, either, by continuing to brush her body against it. Not lightly, or an occasional bump, but like she was trying to smother a fucking fire.

That fire being him.

But the blaze wasn't going out. It was now roaring.

"Caitie..." Her name got caught in his throat. "Need to go sit the fuck down."

She said nothing but continued to move against him, holding him even tighter and he didn't think that was possible.

"Caitie..." He tried to wedge his fingers in between him and her arms. She was having none of that.

He shoved his nose into her hair. "Hangin' by a thread here, baby."

"I know."

"Keep doin' that and I'm gonna embarrass the both of us."

She face-planted into his chest and giggled.

"Ain't funny, baby. Got a load buildin' with nowhere for it to go." And his cock was pointing in a direction it wasn't meant to point. Which meant he needed to adjust it.

"Is it comfortable where it's at?"

"Fuck no."

She quickly turned them away from most of the crowd, slipped one hand between their tightly sandwiched bodies and...

Grabbed his fucking dick.

Just like that.

On a dance floor. On a fucking boat. Amongst a shitload of people she knew. She just reached down, grabbed his hard-on and adjusted it for him.

Like she did it every fucking day.

"That's a handful," she whispered.

He didn't know if he should laugh or fucking cry. "No shit."

"Actually pretty impressive."

"Glad you fuckin' think so. Can you fuckin' let go?"

Her body shook against his. "Do I have to?"

"Yeah. Remember that embarrasin' thing I mentioned? You got about five seconds."

Thank fuck she let go just in time.

He released a breath until the DJ began to play a fast song. They needed off that dance floor. *Hell*, they needed off that fucking boat.

"Do I need to walk in front of you?" she asked with a naughty glint in her eye.

"Might be good."

She giggled again and he followed her. Only she kept walking right past their table and out the nearest exit into the night.

He kept on her heels as she hoofed it up the stairs to the top deck—which was currently deserted—giving him and his suffering dick a perfect view of that ass of hers rocking and rolling.

Which was not a good fucking idea.

Not with her in that fucking loose skirt. Not with the current state of his aching, leaking cock.

He was not fucking Caitie for the first time in some goddamn dark corner against a wall.

Fuck. He wasn't fucking Caitie at all.

He wasn't fucking Caitie at all.

He wasn't.

"Caitie..."

"I just need some air. So do you."

He needed a fuck of a lot more than air.

She stopped suddenly and he just about slammed into her. She spun, and he got distracted by her skirt kicking out around her and her blonde hair swirling about her face in the wind. Before he could pull away, she was up on her toes, grabbing his face and yanking his head down.

His mouth opened to stop her but she took it before the first syllable even escaped.

Her tongue swept deep, took control of his mouth, tasting him everywhere. That did not reduce the blood flow to his dick.

In fact, it kicked it up a notch.

He pushed her tongue out of his mouth, planning on ending the kiss. He didn't. Instead, he shoved his tongue into her mouth, swallowed her groan, dug his fingers into her hair and yanked her head back so her mouth opened wider on a gasp.

He couldn't get enough of her. That kiss wasn't enough.

And never would be.

But it needed to be.

It *needed* to be.

Goddamn it.

He twisted his head, found his breath, then pressed his forehead to hers as they both panted.

And it had only been one kiss.

Like that day in the hidden corner of the DAMC kitchen.

The hardest thing he'd done in a long time was walk away from her that day. To tell her no, when every cell in his body screamed yes. Just like it was doing now. "Don't do that again."

"The kiss?"

"Makin' me hard. Touchin' my dick."

"You didn't like it?"

"Not smart. Strugglin' here, Caitie."

"You're not the only one."

"Then stop makin' it hard for me." Both his cock and his willpower. "There's no easy way to do this."

Which was so damn true, it was killing him. No matter how much he wanted things to be different, they would never be.

Then her hand was there again, between them, grabbing his dick and squeezing it. "No, it won't be easy. But doesn't mean I don't want to try."

"Dyin's the easy part. It's the rest..."

"All the rest is in Shadow Valley. We're not there. We're here."

Jesus fuck. He closed his eyes and sucked in a breath. "We're on a fuckin' boat, Caitie. With your boss and your co-workers."

"I'm on a boat with you."

Christ.

"You got on a boat for me." She leaned into him, not helping out his situation at all and whispered again, this time very slowly, "You got on a boat *for me.*"

He had nothing to say to that. There was nothing he could say that wouldn't reveal how he felt about her.

And that was not smart.

"You came along on my work retreat, Magnum. Something you probably never thought you'd do in a million years, but you came anyway. You're surrounding yourself with people you'd never choose to be around. You're doing things you'd never do. *For me.*"

For fuck's sake, everything she just said exposed things he was trying to keep hidden. "Asked for my help."

"But I didn't ask you to come along on this retreat. That was on you. Your choice."

"You didn't have a choice to come on this fuckin' retreat, Cait. Said so yourself."

"And I would've been more vigilant. I would've been fine."

Again, she was digging deep within him and ripping things to the surface. "You wanted me to find out who was on that goddamn video." That was why he was there. That was why he was on this fucking retreat.

"Yes, I did. But I didn't ask for this."

"Could've told me no."

"Could I have?"

He went solid. "Don't say that kind of shit. I'm not him."

"I didn't mean it like that. You've been nothing but a gentleman..."

He grunted. *A gentleman. Right.* Filling up a drain with cum while jerking off to thoughts of her was not being a fucking gentleman. Neither was the thought of flipping her around, throwing her skirt up over her head and fucking her so hard everyone downstairs would be able to hear her over the DJ.

"Way more than what I want you to be."

"What does that fuckin' mean?" He knew what that meant. He knew. And it made all of this even more difficult.

"You know what I want."

A burn seared his chest. "Can't give it to you, Caitie."

"You can. You choose not to."

"For a good goddamn reason."

"Keep telling yourself that." She pulled away from him and headed to the very front of the boat.

To the railing. Somewhere she didn't think he'd follow her.

Fuck.

Fuck.

Fuck.

But she was right. Now she knew there was a snake in the Gallo agency, she could've gone on the retreat alone and had been very careful. But he couldn't let her do that.

There had been no fucking way he would've let her do that.

Him being there was all on him.

All because of that strong pull to protect her. That need to protect what was his. Or what should be his. To make sure she was safe.

Because what happened to her had destroyed him. Not just from seeing the video but from hearing it the second it passed her lips back at his house.

Which proved just how strong she was. She was not letting it destroy her. She was dealing with it much better than he was.

But it pissed him the fuck off that she had to deal with it at all.

He sucked in a breath, then another. And one more. Then he grew a set and went to her.

Her hands gripped the railing, her eyes were closed, and her face was in the wind. The soft lights of the steamboat emphasized how goddamn beautiful she was. But it was more than that for him.

It was her confidence. Her resilience. The way she was grounded.

How she grew up in an environment totally different from his but still was completely accepting and open to it.

It had impressed him how she slipped so easily into the DAMC life. And if she could accept her real father, his family, his club, then she could accept him, his life and his club, too.

But again, it wasn't just her acceptance he needed. There were so many more speed bumps that would need to be dealt with.

And he wasn't sure how to handle them.

But that wasn't why he was on this retreat. Those speed bumps would have to wait. He had another issue to handle.

He also had a woman to claim.

And once he fucking claimed her, he wasn't sure he'd give her back.

He stepped up to her, wrapped his arms tightly around her waist, trying not to think about the water rushing by them below. Pressing his mouth to her ear, she shivered when he growled, "Remember when I said I was hangin' on by a thread? You just snapped that fuckin' thread."

Chapter Nine

OVER THE YEARS he'd watched her playfully flirt with Crash and Rig, Rooster and Coop. Even some of the DAMC prospects. And they ate that shit up. But none of them, not fucking one, had been stupid enough to touch her.

For them to do that, out of respect, they would have to approach not only her father, a fellow club member, but they'd also have to get the okay from Z, the club president.

With Magnum, he'd also need to approach his own president, who'd need to meet with the DAMC president and negotiations would have to take place.

Because Cait was DAMC property.

One did not just take property from another club without permission. That was a mortal sin.

And he was about to do just that.

"Tell me to stop," he murmured against her lips as she had him pressed to the outer door of their room. The second that door closed, she had shoved him back and once again took his mouth, ripping a groan from him and causing his fingers to grip her waist tightly. The intent was to push her away, instead he pulled her closer.

"Go," she moaned as she took his mouth again.

He twisted away, because he was having a hard time keeping his head on straight. "Caitie. Got any idea what you're doin' to me?"

Her green eyes flashed as they met his. "I have a pretty good idea."

No shit. His dick was hard and heavy, caught between them.

That thread that snapped? If they continued on their current path, it could never be repaired.

"If we do this, should be worried about bein' taken out by D or Dawg. Instead, worried about where this will take you."

"I'm not."

No shit.

"It's just sex, Magnum."

If only that was true.

It wouldn't be just sex. At least, not for him. She wasn't a sweet butt or some random hookup. And that worried him.

Even more importantly, it wasn't just sex on that video. It was more. That also worried him.

Yes, they both wanted it. But having sex with her was now much more complicated than the issues it would cause between the clubs.

"How do I follow that and not fuck it up, Cait? Tell me. How do I not fuck it up? Fuck you up?"

"You won't."

She couldn't guarantee that. She hadn't been with anyone else since that night. "How do I take you back from him?" His voice came out almost hoarse. "How do I take back what he took from you?"

He had no idea how she would react. Maybe on the surface she was coping fine with it. Maybe deep down, she wasn't. Would his actions flip that switch?

He wanted nothing but good for her. And he was afraid he wouldn't be able to give her good. He didn't want to be the one to cause her pain or any kind of distress.

Not fucking ever.

"You don't. He took nothing from me because I didn't allow him to take it. I didn't give him that power. But I'm giving myself to you. My choice is my power, Magnum."

"Think it's that easy." He wished to fuck it was.

"It's that damn easy."

Fuck, he wanted to believe her.

Suddenly, her eyebrows pinched together, and she stepped back, her fingertips to her swollen lips. Puffy because of the kisses on the top deck of that fucking boat. The ones that almost made him lose his mind and lose his load. Also from the kiss against the door.

Her eyes and expression were troubled.

Had he somehow fucked up already?

"Is it because... you see me differently now?"

Oh fuck no, he wasn't going to let that motherfucker fuck with her head. Not even a little bit. Not if he could help it.

The uncharacteristic insecurity in her voice made his temper flare. That was not Caitie. She was never insecure.

He rushed from the door, bent his knees, caught her in her middle and threw her over his shoulder. Her squeal filled the room. Within a few long strides, he kicked open the bedroom door and threw her on the bed, falling over top of her, but careful not to crush her with his weight.

He caged her in. He gripped her cheeks. And he took her mouth.

He claimed it. He made it his. And his alone.

That was *his* mouth. He would make her never doubt that or herself.

He just needed to push any of his own doubts out of his fucking head. They had nothing to do with her, but everything to do with who she was.

Who he was.

Her tongue tangling with his pushed all those doubts away for the moment.

He needed to concentrate on Caitie.

He wasn't afraid of much. But what he was about to do with her scared the fucking shit out of him.

But he was still going to do it.

He was still going to claim her.

No, this wouldn't just be about sex like she said.

It never was.

With a groan, he pushed up and away from her, getting to his feet. Standing at the end of the bed, his eyes not leaving her flushed face, her heaving tits, her red, swollen mouth. And her eyes...

Those fucking green eyes held his. Her confidence was back, and so was her smile.

That smile twisted something inside of him. It broke off a piece of him, a piece he was about to offer her.

He was giving her her power. Giving her her choice.

Which was him.

She rolled up and as her hands grabbed the bottom of her shirt, he barked, "Don't fuckin' move. Don't get naked. Leave that to me."

HE WAS GONE. He'd walked out, leaving her alone on the bed, wanting and needing. Leaving her blood rushing, her body humming and her pussy getting wetter by the second.

Her panties were already soaked from the dirty dancing she had done against him earlier. From touching him in public, even though she was careful so no one would see it. Then that kiss on the top deck before the endless kisses at the bow of the boat with him pressed hard and hot against her. With her touching him as much as he'd allow.

Which wasn't a lot but enough to get them both

desperate to get off that damn boat, get back to the resort and up to their room.

And neither of them had delayed. They ignored everyone else who were chattering and making plans to hang out at the bar. They ignored everyone who suggested a night swim in the heated pool.

She wasn't even sure she said goodnight to anyone.

And she definitely didn't make any excuses as to why they were on a direct path to their room and God help anyone getting in their way.

This was happening.

It was.

If he backed out...

If he walked out of the room and the reality stick beat him the fuck over the head...

If he kept moving out the front door to cool off and find his common sense.

If any of that happened...

No, it couldn't.

Please... It couldn't.

"Magnum," she called out, suddenly worried.

But then he was standing in the doorway, a huge dark silhouette, since the light of the living area was behind him and the bedroom's light hadn't been turned on.

He was massive. There was nothing small about the man. Not only physically but his presence, too.

She quickly leaned over and hit the switch for the lights above the bed.

And she lost her breath.

He had removed his shirt, his boots and his socks. He stood in black jeans that made her wonder how they fit his thick thighs. He was barefoot, bare chested, with his belt removed, the jeans unfastened, giving her a hint of how thick that dark hair that circled his navel got as it went lower.

He had something in his hand. A box.

And even across the room she could read it.

Magnum Bareskin Condoms.

"I shouldn't be surprised," she said as she tracked him moving into the room, around the bed and tossing that box onto the nightstand.

"How d'you think I got my name?"

She'd never really thought about it.

"Started out as a fuckin' joke when I was a prospect. It stuck. Decided to keep it."

"I wondered about the stereotype," she half-joked.

"Ain't always true. Got some brothers with the tiniest fuckin' dicks. Sucks to be them."

She wasn't sure if she wanted to know how or why he knew that. "Well then, it does not suck to be me."

"Let me know after."

She chewed on her bottom lip as her gaze slid back to the box where he was ripping it open. Not neatly, either. "It's only a ten-count," she whispered.

His fingers stilled and his dark eyes shot to her. "Plan on not goin' to anymore activities durin' your retreat?"

She *hmm*'d. "Depends..."

"Fuck, woman."

"Speaking of fuck... you need to take those *fuckin'* jeans off."

His grin made her heart thump a little faster. Every grin or smile he shot her way made her fall a little deeper.

Every damn one.

They were rare. So every one of them was precious.

"I want to see you smiling at me when you're naked." Her words caught in her throat and they also made that grin flatten out and his eyes turn dark and heated.

"Caitie..."

The hesitation in her name was clear.

Oh shit.

She hurried to the edge of the bed and onto her knees, her skirt bellowing around her as she pressed her finger to his dark luscious lips. "Don't you fucking dare let anyone else into this room. Don't. You. Dare." She couldn't hide the tremble now in her voice.

She never wanted anyone as much as she wanted Magnum right now. He was

not going to screw it up. She refused to let either of them screw it up.

"Magnum. I want to see you." Not heeding his earlier order, she ripped her shirt over her head and threw it onto the floor at his feet. "I want you to see me, too." In person, in real life. Not only from in that damn video.

He said nothing, did nothing. Only stared at her as she unhooked her bra and threw that, too.

She cupped her aching breasts for just a moment, sweeping her thumbs over both hard nipples, then she moved her hands down to her waist, hooked her fingers into the elastic waistband of her skirt and shimmied out of it. She dropped to her ass on the mattress, ripped it over her feet and tossed that next.

As she reached for her panties, a guttural noise came from deep within his throat, making everything clench on and in her, making her even more impatient.

His chest was heaving and his eyes searing her every-where they touched. But he still hadn't moved.

He was frozen in place and she *needed* him to move.

She wanted to erase that horrible video which replayed when she least expected it inside her mind and replace it with something good. Something great.

She wanted that power back she spoke of. That man, whoever he was, tried to steal it from her and it was time to take it back.

It was hers and now she wanted to share it with the man who was finally, *finally*, shoving his jeans over his hips and down his massive thighs. She licked her lips as he took his cock in his hand, sliding his fist back and forth over the hard, thick length. With each stroke, his thumb swept over the crown.

"Caitie."

Again, doubt colored her name, so she scrambled to rip her panties down her legs and over her feet. But she didn't throw them.

Instead, she lifted them, showing him how soaked they were. Her throat convulsed and she swallowed hard so she could say, "You did that to me, Magnum. *You.*"

His throat worked and, again, nothing but a mix of air and a groan escaped his now parted lips. And his reaction to her somehow made her want him even more. She didn't think that was possible.

She held out her hand to him, the one with her panties and whispered, "Please." She wasn't above begging. They couldn't get this far and not continue. It would be pure torture and a huge disappointment.

He snagged the panties off her fingers and did something that made her thighs quiver and her breath shudder. He pressed them to his nose and inhaled, his eyelids heavy, the fist wrapped around his cock moving even faster.

His whole body jerked as if someone had pushed his start button, and the panties dropped from his fingers and he focused on her.

Suddenly the look in his eyes became almost feral. Dangerous.

Determined.

Not one ounce of doubt.

A shock of lightning shot through her and goosebumps broke out over her body as he put one knee on the bed, making it dip.

Then everything happened quickly, making her heart skip, then race like a runaway horse.

His big hand fisted her hair as he took her mouth, only breaking the kiss as he yanked her head back, his lips moving from hers, down her throat, over her collarbone and to her nipple.

His lips wrapped around it and sucked it so hard she whimpered. Her fingers curled around the back of his neck, her other hand grabbing his shoulder for balance, her nails digging into his flesh.

His deep, guttural groan vibrated around her peaked nipple, his other hand clenching her hair even tighter.

Oh. My. Fucking. God.

She might come from what his tongue and mouth were doing to her nipples alone.

"Don't hold back," she urged.

His teeth scraped the very tip before sucking it even harder. To the point of almost pain. Almost but not quite. No, it was perfect.

She wobbled. With what he was doing, which was now sweeping his wide hand down her belly getting closer to where she really wanted him, it was going to be impossible to remain on her knees much longer.

"Whatever you want to do to me, do it. *Please.*"

He lifted his head, took her mouth hard one more time and then pulled back until they were almost nose to nose and in a low, gruff voice said, "Everything."

Unable to control her breath, she could barely whisper her demand. "Then do it."

The little air she had left in her lungs escaped when, with a palm to her chest, he pushed her, and she fell backwards to the mattress. Then before she could catch her breath, his hands captured her ankles and pulled her ass to the edge of the bed. He slipped off the bed and to his knees, placing her feet on his broad shoulders and spreading her thighs wide with his fingers.

"Fuck, baby," he said softly, his smooth, dark head a startling contrast between her barely-tan thighs.

"Everything. Give me everything."

His dark brown eyes tipped up to her. "Can't give you everything, Caitie. But can give you me."

And to her, that *was* everything.

He leaned in, her knees dropped outward, and his mouth found her.

He was gentle and he wasn't.

He was thorough and he teased.

He knew exactly how to draw an orgasm from her with just his mouth.

He did it again adding his fingers.

When it got to the point she almost begged him to stop since the orgasms were so intense that she'd been reduced to a quivering mess, he surged to his feet and snagged a condom off the nightstand. Ripping the wrapper open and rolling it on.

And not once had his eyes left her.

Not once.

Almost as if he thought she wasn't real and if he looked away, she might not be there when he looked back.

But she was real. He was real.

And she wasn't going anywhere.

"Gonna take you while you're on your knees at the edge of the bed. But not this time. Need to see your face when I'm inside you the first time."

The first time.

She raised a hand and he grabbed it, their fingers lacing together. She offered her other one, and they did the same. Using their clasped hands, he slid her up until she was back to being completely on the bed and he followed her until his knees were between hers and their joined hands were pressed into the mattress on both sides of her head.

He leaned down, capturing her lips, dragging his tongue through her mouth, his cock pressing against her thigh.

"Baby?" he whispered against her lips.

"Before you ask it, the answer is yes."

Using his knees, he spread her thighs wider, his cock sliding up her thigh, getting closer until she felt the tip pressing against her sensitive flesh. But it wasn't where it needed to be.

She untangled her right hand from his, reaching between them and lining him up. But he hesitated.

"Please," she breathed as he buried his face in her neck, his hot breath sweeping over her throat.

She continued to hold him there, until finally the tip parted her slick lips. She released him and he immediately interlocked their fingers together again.

Then he lifted his face from her neck, stared right into her eyes, and slowly, ever so slowly took her.

MAGNUM CLOSED HIS EYES, but only for a second. Only long enough for him to gather himself. To get his shit together.

Because the second he slid inside Cait, he almost lost it.

Being inside her shouldn't be any different than any other woman he'd ever been with.

But, *fuck him*, it was.

She said it would just be sex.

This was proof it wasn't.

Her tight, wet pussy pulsed around him, making it even harder for him to think. To breathe. To remember what a bad idea this all fucking was.

Because right now, thinking and breathing weren't important. The thought of dying, the fear of war, had temporarily disappeared.

And all that mattered at that fucking moment, and for those next moments, was Caitie.

When he couldn't go any deeper, he stilled and asked, "Okay?"

And that was when a tear slipped from the corner of her eye and her lips trembled as she smiled. "Yes."

"Baby," he breathed.

"I'm good. Don't stop."

Thank fuck.

Because if she wanted him to stop, he would, but it would rip him apart. Because right now, being deep inside her, being a part of her, being connected with her...

After years of wanting her. Of thinking he'd never have her.

That he *couldn't* have her.

All those years... All that waiting...

It was worth every goddamn second.

This had nothing to do with sex. It had everything to do with Cait. It had everything to do with the shit he'd kept buried deep inside him.

It had everything to do with his fight to keep it there.

He knew this would be a mistake. And he knew it still was.

Not because of the shit that would be stirred, the issues that would arise.

But because she now owned his soul.

He couldn't give her everything, but he could give her him.

And he did.

Kissing away the first tear and then the second, he began to move. Slowly. Gently. Taking his time, making sure she was okay, making sure not to hurt her in any fucking way.

He watched her face for any sign of a change. Good. Bad. Anything.

But it was all good. And only got better.

Even though her eyelids got heavy and her sight became

unfocused, their gazes remained locked. He didn't want to miss even the slightest change.

Her expression went slack and her lips opened as the smallest sounds escaped her. But those little sounds made the biggest impact on him.

Her hips began to surge to meet his as he drove himself to the hilt each and every time.

She welcomed him, encouraged him, her wet heat pulled at him. Her hips rose higher and faster, almost frantic, and he knew if he matched her pace, he wouldn't last, so he tried to slow her down.

He ignored her noise of complaint and paced himself with long, steady thrusts. Because he couldn't blow his load before she came. He wanted her to explode around him. He *needed* to feel it.

He was desperate to feel it.

"I want to let go."

He loosened his fingers. "Then let go."

She disconnected their hands and her nails scraped down his back all the way to his ass and she grabbed the cheeks, digging her nails in, squeezing them, trying to pull him even deeper.

He could go no deeper.

But he understood what she needed. Because he needed it, too.

To be connected so deeply that they wouldn't know where one began and the other ended. To be connected body and soul.

He never had that with anyone. Never thought it was possible.

But, *for fuck's sake*, it was.

And it was with someone so wrong for him in so many ways.

One hand released his ass and grabbed his face firmly,

forcing him to open his eyes, which he wasn't even aware he'd closed.

"Hey," she breathed. "Don't hide those beautiful eyes."

His nostrils flared as something so intense stirred inside him. "Maybe your beauty is blindin'."

Everything shook around him as she silently laughed, and her pussy clenched him tight. Her lips curved up and her eyes crinkled at the corners. "You already got in my pants, no need for compliments."

"Baby, you're worth every compliment I give you."

That smile faltered and he was worried she'd start crying again. And every fallen tear shredded him. So, he needed to avoid that.

With one hand planted on the bed to hold his weight, he dipped his head, took her mouth and shoved one arm under her hips to tilt them.

And then he drove home.

Over and over until her legs were squeezing his hips, her groans muffled in his mouth, her fingernails tearing at his skin.

He felt it coming, building, sweeping through her.

Her head jerked back, breaking their kiss, as she let out a wail as every part of her body tensed, then let go.

The climax that exploded around him broke his concentration, broke his will, broke everything inside of him until he, too, had to let go.

The ache became intense, his balls pulled tight and with a grunt he powered deep one more time and came, imagining he wasn't wearing a goddamn wrap. Imagining his cum filling her. Imagining leaving a piece of him inside her.

He buried his face into her neck and breathed as his dick throbbed and his balls emptied. And Cait stayed wrapped around him, her breathing as hitched as his.

Warm fingers curled around the back of his head, her other hand sliding slowly up his back.

And they just remained.
Together. Connected. Sated. Satisfied.
He didn't want to move. He didn't want to let her go.
He couldn't let her go.
He just didn't know what to do about it.

Chapter Ten

MAGNUM CLOSED the door behind her, making sure it was locked. As Cait turned to head down the hallway toward the stairs, the couple in the next room stepped out, took a look at them, and averted their eyes as they hurried away.

Oh shit.

She grabbed Magnum's arm and whispered in horror, "Holy crap, were we that loud?"

"Nope. We weren't. You were."

Heat rose into her cheeks. "I work with him."

"Yeah."

"He heard me having sex."

"Yeah."

Yeah?

YEAH?

"We're going to have to be more quiet."

He only grunted, but grinned, tucking his hand under her hair and grabbing her gently by the neck to steer her toward the stairs.

"We just eatin' this mornin' or we sufferin' through some other bullshit?"

She wrapped her arm around his middle, though it was

too wide to encircle it completely. "If you only want to eat, we can just head back to the room."

He raised a dark eyebrow. "Need to get info, Caitie. Need to find out if the youngest Gallo was the one."

The one. "That's right. That's why you're here." She waited for him to dispute that, but he didn't. "Well, sorry to tell you but this morning's agenda includes a motivational speaker while we stuff our faces."

"Great," he grumbled.

"But maybe you'll get something out of it."

"Right."

"The topic is how to manage difficult people. You might need that soon. If you want, I can grab you a notebook and pen to take notes."

"Goddamn smartass," he griped as he steered her into the main restaurant.

What surprised her was when he directed her to the front of the room by the podium. To the very table where all three Gallo siblings were seated, sipping coffee and chatting.

She put on the brakes. "Mag—*Malcolm.*"

"Gotta spend time with those fuckers if I'm gonna find out any shit."

She turned her eyes up to him. "We got distracted last night so I forgot to mention it, but while on the dance floor, Hank asked me if I was okay. He was concerned about you. He was worried you have a temper and was taking it out on me."

"Fuck. That why he was whisperin' in your fuckin' ear?"

"Yes. Now I'm worried he's going to mention you... *us* to Paul."

"Fuck."

And if it got back to Paul, he would tell her mother and then who knew what the hell would happen. Her mother was never rational when it came to Cait being involved with her father and the MC. And Magnum was a part of that life. That *was* his life. "I'm twenty-five years old. I'm not a damn child," she spouted in frustration.

"Caitie," he murmured, giving her neck a squeeze. "Can't fault the man for carin'. If someone thought my daughter's man was abusin' her, I'd wanna fuckin' know. And then I'd deal with it."

And then I'd deal with it.

Cait's heart skipped a beat. "*Do* you have a daughter?"

His eyes dropped from their destination to her. "Hungry. Let's grab a seat an' get grub."

"Why can't you answer that? It's a simple yes or no."

"Answer ain't simple. Later." He jerked his chin toward an open chair at the table where Drew and Nate sat with their sister, Natalie.

She sighed but glued on a smile as they stepped up to the table and greeted everyone. Magnum pulled out a chair and helped her settle in it, before taking the seat closer to Nate, after shaking the men's hands. Though, she could see he was fighting a grimace when he did so.

While they ate, he did nothing but have conversation with all three Gallos, which surprised the shit out of Cait.

Who the hell was this man?

He spoke without cursing once—though he almost slipped a couple times—he held his own with various topics and never once, during the complete meal, did he not have a possessive hold on her somewhere. Her neck, her thigh, or even simply holding her hand.

That did not go unnoticed by Drew or Nate.

Or even Natalie, who was actually flirting with him. Right in front of her.

Recently having gone through a long and rough divorce, she had said many times, and quite loudly, she was swearing off men. Apparently, the big man next to Cait wasn't off Natalie's menu.

But, sorry, the kitchen was closed. The woman wasn't going to get a taste of Magnum. Not now, not ever.

And if Hank's only daughter knew Magnum wasn't what he appeared to be, she'd probably turn her nose up at him, anyway. Just like she was afraid they'd all judge Dawg, Cait's father. Because Natalie's tastes ran toward men with power and money.

Which made her wonder if that was why Nate chased her so hard. Maybe he thought Cait had power and money because of Paul and her mother. She didn't and never would because she walked away from all of that as soon as she was old enough to make that decision. As soon as Dawg and Emma let her move in with them at seventeen, immediately after her high school graduation.

As soon as she realized she much preferred people who were genuine and down to earth. People who weren't pretentious and whose goal in life was to live a good one. Not necessarily one filled with money, but more with love and loyalty.

That was the life she chose.

That was the life she wanted for her future. For her children.

And from her future spouse.

She didn't need a lot, but she needed something real and solid.

She wanted to love a man who could love her back with both his heart and soul.

One as fiercely loyal to her as she was to him.

Magnum's fingers squeezed hers and she pulled herself out of her thoughts to concentrate on the conversation around the table.

Suddenly, she wished she'd stayed in her head.

"Never seen her like that before. Had a bad reaction to the liquor. Appreciate you gettin' her home safely. When she wouldn't answer her cell, got worried and went over to her apartment. Her car wasn't there and she wasn't inside, either. Pinged her phone and located her at a motel a few miles away. Luckily, she was safe. But she doesn't remember how she got there."

Cait tensed. This was not a topic she was expecting this morning. Why was he discussing this with a table full of people?

Nate's brow furrowed. "That's strange. I unlocked her door for her and helped her inside. Then I left, thinking she'd sleep it off. Are you saying she went somewhere? Her car was left at the club."

"Know it because I got it the next day. If you took her home, how'd she get to the motel? Doubt she walked that five miles in the condition you're sayin' she was in."

Nate rubbed his chin. "There's no way she could've walked five miles. She could hardly walk a couple steps."

"Then how'd she get there, Nate?" His question was a low rumble but it had a sharpness to it.

Nate shrugged, appearing thoroughly perplexed. "I have no idea. Do you think she called someone?"

"Checked her phone. No calls except me tryin' to get ahold of her. Also checked with the motel's office, but they refused to give me that info. It would have to be requested from the pi—*police*."

Damn, he was good at telling stories. She didn't know whether to be impressed or disturbed that lies could slide so easily off his tongue.

"That's very strange," Drew said. "And worrisome. Was... everything okay? When you found her, I mean."

Cait's attention fell on Drew and her heart began to thump, unsure of what Magnum would say next. She dropped her hand to his thigh and squeezed hard. "I was fine."

"Had a bad hangover and couldn't remember sh— *anything*. She normally doesn't drink like that. I forbid it."

He *forbade* it?

More than one set of eyes around the table went wide.

Shit. Shit. Shit.

"Gotta understand me," Magnum continued, ignoring that reaction. "Love this woman to death. Will do anything to protect her. That means I'm lookin' out for her. I can't be with her when she goes out? Then she needs to curb her drinkin'."

Uh. Cait leaned forward to quickly say, "I don't drink that much. I only had one drink that night."

"I remember," Nate said. "You only had that one margarita."

"Then how does she not remember what happened? Why'd she end up at a motel she only lives five miles away from? Someone knows somethin' and I'm wonderin' who."

Oh fuck. She squeezed his thick thigh even tighter and his hand reached down to interlace their fingers.

"Maybe you need to go to the police, Cait," Drew spoke up. "It's scary to think that someone may have slipped something into your drink." His eyes landed on his own brother. "Very scary."

Natalie leaned forward, a concerned look on her face and squeezed Cait's arm. "That *is* scary. Maybe someone roofied you! But who would've done that? The club was closed to everyone but us. And the party only consisted of our employees and some significant others. I can't imagine anyone in our workforce would stoop to something like that. If there is someone among us who would do that..." Her gaze swept the restaurant, which was full of eating and chatting employees. Funny how she didn't look at the men sitting at her own table. Her own brothers.

"Has anyone shown you more interest than you'd like, Cait?" Drew asked, his eyes narrowed on her.

It wasn't surprising he would ask that, because every time Nate had asked her out, he'd done it with no one else around. So, no one probably knew how persistent he'd been.

Was she supposed to out Nate right there at the table? Speak her suspicions out loud at the breakfast table to his siblings?

Her mouth gaped open and she couldn't push the words up and out of her throat.

"Nate," Drew started, focusing on his brother. "This sounds like something your department should handle. If one of our employees drugged Cait during a work function, this could be a crime, as well as an HR nightmare. You need to handle this."

Now it was Nate's mouth that gaped open as he stared back at his older brother. "It didn't happen at work."

"It happened during one of our sponsored get-togethers."

"Drew..."

"Nate, you need to get with the authorities and not only report this but do an investigation on your end. So we can find out who he is and terminate him... Or her."

"I—"

Drew leaned forward and hissed at his brother, "It's your damn job. Do it."

Nate's jaw became set and as he turned to Cait, Magnum said, "No cops. You find out who it was, you come to me."

Natalie raised her palms. "No. The police need to be involved. Especially if..." She turned to Cait, concern in her brown eyes. "Did you wake up alone?"

All eyes landed on her.

She struggled to breathe. Her brain was spinning since she had no idea what to say or how this would play out.

"Yes... Yes, I was alone and I was fine." She waved a hand in the air. "It's just a mystery on how I got from my apartment to the motel, as I don't remember going there.

Mag—" She swallowed his name. "Malcolm came and picked me up. I only had to deal with a pesky headache for a while afterward."

God, she could lie as easily as Magnum.

"Well, that's a relief," Natalie whispered, sitting back and relaxing a little more. "But still, if you were drugged by someone who had nefarious intentions, we still need to know that. Good thing Nate was there to get you home safely."

"Thank fu— *God*," Magnum bit off next to her.

"Yes," Cait leaned forward, caught Nate's gaze and forced out, "Thank you, Nate."

"My pleasure. Anything for you, Caitie."

Magnum tensed next to her and a low growl slipped out.

"Cait," Nate corrected quickly. "Cait. Sorry. I know you don't like being called that."

She also didn't like being drugged and violated while she was passed out. Him calling her Caitie was harmless and excusable. The rest was not.

But if he was the one, he showed no signs of guilt during the whole conversation. None at all.

Which could be a sign the man was a psycho.

Or it could also be an indication of innocence.

Maybe this whole thing was just a bad idea. Maybe she never should have considered getting Magnum involved. Just let it all go. Forgot about it and moved on.

But what if whoever did it, did it to someone else? And she did nothing to stop him?

That's what ate at her the most. She didn't want any other woman to go through what she did. Maybe she didn't remember it but that didn't mean the next woman wouldn't.

And maybe the man wouldn't be gentle with his next victim. Maybe he'd be emboldened because of not being caught the first time—if it was his first time—and would hurt the next woman badly.

No.

No, she needed to find out who he was, and something needed to be done about him. So, she was back to square one. And the reason she got Magnum involved in the first place... because she had nowhere else to go. And while she'd originally been worried about being blackmailed, no further contact from whoever sent her that video had been made.

That made it even more confusing on why the video was sent to her in the first place.

What a damn mess.

She was glad she had finished eating because after all of that, she lost her appetite. She no longer wanted to sit at the table with the Gallos for the rest of the morning. She was also not happy with Magnum for not warning her that he was going to bring that subject up. Not in private, but right there at the table. In front of the person she suspected was the one who did it.

At least he hadn't mentioned the video. And he also made it sound like she had only gotten "lost" instead of raped.

He apparently wanted them to concentrate on who drugged her. Because that would tell him who did the rest. And again, it pointed at Nate Gallo since he had been the one near her drink before she went to the restroom. He'd sat with her and never left her side. He was also the person who "helped" her home. If she even got home. She had no evidence of that, either. Nate could be lying and had taken her directly to the motel.

She chewed on her bottom lip, staring at her now cold cup of coffee.

Magnum pulled her bottom lip from between her teeth with his thumb, leaned over and gave her a firm kiss, then said softly, but loud enough for everyone to hear, "Love you, baby."

He then kissed her again on her temple while her heart pounded so hard in her chest, she swore everyone could see it. When he sat back, a satisfied look on his face, she whispered, "Love you, too."

He gave her the biggest smile she'd ever seen from him, before lifting his coffee cup and downing it.

When he put the empty cup on the table, he was still smiling.

———

Magnum sat under an umbrella by the pool as a bunch of Cait's co-workers played water volleyball in a "team building" exercise. It didn't go unnoticed that a few of the men had done a quick, and not-so-quick, inspection of Cait in her fucking bikini.

Knowing she would be jumping around in the fucking pool, hitting a ball while getting up close and personal with some of her male co-workers made him ask her if she had brought along another bathing suit that covered her more.

She had not.

Then he strongly suggested she skip that exercise in fucking team work.

She did not.

And now he sat there watching her laughing, smiling and splashing around, wanting to throat punch every fucking male in that pool as they watched her tits bounce as much as that fucking ball.

He was also starting to wonder if they were purposely hitting the ball to her more than her female co-workers like Angie, who was about five feet tall and the same width around. Or Petra, who had zero tits and an allergy to shaving her pits, which, with her hands in the air, only made it too obvious.

But, *hell*, maybe those women did it for someone else. Just not him.

He got it, though. A twenty-five-year-old, curvy blonde

with big green eyes and even bigger fucking tits was hard to ignore. Unless you were fucking gay.

He doubted any of them were gay. Petra, maybe, but since she didn't have a dick—from what he could tell—he didn't care if she checked out Cait.

He squeezed the lounge chair's armrests to keep himself in his seat and clenched his teeth to keep from yelling out that those were *his* fucking tits and to stop eyeballing them, otherwise he was going to make sure those fuckers couldn't see anything after he was done.

But he was also pretty fucking sure Cait wouldn't appreciate that outburst or those busted eyes, so he suffered in silence.

However—and it was a big fucking *however*—they were going to have a conversation later about her buying a one-piece bathing suit. Or a damn tent. Or better yet, banning her from pools all together.

Fuck.

As soon as Nate Gallo exited a building on the other side of the pool, Magnum released the armrests which were anchoring him in place and surged to his feet. That motherfucker's eyes went directly to Cait who just hit the ball high and whose tits bounced even higher, almost right out of her top.

"Fuck no," he growled as Nate approached the pool.

Fuck no, screamed in his head. As did, *get the fuck outta the pool, Cait!*

But somehow he managed to choke all of that back and, instead, tried to be casual as fuck as he stalked his way around the pool, staying far away from the edge. Because right now, if he knew how to fucking swim, he'd be in that pool, throwing her over his shoulder and hoofing it right back to their room.

But, *fuck him*, he couldn't, so he didn't.

Instead, when he got close enough to Gallo, he cleared

his throat loudly and gave that fucker a smile. Whether it appeared deadly or not, he didn't fucking care.

"Malcolm," Gallo greeted, also clearing his throat, but not in a *gonna-fuck-you-up* way, but more of a *please-don't-slice-off-my-balls-and-shove-them-down-my-throat*.

"Gallo. Got a sec?"

"Uh... Sure."

Magnum turned to see Cait staring at them from the water. "Be back, baby. Don't leave this area without me."

He ignored her frown and the worry in her eyes, and jerked his head toward an empty pavilion away from the pool area. Gallo followed him and once they were out of hearing range, he turned and towered over the fucker, hands on his hips.

Magnum wondered if the man's asshole was as puckered as his lips. If not, it should be.

"Need to talk to you about that night. Without Cait. Without other ears hearin'. Since you're head of the HR department and are supposed to handle this sh—*stuff* accordin' to your brother, comin' to you with more info no one knows about 'cept me and Cait."

"Uh... okay. I think we need to get police involved."

Magnum frowned. "You want cops involved?" That surprised the fuck out of him.

"Well... I'm not sure I could do a proper investigation and if Caitie... uh... Cait was drugged, that's a crime."

What the fuck!

"Yeah, it's a fu— a fu—" He huffed a breath through clenched teeth, then tried again. "Right. But I got evidence no one else knows about. And... Caitie doesn't want anyone going to the pi— *cops*."

"Why?"

Because I'm gonna kill the fucker so he never does it again to anyone else. "Because she's embarrassed about what happened. She blames herself for being careless. And if her father finds out, which he will if you go to the cops, it's gonna cause a major issue."

And that issue would be caused by more than just Dawg.

"You'd think Paul would want her to go to the police."

Jesus fuck. He kept forgetting they thought that fucking stepfather of hers was her real father. "He's got a temper." He never met the asshole so he had no idea if that was true or not. "A bad one."

"I've never seen it."

"Just be glad you haven't."

"But—"

"Look," Magnum cut him off. "Need your help. We can work together. Get me a name and I'll handle whoever it is. If I find out who it is, I'll give you his name so you can fire his— *him*." Though that last part would never happen because he'd never share that fucking name with anyone but maybe Cait. That name would go to his grave with him, just like the fucker who did what he did to her.

"How?"

Fuck. "How what?"

Gallo's Adam's apple bobbed. "How are you going to handle it... him? If it even is a him."

Oh, it was definitely a him. Magnum had seen the hard proof. "You leave that to me."

"How about we just leave this to law enforcement, I fire whoever it was and you can sleep easy he was caught?"

"Lemme tell you somethin', *Nate*. I love that fu— *woman*. I don't like that someone drugged her with the intent to hurt her. She also doesn't wanna make a big deal out of it, but I'm makin' it a big deal 'cause I can do that. She's mine. She's mine to protect. How 'bout I make a deal with you? You find out who it is before me, just let me have a few words with the fu— *guy* and then we'll let the p—*olice* deal with him."

"Okay, but I'm still not sure how I can help. I didn't see anyone slip anything into her drink and I was..."

"You were what?" *Stalking her ass? Pressuring her? Knockin' her the fuck out so you could steal a piece of her 'cause she wouldn't give it to you willingly?*

"There," he finished lamely. "You keep saying it's a guy. We don't know that. It could've been anyone."

It wasn't just anyone. "She wasn't alone in that motel room."

Gallo looked up at him in surprise. "She said she was."

"She woke up alone but wasn't alone while she was unconscious."

His face twisted in confusion. "How do you know?"

The man's reactions and words were throwing Magnum off. The more he talked to Gallo, the more he was doubting it was the slimy bastard who raped Caitie. And if it wasn't him, then who the fuck was it? "Know 'cause whoever was with her took video."

Nate's throat convulsed and his words were choked. "Video of what?"

"You know of what."

"Are you saying she was raped?"

Jesus fuck, he had a hard time saying that word out loud. "Sayin' someone did somethin' to Cait she did not consent to. Was not *able* to consent to."

"That's rape."

"That's right."

Now he was done jawing and needed to start asking the hardball questions while watching Gallo's face closely as he did so.

"Want you to watch the video." He didn't. He really fucking didn't. He had zero fucking investigative skills. This shit was so far over his fucking head. But he was going to do the best he could with what he had.

He yanked his cell phone out of his pocket and stared at

it, his blood already boiling, hoping he didn't explode this time when he showed it to Gallo. Because if Gallo did it? If he was the man in that fucking video? If he was standing right next to the man who did that shit to Cait? And if he was in arm's reach?

Magnum's life would be fucked. Her life, too. So he needed to keep his shit together. He needed to remain wound tight. Because if he began to spin out of control...

Yeah, killing the fucker would be the last thing he did as a free man.

And he'd only had one night with Caitie. That would never be enough.

He pulled up the video he'd transferred to his phone and deleted from Cait's. He sucked in a deep breath and braced himself. But as he started the video, he made sure to use his fat fingers to block Cait's naked, lifeless body, leaving only the man and motion visible to Gallo.

Gallo sucked in a sharp breath and Magnum pinned his eyes on the man's pale face when he asked, "Recognize that man?"

"I... No. I... I can't see his face."

"Yeah, whoever it was was smart." After checking once more to make sure Cait's body was covered by his fingers, he narrowed his eyes on Gallo. "You took her home, Nate."

"Yes... I took her home, not to a motel. I swear." The man's neck muscles tensed and his Adam's apple lifted and fell. "I would never..."

"You asked her out."

"Yes," Gallo hissed. "But I didn't know she was seeing anyone."

"She said no. And you asked her repeatedly."

"Yes, but..."

"That go against HR policy, Nate?"

"Yes... but—"

The video was now past the five-minute mark. Past the

part where Magnum had lost it when he watched it the first time. He needed to watch the rest in case the man had slipped and showed his face or the video showed some sort of clue. Like clothes or jewelry. Or something he could work with. Or maybe something Gallo could identify. *If* it wasn't him.

"You were alone with her while she was drugged."

"I'd never hurt her," Gallo said on a rough whisper.

"But you want her."

"Not like that." Gallo jabbed a finger toward Magnum's phone.

"You get off on screwin' a woman who can't say no? Who can't fight back? Who doesn't want you and made that clear?"

"No! I would never—"

Magnum kept pressing him. "Then who would? Who got that opportunity?"

"I don't know."

"You were the only one with her alone while she was drugged."

"It wasn't me. Maybe it was a stranger. Someone who broke into Cait's apartment after I left. Or maybe she didn't lock the door."

"Was she capable of lockin' the door?"

His throat worked again. "No. I should've made sure it was locked."

They were getting close to the end of the video. And close to the end...

A loud groan came from the phone as whoever it was... finished. Something dark came into view but quickly disappeared.

He hadn't quite caught what it was.

He forced his mind back to Gallo. To grilling him. Putting pressure on him to see if he would break. "And why would someone who was gonna do that to her take her to a motel? They could've easily done what they did right there. In her apartment. Don't make sense, Nate."

"I don't know. I have no idea how crazy people think. I know you think I did this, but I didn't. I..."

"You what?"

"I love Caitie," he finally whispered.

Christ. His upper lip curled in a snarl. "Weird way of showin' it, Nate."

"I swear..."

"Yeah," Magnum grunted, "me, too. Swear I'm gonna find out who did it. And if it was you..." He shrugged.

"I don't know who it was in that video, but it wasn't me."

"Better hope not," he said under his breath as Gallo rushed away.

But right now he was really doubting it was. And he had no fucking clue how to find out who it was. He felt like he was helplessly holding his dick in his hand, not knowing what to do with it.

As Gallo walked away, Magnum rewound the video to the spot where he'd noticed something strange. A possible clue. After the man shot his load, he bent over slightly to pull the condom off, but enough so a flash of dark hair came into the frame.

He paused the video and compared the color to Gallo's hair. It was close if not exact. But he couldn't be sure since the lighting was different. Though, whoever it was had dark brown hair. So did Gallo.

Coincidence? Could be, since a lot of the men who worked at Caitie's agency had dark hair. And he had no way to know if it was someone who even worked with her.

Gritting his teeth, he pushed Play once more. The man slid his hands over Cait, again gently, almost as if worshipping her, but they continued to slide lower.

And lower.

Magnum closed his eyes, his heart pounding in his throat, and hit the power button on his phone. He couldn't watch anymore. He couldn't see that. Because if he did, he could never unsee it.

A searing rage rushed from his gut into his chest and he forced himself to put his phone back in his pocket before he dropped it to the ground and stomped the fuck out of it, imagining it was that man's face.

Chapter Eleven

CAIT'S back arched and she threw her head back, her blonde hair spilling around her shoulders. Her hard nipples played *peek-a-fucking-boo* through those long silky strands as she ground herself on him, her hips wicked and wanton.

And he loved every fucking second of it.

She had sat on his face after demanding he lie on his back and barked out orders at him, and he tried to control his grin as she did so.

But he listened. Because what fucking man in his right mind wouldn't?

The woman had been horny after a few drinks while he suffered through an evening of bad karaoke where he wanted to poke his fucking eardrums out, and she point blank told him he needed to handle her horniness problem for her.

That's what she actually fucking said as she got naked.

He didn't argue.

Instead, he just grinned wider as she straddled his face and planted her slick pussy on his mouth, squeezing his goddamn ears so tightly with her thighs he figured that was what it would be like to be deaf.

She rode him until his face and lips were covered with her juices, and then after her climax, she slid down his body and right onto his already wrapped and waiting cock.

And was still riding it.

His fingers dug into her ass as her wetness dripped down his balls and into his fucking crack. As he ground his molars to keep from coming—since he didn't want it to end—he couldn't keep his eyes from her as she worked him hard, making him even harder.

And the harder he got, the closer he got.

If she was concerned with the co-worker next door hearing them, she must have forgotten that concern because she wasn't holding back. Not a sigh, not a moan, not a cry, not a whimper, not a drawn out, ear-piercing wail, either.

And, even better, not his name, which she said often and not very quietly.

Her nails now dug into his chest hard enough to almost draw blood as she rose and fell—her body swaying as she moved—all the way to the top and driving herself deep until she hit bottom.

Fuck, this woman!

The curve of her exposed delicate throat as her head tipped back called his name as much as she did. He needed to taste her there. Her pink puckered nipples screamed for his mouth, too.

But again, he couldn't stop watching her. He'd concentrate on those other things another time. Next time when she was under him and he was setting the fucking pace, making her squirm, making her explode around him, soaking him, then those tender, tasty spots would all be fucking his.

Right now, he was all hers.

All of him.

And that should scare the fuck out of him.

No *should* about it, it did.

He had told her he couldn't give her everything and that was still true. Would always be true. So, as much as he wanted to keep her, to claim her as his—not just for this week, but for forever—he knew... he *knew* he couldn't.

He was over forty and his life was settled. It was what it was. It wasn't changing. Not ever.

Being in her mid-twenties, she still had a long road to travel. So many things to achieve. And she deserved everything in life she could grab.

He wasn't going to let her settle on him and not get what she deserved.

It wouldn't be fair to her. And the possibility of her having even the smallest fucking regret would eat him alive.

But for now, he had her. He could pretend it could be fucking different. But at the end of the week, he'd make sure she saw the truth. The reality.

And he would have to accept it just like her.

Until then, though...

Fuck. Until then...

They had two more fucking days and two more long nights...

He needed to lock the sight of her, just as she was right now, into his memory.

He had to store the memory of her on the dance floor, at the front of the boat, in the pool—all of it—away for the future.

Dropping her head forward until her chin hit her chest, her green eyes opened, searching his, drawing him out of his thoughts and back to her. She circled her hips while her thumbnails scraped sharply over the tight tip of his nipples.

"Mag..." she whimpered.

"Yeah, baby?" he forced up his tight throat.

"Mag... I'm going to come."

He couldn't stop his smile, even if he wanted to. "Yeah, baby." He was beginning to recognize the signs of when she was there. And it wasn't because she announced it. Her pussy would tighten, begin to ripple, get even hotter and definitely get slicker around his dick.

All of that, along with watching her reactions, pushed him closer to blowing his load, too. Usually, he wasn't far behind. He was a fucking man after all, and the woman he wanted for years was riding his cock. Or sucking it dry, like she did that morning in the shower.

Remembering the stretch of her lips, the way her tongue teased him, the way she squeezed his balls as she sucked him as deeply as possible while he did his best to stay on his feet along with watching what she was doing now, made his hips surge up, while holding hers down, slamming once, twice...

She cried out his name again and he came at the same time she did.

Thank fuck. Because it had been damn close.

But if he would've blown the timing, he would have flipped her onto her back and powered through it until she caught what she was chasing.

She rode out her orgasm, milking his dick with her hot fist of a pussy, then collapsed onto his chest with a loud, shuddered sigh.

Their skin was slick with sweat, their breathing out of control, but she still tipped her face to his and gave him the biggest lazy, satisfied smile.

And, *fuck*, if that didn't pierce him in the gut.

He fisted one hand in her hair, and drew his thumb over the upward curve of her bottom lip. "That right there, baby, is the most beautiful fuckin' thing in the world."

That big smile became even more blinding. "No, you're wrong."

He wasn't, but he'd play along. "Then what is?"

"It's yours."

"No, baby," he murmured.

"Yes. You know why?"

Again, he'd play along. He loved these moments with her where she'd tease and joke with him. At home, he didn't get a lot of those. "Why?"

"Because your smile is so rare, every time you give me one, it's like a precious gift. It not only lights you up, but it lights me up inside, too."

His nostrils flared and his fingers tightened in her hair. He didn't know what to say to that, so he didn't say anything at all.

She was right. He hardly smiled. Mostly, it was due to his serious responsibilities. He ran a biker bar, he protected his club, he enforced the rules. His brothers kept their asses out of slings most of the time, but there were plenty of times they didn't.

They also tended to do stupid shit when it came to pussy. And sometimes they entered territory they shouldn't, chasing that pussy. Then he had to deal with another club, making sure his brother kept breathing and making sure that brother remembered the rules.

Stacy, his former ol' lady, made him happy for a while until she began to pressure him.

Even though he'd given up, his thoughts would sometimes also slide sideways and thinking about his kids would ruin his goddamn day. So, he tried not to think about them. And that also ruined his goddamn day.

Since he hadn't seen them in over fifteen years—that last day he walked out of the courthouse with his thoughts dark and his heart even darker—being happy became a rare thing.

But for some fucking reason Caitie made him happy. She was like a sliver of sunshine in the midst of a torrential rainstorm. A warm ray he could see, he could feel, but he couldn't keep or hold. Eventually the sun went down or the clouds moved in and it began to pour again.

This week, she was his ray. This week, she was his everything.

But that wasn't why he was there.

He was there to deal with the person who tried to steal that warmth, to darken that beam of sunshine.

And he was having none of that shit.

Her breathing had slowed, and he was starting to soften and lose her, which meant he needed to do something about the wrap soon.

But he didn't want to move.

"Am I crushing you?"

Her weight on him felt good. "Never, baby."

"I don't want to move. I love you being inside me."

He loved being inside her, too. "Can't stay there forever."

When she leaned forward, he slid from her and quickly grabbed the wrap, slipped it off and held it until she finished kissing him.

Which took a while. And he didn't rush it.

Once she was done and had burrowed under the sheets, he rolled from the bed to clean up and get rid of it, and also grab a wet washcloth to clean her up, too. He enjoyed taking care of her, even though she hadn't asked it of him once.

But it felt right.

As he headed toward the bathroom, his eyes fell on the nightstand. He was down to two wraps and they had two days and nights until they left early Saturday morning.

That wouldn't do.

Two would never be enough.

He decided they needed to go for a drive since it was quite possible, those two would be gone by the morning. And he was not fucking her without one, even though she'd insisted she was on the Pill.

He trusted her. But still...

He couldn't risk it.

One mistake and she'd be tied to him forever.

And though he wouldn't hate that, he knew it would be for the wrong reason.

If Cait was going to be tied to a man, it needed to be for the right ones.

———

Cait's phone beeped loudly. Once, twice, three times in quick succession. She groaned and unwrapped her tangled limbs from Magnum's. Though as she did, his big paw reached out, snagged her waist and pulled her back into him. But luckily, she'd had enough time to snatch her phone.

She kissed his bare chest, brushed her fingers over the short, wiry, black hairs trailing down his belly and held her phone in front of her face.

She sat straight up. "Fuck!"

Magnum's head lifted from the pillow and he rose to his elbows. "What?"

Three texts.

It only took three texts to scare the shit out of her.

She should've known.

She should've fucking known!

But she was currently living in a comfortable, very pleasurable bubble, forgetting about the real world. Forgetting about Shadow Valley. Her father. The DAMC. And the Dark Knights.

But the real world had found her.

Those texts had popped that bubble like a sharpened knitting needle.

"Who they from?" Magnum's voice was rough, because they had both drifted off after their last round of totally mind-blowing, but exhausting, sex.

And it was two a.m. Why the hell was she getting these texts now?

"Regan."

"Who the fuck is Regan?" The sudden sharpness in his tone made her wonder if he was jealous.

"My mother."

His head flopped back onto the pillow and he covered his eyes with his hand. "Motherfucker."

"I agree. And that's being kind."

He dropped his hand from his face and yanked her phone from her fingers. He read the three texts out loud in his deep voice even though she could hear her mother's shrill voice screaming out those words instead. "Who are you with at that retreat? Who is Malcolm Moore? Call me immediately."

He handed her back the phone and she tossed it back on the nightstand.

"Ain't callin' her back?"

"At two a.m.?" she shouted, her nerves about to unravel.

"Baby," he said calmly, running his fingers down her bare spine, then running them back up.

She forced herself to whisper. "I can't."

"Guess you were right. Fuckin' Hank talked to your stepdad."

"Of course. Because again, they forget I'm a fucking adult!" she shouted.

"Yeah. Now everyone at this resort knows it."

She buried her face into his chest. "Sorry."

"Tell the neighbors you're sorry in the mornin'."

"Ugh," she groaned against his skin. "This is a disaster."

"So, you call her in the mornin' and you tell her."

"Tell her?' She lifted her head and bugged out her eyes at him. "Tell her what?"

"That a friend came the fuck along with you."

"Right. You don't know Regan."

"Glad I don't. Heard she's a fuckin' nightmare."

"You heard right."

"But she's your mother."

"One thing I learned in the last ten years is blood isn't always family. She lied to me, Magnum. *Lied*. For almost fifteen years."

"Yeah, baby, fuckin' get that. But she had her reasons."

She had her reasons? "How would you feel if you were Dawg and you found out the mother of your child didn't tell you you had a daughter? Reason being, she didn't think you were good enough to know. I'd be pissed. I *was* pissed."

"Yeah, baby, I'd be pissed," he said softly. "I get it. People fuck up tryin' to protect the ones they love. Sometimes they'll do anything to do that, even lie."

While that may be true, it didn't make what her mother did right. "Dawg's a good man. She just refuses to see it, to believe it. She only sees who he is and what he is on the surface. She only knew him for a split moment, just long enough to get knocked up with me. She never got to really know him. She's embarrassed by her 'mistake.'"

"Yeah, get that."

Cait was the result of her so-called mistake. One she had been reminded of again and again during the awful visitation fight. "So, don't defend her."

He said nothing.

"She stole me from my father. She stole him from me."

His chest surged up abruptly and then fell. "Gonna say this one last time. She thought she was doin' what was best for you."

Her fingers curled against his warm skin. "But it wasn't."

"Yeah, it wasn't. She was wrong."

"I'd never do that to my kids."

Again, he said nothing.

"Would you lie to your kids like that?"

More silence.

She lifted her head and met his eyes. "Magnum, would you lie to your kids like that?"

It took him way too long to answer. "No."

She jumped as her phone rang. It was Magnum who reached out with his long arm and snagged it off the nightstand. He hit the power button, silencing it. "Mornin'. It can wait 'til mornin'."

"It can wait until I get back."

"Do what you need to do, Caitie. Do it on your time, but eventually you're gonna have to deal with it. Like it or not."

She burrowed herself against him and his arm curled around her. "Does anyone know your real name?"

"Doubt it."

Well, that was a relief. "Good. Then I'll think of a story."

THAT RELIEF WAS SHORT LIVED.

Because even if no one knew his real name, everyone in her personal life revolving around the MC world knew what Magnum *looked* like.

She ignored the endless texts and the phone calls that started as soon as she had turned her phone back on earlier, letting all the calls go to voicemail. Though, each message from her mother got shorter and angrier.

But it was the photo her mother texted of her and Magnum together on the steamboat's dance floor that made the phone fall from her fingers.

She didn't even try to catch it.

Instead, she sank to the ground next to it.

Hank! It was all Hank's doing for not minding his own damn business.

Between this and what happened to her that night a few

weeks ago, her dream job was quickly turning into a damn nightmare.

Unfortunately, because of that picture, she couldn't wait until she returned to Shadow Valley to deal with this. She needed to try to at least minimize the damage before it got to the point of no return.

Which would be Dawg finding out. And if he saw that picture...

Regan normally didn't talk to Cait's father. But if she was pissed enough, she wouldn't hesitate. And right now, the way her voicemails sounded, she was at that point.

For a woman who hadn't wanted to admit she slept with a biker, she sure used him when convenient to try to control Cait when she couldn't.

Dawg hated it. And he rarely agreed with anything Regan wanted.

Like when Cait decided to go to the University of Pitt instead of the Ivy League school her and Paul had donated money to.

Cait never saw a vein pop out that far on a forehead as much as Regan's had the day she announced that U of P was the college she selected.

Regan had immediately blamed Dawg for that. Blamed him for encouraging her to stay close to home.

He hadn't. He supported whatever decision Cait made. Unless she had decided not to go to college at all, then her father might have put his biker boot down firmly.

He wasn't poor. He'd run the MC's very lucrative strip club for almost twenty years, and now managed a very successful gun shop and shooting range, also owned by the MC. The club was flush and so were their members.

Rich? No. Doing well? Very much so.

So, it *really* stuck in Regan's craw when the threat of not paying for Cait's college degree—unless she went to her mother's choice of school—went ignored and Dawg stepped in to help.

Dawg didn't like to be manipulated and didn't like his daughter being manipulated, either.

The only thing she had to do for him to afford her education—even with her scholarships—was live at home with him and Emma so she could commute. But that wasn't a hardship since it also gave her the chance to help out with her two younger sisters, Lily and Emmalee, which she enjoyed.

But that also meant Dawg kept a close eye on who she was dating.

A very close eye.

Or would have if she'd brought anyone home, which she didn't. It wasn't because he was a biker, but because he was overly protective and she wanted to give anyone she was dating a chance before he was scared off. Because of that, she never mentioned her dates, only saying she was going to hang out with her girlfriends or had to stay on campus late to study.

Emma mentioned a few times—when Dawg wasn't around—about finding it curious a "pretty and smart girl" like her wasn't going on dates. But she would also give Cait a knowing look. Which meant her stepmother knew Cait was dating and most likely having sex, but said nothing to her ol' man.

But then, Emma was cool like that. There were too many times Cait had wished Emma had been her mother instead of Regan.

She wasn't.

And now she had no choice but to deal with her mother who hated her father and was bitter about Dawg "stealing" her away. Every time Cait heard her say that, one word would come to mind: karma.

She loved her mother, but there were days she hated her, too. She already knew today would be one of those days.

She picked up the phone when she saw her mother trying to video call her.

Oh no. That wasn't going to happen, especially since Magnum was sitting out on the balcony smoking a joint and could walk into the room at any time.

She swiped her finger across the screen to ignore the video call and then immediately dialed her mother back.

"I'm so angry at you right now!"

Yep. That should set the whole tone of the conversation. "Hi, Mom," she answered on a sigh.

"Cait—"

"You forget I'm twenty-five," Cait interrupted her. "I have my own apartment, pay my own bills, and have a job."

"I don't forget it. But you are still my daughter and my child."

Cait rolled her eyes. "*Your* child, not *a* child."

"You still make foolish decisions."

"Because they don't align with what you want or expect?" Cait did her best to tamp down her bubbling temper.

"I know what's best for you. I made mistakes that I want you to avoid. That's my job as your mother."

Cait pinned her lips together and sucked a deep breath through her nose. After a second of blessed silence, she asked, "Hank send you that photo?"

"Of course. He's worried about you and also said this man you're with has a bad temper. He trashed the room you two are staying in. You're sharing a room, Cait, with a man I've never met. With a man I've never even heard about!"

"And I'm an adult and can make that decision. I also don't need to announce that decision to either of my parents. That's private."

"Hank has me worried this man may hurt you."

"He hasn't and won't. So, don't." That would never be a fear. That was one thing that impressed her about the biker community, the men didn't usually abuse their women. If anything, they'd hurt someone who hurt or threatened their woman, instead. There were a few exceptions, of course, but abusers like that were in the minority. And she knew Zak, Diesel and the rest of them did not tolerate that kind of thing in their club. She figured Magnum was the same way with his.

"How do you know he won't?"

"Mom... Honestly... You should've studied the dramatic arts in school."

"Not funny, Cait."

"No, it's not. Now you get my point."

"Does your father know about this? Does he know him? Has he met him? Why haven't I heard about him?"

"We only recently started seeing each other," Cait lied since they weren't technically seeing each other, just having sex.

"Not according to Hank! That man said he's been with you for eight years!" Regan's voice had risen to dog whistle level on the last part.

She winced. *Shit.*

"Eight years ago, Cait, you were only seventeen and living with that damn..."

Oh. No. Her mother hardly cursed and hated when Cait did since it wasn't "lady-like." That could only mean things would spiral out of control sooner than expected.

"That *damn* what, Mom? My father?"

"Does he know about him?"

"No. And Malcolm only said that as a joke."

"Being with an underage girl is not a joke. And Hank said he's old enough to be your father, Caitlin."

Oh fuck, she was pulling out the use of her full first name. "He's not."

"The hell he isn't. I can see it clearly in the picture. He's not in his twenties. He's not even in his thirties. Who is he? What does he do? Why did he go with you?"

"Mother."

"Don't *Mother* me. Hank is worried and so are Paul and I."

"It's none of Hank's business. He forgets I'm his employee."

"He's looking out for you."

"Bullshit."

"God, your language! Ever since he..."

"*He*? Who? You mean my dad?"

"Ever since he forced himself into your life... Your language, your attitude... Your hopes and dreams. Everything changed. I had such high hopes for you, Caitlin. That you'd break the mold of your DNA."

She meant Dawg's half of her DNA. Certainly not hers, since Regan was apparently perfect. Oh, except for that one big mistake she made named Dawg.

Cait's chest compressed to the point where it was getting hard to breathe. "Holy shit, Mother, why do you have to be so fucking dramatic? There's nothing wrong with my DNA."

"I did my best to give you a fighting chance."

Oh no, she didn't... "I'm hanging up now."

"You don't warn someone you're hang—"

She hit the End button, cutting off her mother's voice.

Sitting cross-legged on the floor, she tapped her phone against her forehead, trying to calm her raging blood.

"Probably not a good idea to piss off your mother."

She inhaled deeply and glanced up at Magnum from the floor, who was now standing over her, his booted feet wide, hands on his hips and his face, masked with a blank expression, tipped down to her. But his eyes were searching, assessing. Also, not holding any kind of happy.

"She has a photo of the two of us."

"Fuck," he growled, his eyebrows dropping low. "Yeah, not a good idea to piss her the fuck off when she's got that shit, Cait. Call her back and make fuckin' nice."

"I'm not making *fuckin' nice*."

He stabbed a finger toward her. "If she's got a goddamn picture, then you make fuckin' nice. She sends that photo to your father, I'm fucked. You, too." He grabbed his crotch. "Say goodbye to my fuckin' balls, Cait, because they'll be sliced the fuck off, shoved down my throat and, if I'm still breathin', shittin' them out the next day. You get that?"

"My father... Diesel... all of them like you."

"None of 'em are gonna like that *I fucked you.*" He raised a palm to stop her next words. "Stepped in their territory, which is you, without permission. Touched their property, which is you, without permission. Can't believe I'm explainin' this shit to you again."

"I don't need to hear it again." She was tired of hearing it. Sometimes she hated the archaic rules of an MC. This "women as property" shit was one of them.

"Then pay the fuck attention."

Cait surged to her feet, snapping, "Pot should've mellowed you out, not turned you into a damn asshole."

"Always been an asshole, Cait, it's a part of the job. And ain't enough pot in the fuckin' world to prepare me for the shit that's gonna land on me if Dawg gets that picture. Call your fuckin' mother back and eat your pride."

"No."

His lips thinned out, his nostrils flared wider, and suddenly he seemed a hell of a lot bigger than he was. "You're actin' like a goddamn spoiled brat right now, Cait. Not likin' it. Not likin' it at all."

"I'm not a spoiled brat, I—"

"Really? What the fuck do you know 'bout growin' up poor? Grew up with a goddamn silver spoon in your mouth. Your 'daddy' was rich—"

"Stepdad."

He cocked a brow. "You know he was your stepdad all those years?"

She didn't bother to answer, because he knew the answer.

"Right. Know nothin' about scroungin' for survival. For food. For money. For a minute of your mother's fuckin' time 'cause she's bustin' her goddamn hump for her kids, workin' two jobs and also workin' a side hustle to try to make ends meet. You wore goddamn plaid skirts and knee-high socks to go to private school. You probably didn't walk to school or ride a public bus. Bet you got dropped off in a fuckin' Benz."

Cait closed her eyes at the truth he was saying.

She didn't want to fight with him. She also understood his concern. She had it, too. But she was tired of people trying to make her life decisions for her when she was damn well capable of making them—and screwing them up—on her own.

The point of making mistakes was to learn from them, right? Just like that night a few weeks ago. It was a hard lesson to learn, but she had and now she was dealing with it. Maybe not perfectly, but she was.

She needed to change the tension in the room and between them. "I still have those if you'd like me to wear them while I ride your cock."

She realized it did neither when he said flatly, "Don't got no schoolgirl fantasies."

Cait shrugged. "I thought most guys were into that."

"Babe, first thing you need to learn is, I'm not most guys. Figured you knew that by now."

"Sorry," she whispered, suddenly feeling pressure from all sides.

When the hell was her life going to be her own? When was her mother going to let her live it? When would her boss mind his own damn business? When would her father not be a threat to anyone she might be interested in?

She thought it would be after she graduated college, when she got her own place, when she got a steady paycheck. One she could afford to live off.

Apparently, she was wrong.

It shouldn't matter to anyone who she slept with, who she spent time with, but, of course, the man she wanted also had strong opinions.

She suddenly felt like running away, but then, she would be acting childish.

Even so, she could give at least the two of them space for now. Because she didn't want it to be like that between them. She didn't want them to be angry with each other.

She wanted to enjoy the little bubble they'd created up here. And while it had popped, maybe they could make the best of it for now.

"I need air," she mumbled and turned to head out onto the balcony.

Before she could take two steps, he snagged her wrist and stopped her. He took her open hand and held it against his crotch. "Know you like this and what I do with it. What you do with it. You want more of that, it needs to remain attached to my body. Call your fuckin' mother and make up a goddamn story so she doesn't go screamin' to Dawg."

He released her, stiffly moved away from her and snagged her car keys off the coffee table, giving her his broad back. "Gonna find a store. Better have called her before I get back. You don't leave this room, you don't unlock that fuckin' door for anyone. Get that shit fixed, Cait."

He jerked the door open, and slammed it shut behind him.

Cait stared at the door for the longest time. Then she called her mother.

She made up a story about Magnum she hoped her mother would believe. But knowing her mother, she doubted it would satisfy her.

Her mother made her opinion known, several times, that Magnum was too old for her, that he was close to her and Paul's age, and was probably trying to take advantage of her.

Cait did her best to convince her she was wrong, but the more she tried, the more frustrated she became. So, as soon as she could, she ended the call, sat on the balcony and while waiting for Magnum to return, let the warm sunshine soothe her.

In the end, she realized the smart thing for her and Magnum to do would be to brace for the storm that could hit them head on when they returned to Pennsylvania.

Because Cait had no doubt that was coming.

She just hoped it was a light rain shower instead of a hurricane, destroying everything in its path.

Chapter Twelve

MAGNUM SLOWLY SCANNED THE ROOM, doing his best not to be too obvious. He did it a couple more times, pretending to work the crick out of his neck. He also did it while leaning over and whispering into Cait's ear so he could see behind them. The only thing he told her was what he would do to her when they got back to their room. That was, after whatever bullshit work thing she had to do after dinner, which got her squeezing his thigh under the table way too close to his dick.

The one he was attached to and wanted to keep. So, he was relieved when Cait said she smoothed things over, for the most part, with Regan, but wasn't surprised when she said her mother had a problem with their age difference.

She wasn't the only one.

He had one more day to take action with whatever male he thought was in that video. Up in the Adirondacks, there were plenty of locations to dispose of a fucking dead man. So, if possible, he wanted to take care of that important business before heading home.

Only problem was, he wanted it to be the right dead man. Being wrong, and letting whoever violated Cait continue to breathe would be a fucking shame. It also meant she wouldn't be safe. Once they went back to Pennsylvania, he couldn't stay by her side, protecting her, like he had during this retreat.

He checked out every dark-haired male sitting in the restaurant, seeing who had a brown shade similar to what appeared in the video.

He nixed all the men who had dark hair with gray mixed in. He crossed off all of the blonds and redheads. Then he studied the possibilities. He had them narrowed down to five good prospects.

A spouse who Cait said wasn't at the celebration that night, so he was out. And two married co-workers who'd been there with their wives. He doubted it was either of them.

But his eyes kept slicing back to Nate and Drew Gallo, who sat at the table in front of them. His gut was screaming at him it had to be Nate.

The fucker had the opportunity and even the motive since he obviously wanted Cait, though she shot him down time and time again.

His fingers curled against his thighs under the table, imagining they were tightening around the bastard's neck. He never snapped a man's neck with his hands before. While he knew it was possible, he also knew it took skill. But he did know how to do it with a baseball bat or a club. Unfortunately, he didn't have anything like that with him. Crushing a windpipe would work, too. It just took a little longer and a little more effort.

If he could swim, he'd drown the fucker and make it look like an accident. That was out. If he knew how to drive a boat, he could tie weights from the gym to the mother-fucker's limbs and toss him overboard in the deepest spot he could find.

One good thing was, he had Cait's car and when he

went out to get more wraps earlier, he'd taken it onto several dirt roads into the woods, scouting a couple potential spots. The bad thing was, he didn't have the shit to dig a hole, so that might be out.

He gritted his teeth.

Back home in Pennsylvania there were plenty of abandoned quarries where bodies could easily be tossed and hopefully never found. He'd also found some interesting ways to get rid of Shadow Warriors when he or his brothers had come across them.

But, again, he had none of those tools up here in New York.

He also probably wouldn't have a lot of time. If Nate Gallo wasn't seen or heard from for even a short length of time, they might go searching for him.

For the most part, no one knew when one of those fucknut Warriors had gone missing until weeks later, since they were a nomad club without a home base.

But Gallo wasn't a Warrior. Someone actually gave a shit about him. Which meant they might figure out he was missing sooner than later.

Fuck.

Cait happened to mention she knew how to drive a boat, but there was no fucking way he was letting her help him. No fucking way he'd let her get slapped with an accessory to murder charge, if it came down to it.

No matter fucking what, time was slipping away and he needed to do something soon.

He narrowed his gaze on Drew Gallo as he approached their table. "Can I have a word, Malcolm?"

What the fuck. "Yeah." He leaned over to Cait and murmured into her ear, "Be back. Stay here 'til I return."

She nodded and let her hand slide down his arm as he rose and followed the oldest Gallo son out of the restaurant and outside to an empty patio in one of the gardens.

What the fuck was going on? Did Regan pull some shit?

"What's goin' on, Gallo?"

"Drew, please."

"All right, *Drew*, what the fu— What's goin' on?"

"I got an interesting email today. It was a bit disturbing and—"

Fuck. The video. "Where'd it come from?"

"I don't know. The email address used was one of those anonymous ones and there was a video attached."

Either the younger Gallo sent it to him, or whoever had been in that motel room did. But it made no sense. Why would they send it to Drew?

"A video of what?" He braced, already knowing what.

"She wasn't alone in that room."

Of course that motherfucker watched it. He'd seen Cait naked and vulnerable. His blood pressure began to rise, but he needed to keep his shit together. "Who was with her?"

"I don't know, but I have my suspicions. Do you want to see the video?"

Fuck. He had to play a dumb fuck and see where this all led. "Am I gonna get upset about it?"

"Yes."

"What was happenin' in that video?"

"Cait was compromised."

Compromised. A fancy fucking word for an ugly action. "How was she compromised, *Drew*?"

Gallo lowered his voice to a whisper. "She was naked. And... the person with her was a man."

Magnum wanted to roll his eyes but needed to act shocked and surprised instead. With a sharp noise, he covered his face with his hands. "Was she raped, Drew? Is that what you're sayin'?" Even though his words were muffled behind his hands, he raised his voice to a higher pitch.

A muscle in his jaw popped when Gallo pressed a hand to Magnum's arm. "Maybe you should sit down."

"No." Magnum said between his fingers, playing the devastated boyfriend. "No... Just... say it."

"It appears she was. Either that or... or she was willing and—"

Magnum dropped his hands and his glare stopped Drew cold. "You think she was fuckin' willin'? That she was screwin' around on me?"

Fuck, he didn't mean to curse. But fuck it, he was a man who was just told his woman had sex with someone else, consensual or not. It would be upsetting. *Jesus fuck*, it was upsetting even when Cait wasn't his damn girlfriend.

"Malcolm," Gallo started, sounding concerned.

"You think she was fuckin' willin'?" he asked again on the edge of shouting, making Gallo look around nervously.

"Her eyes were closed, her face was blank... and she wasn't moving. You'd know better than anyone how she..."

His eyebrows shot up and his jaw shifted. "How she what?"

"*You know.*"

"Yeah, Drew, *I know*. What'd you do with the video?"

"I... saved it. For evidence. To show the police."

Fuck that. There was no way they were getting the pigs involved. No fucking way.

"Need you to keep this to yourself, Drew. Don't want anyone else seein' it. Don't want Cait embarrassed by it. She doesn't know and I may not even want her to know. Need you to send me that video and delete the email."

Hell, he wanted to watch Drew delete the fucking email. Though, the man could've saved a copy to his phone. If not other places.

"It just proves that the police *should* get involved, Malcolm, like I said."

"You send me that video and let me decide on that.

She's my wo— *girlfriend.* She finds out some moth— *man* did that to her, it may mess her up. Right now, she's happy. That's gonna make her unhappy. She's unhappy, I'm unhappy. Get what I'm sayin'?"

Gallo's answer was a "yes," but it wasn't convincing.

"Said you've got your suspicions? Wanna share 'em?"

Gallo again glanced around and took a step closer to Magnum. He didn't like it but he tolerated the fucker getting up close and personal since he might be getting a name.

Gallo lowered his voice again. "I fear it's my brother. He's been obsessed with Cait since she started at our agency. He took her home that night. He had access to her drink and access to her."

Play dumb and let the asshole keep speakin'. "If he took her home like he said, why would he take her to the motel afterward?"

"Maybe he took her straight there. Look, I think he has issues and I'd hate to say that about my own brother, but I've been concerned about him for a while."

This whole "concern" thing was feeling like a whole bunch of bullshit. "You take those concerns to your father?"

"Of course, but, again, Nate's his favorite, as well as his namesake, which should've been me since I was the firstborn son. He's always been blind to my brother's behavior, too."

"You wanted Nate to investigate it," Magnum reminded him.

"Before I saw the video."

"What makes you think it's him? Can you see his face?"

Gallo hesitated. "No. But I grew up with him. We're in the locker room at the club together all the time. I know what his body looks like."

"And you think it's him."

"I hope it's not, but I'm... leaning toward it."

"You confront him? Or did you come to me first?"

"You."

There was something so fucking off with this whole thing. So much so, Magnum's skin was getting itchy. "Why?"

"Because if it was my girlfriend, I'd want to know first."

Right. The fucker was throwing his brother under the bus. There was no fucking way Magnum would ever do that to one of his brothers, blood or not. He'd handle that shit himself. But then, Gallo probably didn't have the balls big enough.

Magnum held out his hand.

Gallo stared at it, confused.

"Phone. Unlock it, pull up the email and hand it over."

"I... uh..."

"Pull it up and hand it over," he said more firmly, drawing himself to his full height of six-foot-three. He had a good five inches and about sixty solid pounds on the asshole.

Gallo pulled his cell from the holder on his belt and unlocked it using his fingerprint. "Give me your number and I'll text it to you."

Magnum snagged it from his fingers, pulled up the email app, scrolled down through the emails. "Which email?"

"I... I downloaded the video to my phone and deleted it."

Magnum raised a brow. This fucker was a lying sack of shit. What was his angle? "You deleted the email you were gonna use as evidence for the police?"

"Yes... But I saved the video," he said quickly.

"Ever thought they could've figured out where the email came from?"

"Sorry."

"It in your deleted email?"

Gallo's eyes widened for a second. "No. Sorry."

Something definitely wasn't right. Magnum scrolled through the man's phone until he found the saved video, then sent it to himself, even though he already had a copy.

He wasted no time deleting it from Gallo's phone. "That it? Any other copies?"

"No."

"You sure? I find out differently, Drew, I'm gonna have a problem. No, *you're* gonna have a problem. I'll decide who gets to see it, includin' Cait."

"I'm not sure if that's smart. If it's my brother, something has to be done about him. To stop him from doing this again in the future."

Something was going to be done about it, guaran-fuck-ing-teed. "What would you do about it if it was?"

"Call the police, like I said."

"No name, no face, no identifying marks, right? Anonymous email you deleted. Weeks later, so no DNA to test. What the fu—*hell* do you think the... *cops* are gonna do with that video besides watch it and scratch their heads?" Scratch their fucking balls, more likely.

"I don't know."

"Right," he grunted and handed Gallo his phone back. He spun on his heels and went to get Cait.

He needed to get away from that motherfucker before he killed him, too.

———

CAIT WANDERED through the open slider and climbed sideways onto Magnum's lap, hoping the chair would hold the both of them. It groaned and flexed but seemed to hold as he wrapped his thick arms around her.

She settled her legs over the armrest and put her ear to his chest over his heart. The beat was strong and steady.

He tucked his nose into her hair and inhaled.

He was like a rock. Her rock.

She just needed to convince him of that. She also

needed to come up with a good way to convince her father of it, too.

"Maybe you could approach my father and..."

His whole body tensed under and around her. "And what?"

"Ask for permission."

"For what?"

She pinned her lips together. He probably didn't want the same things she did.

"For what, Cait? What am I askin' Dawg for? Besides a fuckin' beat down?"

She grimaced. If anything, she was sure Magnum could take her father, but there was no way she wanted that.

"For what?" he prodded again, his fingers digging harshly into her thigh. "To be my ol' lady? Or just permission to fuck you?"

"I don't know how it works," she said weakly.

"Yeah, you do. Not lookin' for an ol' lady, Cait. And that's a commitment you shouldn't be lookin' for with me anyway."

"Why not? Because I'm too young?"

"Yeah, baby, 'cause you are way too fuckin' young."

Age shouldn't even matter. Compatibility should. "We're good together."

"It's been a few days. Not enough time to know that."

But it was a good start. "We could give it the time it needs."

"Cait..."

"Tell me about Stacy."

He jerked in the chair and she lifted her head from his chest to see his jawline hard, his eyes focused on the calm, dark lake beyond her.

"The sisterhood mentioned her. They said she was your ol' lady and then suddenly one day she wasn't."

"Told *you* that?"

"Well, they mentioned it when they were speaking in general." But she had paid attention whenever he was mentioned. No one knew what happened. Stacy was there and then she was history. No one ever heard them arguing or anything. And the few times his ol' lady was invited to DAMC events, the women said she never bitched about Magnum. Not once. If they had been having problems, they'd hidden it well.

"Why am I in their mouth?"

"How can you not be? Single beast like you?" She grinned.

His lips finally twitched and his jaw softened. He dropped his gaze to her. "Yeah?"

"Oh, you like that? The women all drooling over you?"

"Right," he grunted.

"They do. Single *and* sexy." She ran her fingertips lightly over his very kissable, very suckable, very skilled lips. "And great in bed, too. But none of them know that."

"Reason for that, Caitie."

"Yes, because they aren't single."

"Not all of 'em."

"Well, no. Annie and Allie aren't. But I don't think either are looking for a man." Both were also a lot older than Magnum. Her mouth got tight. If age wasn't supposed to matter, she couldn't think like that. "So, tell me about Stacy. Was she your only ol' lady? What happened with her?"

Magnum focused on her lips. "Mouth."

A shiver ran through her at that demand. He was trying to distract her. Even so, she tipped her head up and offered it to him.

He took it long and hard. And soon it wasn't the only thing long and hard.

After a while, she twisted her head away and planted her hand on his chest. "I still want an answer."

"Tryin' to demand shit you got no right to demand," he grumbled.

"Maybe. But you're going to tell me anyway."

His eyebrows rose. "Don't got a problem when you're naked and bossin' me around. Right now, you ain't naked."

"I could be if it'll get me the answers," she said lightly, starting to extract herself from his lap.

He tugged her back down, causing the chair to creak scarily.

"Undo your shorts."

"Now who's being bossy?" she whispered, her thighs automatically squeezing at his rough command.

No one was outside on their balconies on either side of them, and the interiors of their rooms were also dark. Either they were asleep or doing some late-night activity somewhere on the resort. Plus, Cait's balcony was dark since neither her nor Magnum had flipped on the outside light.

With fingers trembling in anticipation, she undid the button and slid down the zipper, the noise deafening in the quiet night. He knocked her hand away when his much bigger one slipped into her panties. His middle finger caressed her clit, circling and pressing it a few times, enough to make her twitch, before continuing on to slide between her quickly slickening folds.

He curved his long middle finger and slipped it inside her with ease. "Fuckin' so wet, baby," he mumbled into her hair.

"All because of you."

He worked his finger in and out of her, and she spread her thighs wider and leaned into him, dropping her head back onto his shoulder. When he slipped a second thick finger into her, she groaned and began to move with his motion.

His cock was hard and hot against her ass and she

wanted to grind and thrust against it but was afraid the chair would give out.

Instead, she let him do what he was doing and made a challenge out of staying as still as possible, only encouraging him softly with her words.

"Tell me when you're comin'."

"I always do," she managed to get out.

He grunted. "Dick's so damn hard for you."

"You're just trying to get out of answering my questions."

Instead of responding, his fingers began to move more quickly and he sucked hard on her neck, drawing another moan from her.

His other hand slid into her V-neck tee and into her bra, and using two fingers he twisted her nipple, making her hips shoot up, which drove his fingers deeper inside her.

"Mag," she breathed.

"That's it, baby, show me how much you like me touchin' you. Want you to soak my fingers."

That wasn't going to be a problem. His fingers weren't the only things wet. Her panties and the crotch of her shorts were now damp, but she didn't care.

She whimpered when he added the pressure of his thumb to her clit.

Her breathing became ragged, her hips shot up one more time, and she came, the orgasm radiating out from where his fingers were buried down to her toes and up past the nipple he was tweaking hard.

Capturing her mouth with his, he swallowed her wail so it didn't fill the still night air. Once she came back down from the high of her climax, he released her mouth, her nipple and then slowly withdrew his fingers from her still pulsing pussy.

He held them up in front of her face. "See that?"

What he was showing her wasn't hard to see, even in the limited light. "Yes."

"Lucky goddamn man right now."

She wanted to tell him he could always be lucky, but she bit it back. He wasn't going to accept a "forever" for them. Not now. Maybe not ever.

"Mouth," he ordered again.

She twisted to face him, opening her mouth for his kiss. But he slid his slick fingers into his own, sucking on them for a moment, before taking that kiss, forcing her to taste herself on his tongue. It made her pussy clench and her moan into his mouth as his tongue swept through it.

"Fuck, baby," he whispered against her lips. "Never had a woman who tasted so fuckin' good."

"You taste good, too." She slipped her hand between them and ran her fingers over his erection. It flexed against her palm. "You need relief."

She went to get to her feet again, and like earlier, he stopped her from getting up. "Stay. It can wait."

"Are you sure?"

"Yeah," he grunted, tightening his arms around her again.

But she wasn't sure she wanted to wait. Until his next words.

"She'd had enough." He paused for a long moment, the crickets and the frogs in the distance the only sounds filling the air. "She wanted kids. I didn't want any more. She left."

There were a few things to unpack in his words. She didn't know where to start, so she picked the least important to her first.

"You loved her." She didn't make it a question.

He didn't answer, so she took his silence as one.

"She wanted kids, you didn't. She pressured you, you weren't having it, so she left," she summarized neat and cleanly.

"Just said that."

"I'm just trying to get the complete picture." Cait shifted in his lap, stared into his eyes and asked, "Any more?"

When he once again tensed against her, she waited. She blindly ran her fingers down the two vertical tattoos she had stared at and studied many times over the last few days. The tattoos she figured were the initials and birthdates for his children.

The two that were only one and two years younger than her. Two *children* who were no longer that. They were adults who may not want their father "seeing" a woman their age, since a year or two difference wasn't much of a difference at all.

It shouldn't weird her out, but it did. And if it weirded her out, then the closeness in age probably bothered Magnum, too.

Her mother was right, even though she didn't want to admit it. Magnum was old enough to be her father, *if* he'd been very young when she was born. And there were plenty of teenaged parents out there. He'd been too young when his own children were born. Most likely seventeen for the first one.

Nobody was ready to be a parent of two children at eighteen. She wasn't even sure she was ready to be a mother of one at twenty-five.

"Got two kids."

"The tattoos."

His body jerked stiffly against her again, proving this was a topic he did not like to discuss. "Was a young, stupid fuck. Learned a hard fuckin' lesson. Seventeen-year-olds aren't ready to be parents. Had no choice, lived with it as best as I could, then fucked up again not even a year later. At eighteen, after barely gettin' my GED, it was hard to support a family of four. Really fuckin' hard. Almost impossible."

He hesitated for a few seconds, almost as if he was going back to the past.

"My mother busted her ass to raise me and my sister. All she did was work 'til she couldn't work anymore. Had to tell the woman that I stupidly knocked up my girl. Thought she'd never stop fuckin' cryin' when I did. She hated my girl, too, which made it even worse. She really fuckin' hated I was gonna be tied to her for life. But my father abandoned us so there was no fuckin' way she was lettin' me abandon my daughter. I didn't."

Cait remained silent while his words stopped, but his jaw kept working.

His deep voice, though kept low, filled the night air. "When I told her about my baby's momma carryin' my son, my mother could hardly look at me. When she did, it was with nothin' but disappointment and sadness. Hated that I let her the fuck down. *Hated* it. But promised I'd do right and be there for my kids, hustle to take care of 'em. Against my better judgment, which was already lackin' in that whole fuckin' situation, married their mother. Planned on a life of bustin' my ass like my mother. But what I was doin' wasn't good enough for my wife, not good enough for my kids, not good enough for me. Told me I wasn't man enough..."

Her stomach churned. *Fuck*, that had to hurt him to hear that.

"She left, found someone she thought would do better than me. He gave my kids shit I couldn't. Gave my wife what she wanted. 'Cause of that, I had nothin'. Unlike your father, at the time I couldn't afford the legal fight to see my own fuckin' kids. She shut me out no matter how many times I begged to see 'em. She lied to the pigs, lied to the judge, and got a restrainin' order. For her. For my babies."

He stopped talking, but he wasn't done. She could feel there was so much more he needed to say and hoped he would. Her heart was breaking for him because she could tell he loved his kids, wanted to be a good father and that opportunity was taken away from him. Not by choice.

Cait wanted to kill that woman and she didn't even know the bitch's name.

She squeezed his arm in encouragement and eventually he continued. "Had nothin' 'til I found the club. Found my place within it. Got my shit together and made scratch any way I could. Every dime I made that didn't go to keepin' me breathin' or child support, got stashed away for a retainer and legal fees. Fought that shit, but by then, like you, they were old enough to make their wishes known to the judge."

"So, you got to see your kids?" she asked with false hope, already dreading his answer.

"By then my ex poisoned them against me with all the lies."

"Sounds like what my mom did. Or tried to do."

His fingers squeezed her bare thigh. "But you turned that around, Cait. You gave your dad a chance. Mine ain't willin' and they're old enough to do so. They're old enough to see me for who I am and make their own fuckin' decision. They refuse to." Warm breath forced from between his lips brushed over her cheek. "Can't force 'em, either."

Cait closed her eyes and pressed her forehead against his strong jaw, cupping the opposite cheek, holding him close. "I'm sorry."

He swallowed so hard, she could hear it.

"So, no, don't want any more kids. Feels wrong to bring more into the world when I couldn't do it right the first time. Can't live through losin' any more kids because their mother decides I ain't good enough. Too old for that shit anyway. Now at the age where my babies could be havin' their own babies. Missed out on bein' a father, gonna miss out on being a grandfather."

Cait's throat was tight and her eyes stung. He tried to keep his voice level, like it didn't affect him, but it did. The pain in his words, even though he tried not to reveal it, was clearly heard and felt.

And the unfairness of it all made her angry.

"What made that bitch think she was better than you?" She pulled back and narrowed her eyes. "What made her a better parent than you?" She inhaled deeply, the blood rushing to her ears. "It's wrong. Why do people do that to their kids? It'd be one thing if you were abusive or... or..."

"Caitie," he murmured, brushing her hair back and holding it away from her face with his fist.

"No. It's wrong."

"Yeah."

"They lost out because of their mother poisoning them. It's not to protect them, it's selfishness. This is why I get so angry with my mother. I lost out on almost fifteen years with my father. It hurts my heart every time I think about it. I know it bothers him, too."

"She—"

"No. No excuses. Don't make even one for her. Don't make any for the mother of your children, either. I'm sorry this happened to you and I'm sorry this happened to your kids. They missed out on knowing a great man."

"Nothin' great about me."

She grabbed his chin and yanked his head toward her. "Bullshit. Look where you're at. Here. Now. Look what you're doing to help me. You didn't have to. You could've told me to fuck off. You're here out of your comfort zone dealing with something that wasn't yours to deal with. You were also prepared to bust your ass to provide for your kids. That right there, Magnum, is selflessness, not selfishness like your ex. That's what makes you a great man. Not how much money you make or what material objects you can buy, but true greatness is in here." She placed her hand over his heart. "You were willing to work hard and love even harder. And there's nothing more genuine than that. And that's why

I—" She swallowed her next words and her chest compressed at where her thoughts automatically went. What had been right on the tip of her tongue.

He jerked his chin out of her hand. "You what?"

"I... appreciate you."

"Same. Got a fire in you, baby. You're a strong, capable woman. The shit that happened to you could've broken you if you had let it. You didn't. You wanted to fight back and not let it eat you alive. But glad you ain't tryin' to do it on your own."

"I should've gone to the police immediately." Before she showered, before she washed away any possible evidence. But her confusion and unsurety had ruled her thinking at the time. And it was quite possible they wouldn't have believed her anyway. She'd heard those victim's nightmares all too often.

"Yeah. You didn't. Now we're dealin' with it."

"*You're* dealing with it," she corrected.

"Yeah, baby," he said softly. "I'm gonna deal with it. Promise you that."

Chapter Thirteen

HE WAS OUT OF TIME. If he didn't find out the truth by the end of today, this shit would follow them back to Pennsylvania. And once they headed back home, things could get really fucking messy.

Not just with finding out who was on that video, but with Cait's family. Also, between the clubs.

At this point, he expected a lot of shit to go down. However, Cait hadn't heard a word from Dawg, so he figured they didn't know Magnum was in NY with his daughter. Yet.

He should be crossing his fingers, his toes and his damn balls right now. He needed to get ahead of that situation, if possible. He just didn't know how to go about it.

One reason being, he wasn't sure how things would go between him and Cait.

The best thing would be, after this week was over, if Cait told Regan they were no longer seeing each other. That they had "broken up" and she promised to never see him again. It might squash Regan's concern and possibly stop Dawg from getting involved.

They go home, go their separate ways and no one but her mother and stepfather would be the fucking wiser.

Easy.

But life was never fucking easy. It was rare shit ever went smoothly.

Just like trying to figure out who the fucker was that needed to die.

As he stared at the ceiling with Cait still sleeping next to him, he heard a fucking clock ticking in his head.

Tick motherfucking tock.

Yeah, Magnum wouldn't be offered a spot on D's crew any time soon. He'd suck at being a Shadow. But it was what it was.

And unless he went against Cait's wishes and got D involved...

Hell, there would be way too many questions now if he did.

He promised Cait he'd deal with it. He needed to nut up and deal with it.

If he had to take out both of those Gallo bastards, he would. Just to be sure. To make sure Cait was safe. To make sure any woman those fuckers set their eyes on remained safe.

Would the world miss those two rich assholes?

Maybe their sister and even richer parents.

Fuck.

He hardly slept last night, even after fucking Cait twice. He should've been knocked out cold after draining his balls dry. He wasn't. Instead, he went over everything the Gallo brothers had said to him or Cait during that retreat. He picked every word apart. Every gesture, every reaction. There had to be something there somewhere.

Not a confession, but maybe a clue.

What bugged him the most was Drew Gallo blaming his fucking brother while Nate Gallo claimed his innocence.

The younger Gallo had the opportunity and the motive but he hadn't come across as acting guilty when confronted. He could be a psychopath and be able to hide his guilt. Or truly believe what he did wasn't wrong.

Magnum scrubbed a hand over his bald head and then down his face. The only time he'd felt this out of control over a situation was in that courtroom fighting for his kids. He walked out of there empty and defeated. The pain had been as intense as being kicked directly in the nuts.

He would not leave New York defeated.

Then it hit him. Drew had said he knew what his brother's naked body looked like because they used the same locker room at the fucking country club. If Drew knew what Nate looked like, then Nate would know what Drew looked like.

His heart was pounding as he shot up in bed and glanced at the clock. *Fuck*, it was only four a.m.

Cait groaned as she rolled away from his side onto her back, taking the sheet with her. He leaned over and kissed her awake.

"What?" she asked sleepily once her eyes blinked open.

"You know what room the youngest Gallo is in?"

She stretched her body long, her arms over her head, as she yawned loudly.

So goddamn beautiful, even half asleep with her hair a mess, creases on her face and not a touch of makeup.

And totally naked. The way he liked her.

"Nate?" she asked on another yawn.

"Yeah, Nate."

She turned her head and looked at the clock. When her head twisted back, she wore a frown. "It's four."

"Yeah. Asked a question."

She rubbed at her eyes and sat up, the sheet falling down around her waist and her tits suddenly catching his attention. He forced his gaze back up to her face. He needed to stay on track.

"Why would I know what room he's in?"

Because that obsessed motherfucker invited you? "Think you can find out?"

Her blonde eyebrows shot up her forehead. "Now?"

He ground his teeth and dug for any patience he had left. This whole situation was working on his last nerve. "Yeah, baby."

"No one's awake... except for us." She fell back to the mattress and pulled the sheet over her, yawning a third time. "And I wouldn't be awake if you hadn't woken me. Why *are* you awake?" She reached out and stroked his cheek which was now rough with an overnight growth of stubble. "I'd like to see you with a beard."

Jesus fuck. She was going to soon *see* his dick inside her. She needed to stop being so tempting. "Cait, need you to pay attention."

Her brows knitted together. "Before I have coffee?"

He sighed, dropped his head to stare at his own lap, then shook it. "Cait..."

She brushed her knuckles along his stubble. "I'm teasing. Sort of. But really, you with a beard... Not a long one, but short and tight."

Magnum moved until he was over her, caging her in with his arms and legs. "Baby, c'mon."

Her expression turned serious. "It's too early. I'm not going to wake anyone up." She lifted an index finger. "I can try the front desk, but I'm not sure they'll tell me."

"They might. Not like you're strangers." Magnum grabbed the handset off the receiver by the bed, passed it to her and pressed "0."

She put it to her ear and locked gazes with him. A little smile curled her lips.

"Not growin' a beard," he grumbled.

She opened her mouth to respond, but said, "Yes, hello. This is Cait Nicholson in three-fifteen," instead.

He had no idea if Nicholson was her stepfather's last name or Dawg's. He'd never heard either.

"Yes... Good morning to you, also... I'm sorry to bother you, but I have a problem. Actually, an emergency, which is why I'm calling you so early... I need to find my boss, Nate Gallo, and I forgot to ask him his room number. He's not answering his cell phone, so he must have it turned off... No, unfortunately, it can't wait... Yes, I know... I have information he needs immediately."

She covered the phone with her hand and whispered, "She wants to connect me to the phone in his room." He frowned, but before he could respond, Cait continued, "Yes, that would be great. Thank you." She said quickly, "She's putting me through..."

Cait's face twisted and suddenly she sounded upset and almost hysterical when she cried into the phone, "Nate! Thank God. I... I... I need some help... Yes... Yes, I'm okay... I just need somewhere to go until Malcolm calms down a little..." Her voice was shaky and she sniffled. "He... He... I'm so sorry to bother you. I... don't... Please... Yes, just for a little while until... Where? No, no, I can find it. I'll come to you." She put the handset back on the receiver.

And shot Magnum a wide smile.

But that quickly disappeared as he launched himself out of bed.

Magnum pounded on the door.

The smile Gallo was wearing—not full of concern, of course, that Cait might be afraid of her boyfriend and was coming to him for help—quickly slipped and fear rose into those shit brown eyes.

They should. But not for the reason the man thought.

"She said she needed help!" he yelled and tried to slam the door on him, but Magnum shoved it open, making Gallo stumble back and almost fall on his ass.

Magnum had the cottage door slammed shut and locked before the man could catch his balance. He also blocked that door, hoping there wasn't another way for him to escape. Besides the windows.

"C-C-Cait's not here," Gallo stuttered.

"No shit."

"Then why are you here?" The man was only wearing boxers and a flush rushed up his pale chest into his face.

"Was only gonna wear that when she came to you for help?" he growled.

"I didn't have time to get dressed."

"Bullshit."

"Where's Cait? What did you do to her?"

"Cait's fine and in my bed where she belongs. Now, gonna ask you the same shit. What did you do to her?"

Gallo's Adam's apple jumped. "Nothing. I already told you that. That's not me in that video."

"Finally got a hold of the security video from her apartment complex," he lied.

Magnum's frown deepened when relief passed over Gallo's face.

"Then you saw that I helped her inside and left immediately. I told you that."

Fuck.

"My only mistake was not locking her door behind me. I feel partially responsible for what happened to her because of that."

Fuck.

He pulled his cell phone from the back pocket of his jeans. "Gonna watch the video again, Gallo. You say it's not you, need your help figurin' out who it is." He pulled up the video and shoved the phone into Gallo's face. "Pay the fuck attention."

Gallo scrambled back and Magnum snaked out his hand, grabbing the man's neck to yank him closer. "You feel guilty? Wanna help Cait? Then you're gonna listen to what I gotta say and watch the video again."

"I don't know who it is," Gallo squeaked.

"Yeah, you do." He pressed play, once again covering Cait's naked body with his fingers as best as he could. Gallo was not getting a free show out of it. "Look closer at him. Asked if he looked familiar. You said no. Take a good fuckin' look, Gallo. A good look. Don't look at Cait, look at him. At any marks on his body. They look familiar?"

"It's not me."

"Ain't sayin' it's you, asshole. Look!" he roared in Gallo's face, making the fucker wince and try to take a step back, only stopping short because Magnum tightened his hand on the man's throat. It moved beneath his fingers as he tried to swallow.

It wouldn't take much to crush it, but he needed the fucker's help. "We're gonna watch this goddamn video frame by fuckin' frame until you study every fuckin' part of that motherfucker. You get me?"

"I don't want to see him... doing that to Cait."

"Think I wanna see it?" Magnum shouted. "Think Cait wanted to see it?"

"N-no."

"Gonna get whoever this is."

"I—"

Magnum kept the video playing in front of Gallo's face when he said, "Your brother said it's you."

Gallo's eyes flipped up to him.

"Keep watchin'," Magnum barked.

"Why? Why would he say that?"

"You tell me."

"He's..." Gallo shook his head, his face now even whiter, the flush long gone. He whispered, "I'd never hurt Caitie."

"Why would your brother want me to think it's you? Sort of looks like your body, your hair. See that? Right there? Dark brown hair just like you."

"It's not..."

"Check out that mark. Right there. Raise your right arm. Lemme see if you got that mark."

"I don't. I... Oh my God... *Oh my God!*" Nate covered his face with his hands.

"Who is it?"

"Drew said it was me?"

"Yeah."

"That's proof it isn't me. Look." Gallo raised his right arm and pointed to the same area where the mark was on the man in the video. He didn't have one there. It wasn't huge, but more like a small birthmark or a freckle that was easy to see if you were looking for it.

The youngest Gallo was innocent. At least on this one thing. "You drug her? D'you work with him?"

"No."

"Better not be lyin' to me. Fuckin' swear I find out you're lyin'..."

"I'm not!" Gallo yelled. "I swear it. I love Caitie. I wouldn't hurt her."

"That your brother?"

"Y-yes. It looks like him. He has that freckle on his arm. He..." Gallo sucked in a breath. "He also has a tiny scar on his thigh." He pointed at the video. "Do you see it? It's barely there because it's old. When he was five, he tripped holding a butter knife and when he fell on it, it punctured the skin."

Magnum released Gallo's throat and turned the phone to look carefully. He wouldn't have noticed it until Gallo pointed it out. It was maybe an inch long and faded.

"You didn't see that shit before?"

"Unlike my brother, I wouldn't have assumed it was Drew. Why did he blame me? Was he setting me up? Did he want me to be the scapegoat? Why?"

"He wants you to go down for this for some reason."

"He's jealous," Gallo hissed.

"Yeah," Magnum grunted.

"He's always been jealous. Dad gave me his name. Dad has always favored me. I have no idea why, but that's not my fault."

Magnum didn't give a fuck about their family issues.

"Now what?"

Magnum stared at the youngest Gallo. *Now what* was a good question. Now Nate Gallo knew his brother was guilty. Now Gallo knew Drew was Magnum's target. How was Magnum going to handle the oldest Gallo?

He had no fucking clue. The only smart thing to do would be to take both Gallo's out. The one who did the deed and the one who could point out Magnum as the guilty party once Drew Gallo went mysteriously missing.

"What do you think, Gallo?" Magnum asked, curious to see what he would say.

"I would suggest informing the authorities."

Informing the authorities. "You'd turn your brother in?"

Gallo's face twisted in confusion. "What else should be done?"

Christ, that wasn't fucking helpful.

"He set you up this time to take the fall. Think he won't do it again? He wanted you arrested. Wanted you kicked out of the agency and the family for whatever reason. Doesn't give a shit about you." He emphasized the next point, hoping it opened Gallo's eyes. "He drugged and *fucked* the woman you say you *love* against her fuckin' will."

Gallo took a step back and rubbed a hand over his forehead before drawing it down his face, whispering, "He needs help."

No shit. "I can help him..." *Stop breathing.* "And you're gonna help me."

Gallo's mouth gaped open. "How?"

"Caitie doesn't want anyone knowin' what your brother did. We go to the *authorities* then it's gonna come out. Want the woman you *love* to go through all that?" *Fuck*, he hated saying that shit about Gallo loving Cait.

Which was bullshit anyway. It was an obsession or lust, not fucking love. He knew the damn difference.

He froze. *Fuck.*

Was he any different from Gallo? He'd watched Caitie *for years.* He'd lusted after her, too. And now?

Fuck no, the difference was, if it wasn't for this situation, he would have kept her at arm's length. Which meant, she wouldn't be in his bed.

Or burrowing into his life. And head. And... his goddamn heart.

And... *fuck him...*

Fuck him.

Goddamn it.

He pushed that problem aside to study the one who stood in front of him. He needed to come up with a plan and needed to do it fast.

His fingers itched to call Diesel's head Shadow, Mercy. A man who was merciless when it came to dishing out revenge and justice. Merciless when it came to torturing someone who deserved it. He didn't have to tell the former Delta Force operator it involved Dawg's daughter.

"Need to step outside and make a call. You don't let me back in, I'll bust the fuckin' door in, you got me?"

Gallo nodded.

"It'll be to your benefit to help me stop your brother from settin' you up. Now and in the future."

Gallo said nothing as Magnum went back outside into the dark but out of ear shot. He hoped Mercy picked up even though it wasn't even dawn yet.

That fucker probably slept with one eye open and a machete in his hand.

He scrolled through his contacts, found the one he was searching for and pressed Send.

"Go," was Mercy's terse greeting.

Jesus fuck. "Got an issue. Need advice. Also need you to keep it to yourself."

Magnum took the grunt on the other end of the phone as an agreement.

"Need to take out two brothers but keep clear of any shit splashin' back on me." That should be a given, but he still felt the need to say it.

A long silence greeted him on the other end. Magnum struggled to wait it out, but he did. He figured Mercy needed to process the situation, even though Magnum hadn't given him much to go on. He'd let the expert ask the important questions.

"Two brothers," Mercy said slowly. "They like each other?"

"Thinkin' at this point, not too much. One's tryin' to fuck the other without a drop of lube."

Another pause. "Can you ramp the dislike up to hatred?"

"Possibly."

"Either got a gun? Make it look like murder-suicide?"

"Not sure about a gun. Both are pretty much fuckin' douchebags. Be surprised if either touched anything but a golf club and their own fuckin' dicks." And Caitie.

Another deep grunt. "Still can make it look like it without one."

"How?"

"Knife."

"Jesus," Magnum muttered.

"Poison."

A light bulb went off. Fucking poison. That got his own brain switched into gear. "Got it, brother. Thanks."

"Yeah. Good luck. Need us to do a job, just fucking shout."

"Handlin' this one."

He got an answering grunt before the man hung up.

Magnum wasn't scared of much, but that dead-eyed motherfucker with the icy exterior was someone he thought twice about.

Another reason he needed to keep the fact he was with Cait on the down low. It would just take one word from Diesel to his crew and Magnum would be begging to die quickly to escape a drawn-out torture.

He paced back and forth through the dark, not venturing far from Gallo's cottage, which was in a cluster of other cottages. He figured all the Gallos were occupying them. They were more upscale and private than the rooms like the one he and Caitie were staying in.

He knew rohypnol paralyzed the person who took it, which was why they couldn't fight back. And it also made them not remember a damn thing. He could use that to his benefit, but only if the older Gallo son had brought some with him on the retreat.

If he could convince Drew to roofie Nate and do the dirty deed to his younger brother, he would keep his hands clean on that one. Then he'd only have Drew to deal with.

Maybe not a murder-suicide. But a murder and an accident.

He turned and stared out at the calm water of Lake George.

A boating accident? A drowning? A man paralyzed by a tranquilizer would drown quickly and without a fight.

Problem was, where his mind, and his plan, was leading him involved water and a deep fucking lake.

The biggest handicap in his plan was he couldn't fucking swim. And the fuck if he was getting Caitie involved.

He never got the chance to learn to swim at the local Y because he was too busy taking care of his baby sister while his mother busted her ass for them. He had done his part to help. Which meant he missed out on a lot of shit. Swimming was one of them.

He didn't care at the time. Now he did.

But it was too late to change that. He'd need to figure out how to get around that problem. Boats had those floating bumpers like Cait said.

Christ, that didn't give him the warm fucking fuzzies.

But he needed a solid plan and to do it in the dark. And the way color was tinging the sky at this point, it was too late to do anything about it that morning. But then, everything needed to be well thought out first. He needed a way to cover his ass. He needed to make sure Cait didn't get caught up in any of it, either. At worst, she would have to be his alibi, if needed.

He headed back to Gallo's cottage and found the door unlocked. *Thank fuck.* Because him kicking it the fuck in would've woken up a lot of people.

The asshole was now dressed and looking worried.

He should be.

"Here's how it's gonna go," he began.

Chapter Fourteen

CAIT KNEW Magnum was feeling the time pinch of finding out who was on the video. But something was up.

He had shot out of bed that morning and then returned about an hour later, climbed back into bed with her and held her tight, his face buried in her hair, like he tended to do. She wasn't sure if he felt comfort in that or just liked the smell of her shampoo. She didn't ask because she didn't want to make him self-conscious about it or for him to stop. She liked when he did it, too.

He never said where he went before the crack of dawn. She had a good idea since he'd wanted Nate's room number and when she asked him, he said he wouldn't discuss it with her to keep her "hands clean."

That did not settle her worry. In fact, it ramped it up.

She'd gotten him into this mess. And if he ended up in prison for doing whatever he was planning on doing, she'd never forgive herself.

But she also wanted to know what the hell was going on.

All he told her was, that night after dinner, after whatever the final retreat activity was, he needed to disappear for a bit. She wasn't to follow him, ask who he was with or where he was going.

That night's dinner had ended with a closing speech from Hank, thanking all of his employees for being team players, for being hard workers and for being family.

While all of that should sound good, it turned her stomach.

Because the man sitting next to her at the time, who had his fingers laced tightly with hers, who'd sacrificed all week for her, who'd brought her pleasure like she'd never experienced before, who wanted to selflessly protect her... The man who she'd fallen deeper in love with every day and every night while in New York, was going to do something that night which could risk his future. Maybe even his life.

But he was doing what she had asked of him.

It was her fault by being careless that she'd been drugged. And in the end, it would be her fault if something happened to him because of that.

After dinner, almost everyone had gone to the bar to play trivia. Cait sat there unable to concentrate, unable to stop wringing her hands and her leg bouncing nervously under the small table they sat at.

She also couldn't keep her eyes off Magnum, who sat there calmly, trying to ignore her freak-out, and constantly touching her to try to settle her down. By curling his fingers around the back of her neck and giving it a light squeeze, touching her hair, kissing her temple, holding her hand, sliding his fingers down her arm, her thigh, her cheek...

"Caitie," he murmured under his breath. "Gotta calm the fuck down."

"I can't," she whispered back. "I don't know what's going on. I don't know what you're going to do. I'm worried about you."

"Gonna handle the problem like you asked."

"And I know what that means," she hissed. "Because of that, I'm worried."

"Baby," he breathed, his lips now against her ear. "If you didn't want me to handle it, shouldn't have come to me. You did. I'm here. Handlin' it the best I can."

"I'm sorry that I did. I put you in a spot I shouldn't have. It's all my fault—"

"Stop," he said sharply, pulling away from her. "Ain't your fault. It's the fucker's fault who drugged you. You didn't ask for that shit."

He could say that all he wanted, she still felt responsible. She squeezed her eyes shut for a moment, trying to stop her spinning thoughts. "It's our last night together." Which didn't help her anxiety at all. It only compounded it.

"Yeah, baby. I'll be back before the night's over. Promise."

He thought it had to do with sex. It didn't. It had nothing to do with sex and everything to do with the possibility of things going sideways and her never seeing him again. Never being with him again.

Her eyes began to well up and sting. She was not going to start crying in front of her co-workers. She gripped his hand tighter and raised it to her mouth, pressing her lips firmly against the dark, warm skin of his fingers.

She swept her thumb over the inside of his wrist, knowing if she pushed up the cuff of the long-sleeved shirt he wore, even the slightest bit, she'd be able to see his tattoos. The ones he worked so hard to keep hidden from her co-workers.

For her.

He sat next to her at a resort in Lake George for her.

He might risk everything for her.

Her heart thumped heavily in her chest. "I need to tell you something…"

His dark eyes landed on her and held fast and steady. "No, you don't."

"Mag— Malcolm," she began, her voice catching.

"No," he barked, catching the couple's attention sitting at the next table. A muscle ticked in his cheek, but he lowered his voice. "You don't. Not now. Not here."

With her free hand she swiped at her eyes. "But—"

"Caitie... No."

His tone had changed slightly, his voice became thicker, and she noticed something flash behind his eyes. Something resembling pain. Or regret, maybe.

The last thing she wanted to do was cause him that. Or distract him from whatever his plan was.

She blinked quickly, trying to relieve the sting, and nodded, her throat tight.

"Okay," she whispered, turning to him and cupping his cheek. "Not now."

His lips became nothing but a slash as he pressed them together and she waited for him to respond with, "Not ever." But he didn't.

That gave her a tiny sliver of hope.

He broke their locked gazes and turned to look at the bar's small, low stage, where a few of her co-workers had microphones and trivia questions, and were keeping score on a big whiteboard. "When's this shit gonna end?"

She knew he meant the trivia contest, but she couldn't help read into that question deeper.

"Soon," she murmured and her leg began to bounce uncontrollably once again.

FROM A DISTANCE, Magnum stalked Drew Gallo from the bar over the dimly lit brick path back to a cottage near Nate Gallo's.

He'd sent Caitie back to their room, told her to lock the door and wait there until he got back. To try to ease her worry, he promised to return to her as soon as he could.

As soon as the older brother had the door unlocked and was twisting the knob, Magnum shoved him inside, hurrying to shut the door behind them.

"Hey!" Gallo exclaimed and spun around, only to stop dead at the sight of Magnum. "Malcolm! What the hell is going on?"

"Need to talk to you in private."

"You could've just asked."

Enough with the bullshit. Time to set his plan in motion. "Confronted your brother. He's blamin' you. Identified you in that video by the marks on your body."

Gallo's eyes flashed wide, then narrowed just as quickly. "He's lying."

"Is he?" Magnum cocked an eyebrow and took a step closer to Gallo, drawing himself to his full height. "He's really pissed at you for tryin' to pin it on him. Talked to him earlier and he said he's goin' to the cops once he gets back home. Wants you to go down for not only lyin' 'bout him, but for what you did to Cait."

"What are you talking about? He said nothing to me at dinner or during trivia. He acted completely normal."

Color was rising into Gallo's face, which meant he was getting pissed. But Magnum needed to get him raging. Like Mercy said. Enough so that he'd want to take action to stop his brother.

"Right. He's keepin' it from you so you don't stop him or try turnin' it around on him."

Gallo tilted his head, his eyebrows pinned together. "Why are you telling me this?"

"'Cause I think he's lyin' and it's him, not you."

"It *is* him!"

Fucking lying motherfucker.

Magnum's fingers flexed with the urge to strangle that asshole.

A true brother didn't throw another brother under the fucking bus.

He didn't use a woman as a tool to fuck over that brother.

A true *man* didn't drug and rape a woman.

The Gallo before him was a spineless, spoiled mother-fucker who was sucking air that could be better used on people who deserved to breathe.

He hurt Cait all because of some petty fucking jealousy. Some sibling rivalry which did not warrant the actions he took. He tried to screw over his own flesh and blood and hurt Cait in the attempt.

It was going to cost him. The man just didn't know how much yet.

But he would find out. Hopefully soon, if Magnum played this right.

"I need to stop him from going to the police."

No shit. "Yeah. Could screw up your whole life if you get accused of rapin' an employee. No one will ever look at you the same again. People at the agency, clients, your parents. People at your country club, your friends. Other women will never trust you. Always wonderin' if you're gonna drug them and rape 'em. Your professional life would be fu— *screwed* and so would your personal life. Even if you get cleared of those charges, everyone's still gonna wonder. And you think your daddy loves and favors your brother more now? Just think what'll happen after. Especially when it involved a friend's daughter. Makin' him look bad in front of everyone. Hurtin' his business."

Gallo's face was turning a deeper shade of red as his blood pressure spiked. "I didn't do it!"

Magnum was getting the result he wanted. Playing him

was much easier than he expected. "Even so. It would take a while to clear your name if that's true. And who's your dad gonna believe? His golden boy, Nate, or you?"

"What the hell!"

Wind the fucker up, now push him toward a solution... "Need to stop him before he goes to the cops. Stop him before he causes damage you can't repair."

"How?"

Magnum shrugged. "Dunno. What d'you think?"

"He raped *your* girlfriend."

Magnum's nostrils flared and his lip curled in a snarl. He forced it back down and grunted out a, "Yeah."

"What do *you* want to do about him?"

His fingers curled into his palms. "Want him to get what's comin' to him."

"I know if he raped my girlfriend, I'd want to kill him."

Bingo. "Yeah."

"I can help you do that. You'd get revenge for Cait. It'd stop him from falsely accusing me of rape and ruining my life. This lake is perfect to get rid of a body. It has a lot of deep areas. Some close to two hundred feet. We weigh him down and he'd never be found."

Or make it look like a struggle between two brothers. An unfortunate accident.

But, *holy fuck*, this guy was fucked in the head. He wanted to accuse his brother of the shit he did, then kill the guy to get rid of him to keep him quiet. The nanny must have dropped him on his goddamn head when he was a baby.

"He's your brother."

"And the world would be a better place with one less rapist."

That was fucking true. Magnum was staring at that rapist.

"He'd never be able to do it again to any woman."

That was also true. "How you gettin' him out to one of those deep spots?" Magnum asked.

"We'll borrow one of the resort's boats. We can borrow them at any time during the retreat."

Christ. This shit was easier than he ever expected. The man fell right into Magnum's plan. He only wished it didn't have anything to do with a deep lake and a fucking boat. "Know how to drive one?"

"Of course."

Of fucking course.

"How you gettin' him on that boat? He's gettin' ready to snitch on you, you think he's takin' a night cruise with his brother?"

Gallo chewed on his bottom lip while he thought about it. "I'll roofie him like he did Cait."

"That what he used on Cait?"

"Of course."

Of fucking course.

"How do you know that?"

"Because it'd only make sense he'd use a date rape drug to knock Cait unconscious."

Magnum wanted to roll his eyes at the bullshit spewing from the fucker's mouth.

"I'll go over to his cottage, pretend to confess to him, beg him to reconsider going to the police and I'll slip him the drug. He probably has it in his toiletry bag."

Or you have it in yours. "Then what?"

"Then we get him onto the boat, use the depth finder to find a perfect spot, drop him overboard and because he's knocked out, he'll drown."

Christ, he was a sick motherfucker. His brother had done nothing to him. Abso-fucking-lutely nothing that Magnum knew of and the man didn't think twice about taking the guy out.

"How you gonna slip him the drug?"

Gallo's gaze slid to the side then back. "You let me worry about that. I'll just need your help getting him into the boat."

"You want my help, you don't tell anyone about this. Not a fu— *damn* word."

Gallo nodded. "I want to do this now while it's dark."

"Yeah," Magnum grunted, relieved this was all falling into place. Maybe that Shadows shit was easier than he thought.

"Then go now. Gonna hang outside his place while you do it. Once it's done, gonna get him down to the dock. Need to do it quickly and quietly, you get me?"

"Yes." Gallo nodded again. "I... I just need to grab something first."

Of fucking course he did. Because he was the one holding the fucking drug.

"Gonna wait outside."

And that's what he did.

———

MAGNUM WANTED TO FUCKING PUKE. The movement of the *way-too-small* boat through the dark water, the sound of that water rushing by, the drone of the outboard, everything about it was churning his stomach.

Somehow, he needed to get both Gallos over the side of the boat once they got to their destination and get himself back to shore without dying.

Right now he was questioning his plan, his decision, the whole fucking thing.

He was gripping the side of the boat with everything he had. He could only imagine the ride would be worse if the water had been choppy. Thank fuck it wasn't.

Thank fuck Drew Gallo knew how to drive a boat.

Thank fuck Drew Gallo was also a gullible stupid fuck.

Thank fuck Drew Gallo hated his own brother.

Otherwise, Magnum would be yanking on his own dick trying to figure out a better way to get rid of them both.

Gallo had also thrown some fishing equipment into the boat, saying if anyone questioned them as to why they were out there in the middle of the night, that they could claim they were going night fishing.

Night fucking fishing.

He'd shaken his head but was glad the fucker had an evil mind. He never would have come up with that idea since he never fished in his fucking life. He never planned to, either.

He breathed easier when Gallo pulled back on the throttle, slowing down the floating deathtrap and drifting to a stop.

"Where we at?" Magnum asked when the boat's engine went silent.

Gallo jerked his chin back toward shore. "A spot not too far from the resort."

He was surprised when he noticed they hadn't gone very far from the dock. But even a foot was still too far for Magnum. "A deep one?"

"Yes. About seventy feet."

Seventy feet was not two hundred.

"Gotta make it look like an accident," Magnum reminded him.

"I've been thinking about that."

Thank fuck the man could think. Right now Magnum couldn't think about much except how to avoid drowning.

"If we loosely tie the boat's anchor around his ankles and make it look like he got caught up in it and fell overboard, it will cover our tracks. He tripped, he fell over the side and got dragged under from the anchor. It was dark and even with the spotlight we couldn't find him. We head back to shore and notify authorities, telling them it was an unfortunate accident during our night fishing. I'll act upset, even panicked. I'll even get wet like I went in after him. It could be believable."

Could be if that story was ever told, which it wouldn't be.

"Yeah. Sounds like a plan," Magnum murmured, watching the fucker grab the thick nylon rope attached to the small anchor and loop it loosely a couple times around his unconscious brother's feet and ankles.

When Gallo was done, he straightened. "Help me dump him over the side."

Magnum frowned. "This shit don't bother you? Got no hesitation on offin' your own brother?"

Gallo pursed his lips and tilted his head. "Do you?"

"He ain't my brother."

"And soon he won't be mine."

Damn. The fucker was cold. "Hate him that much?"

Gallo said nothing and waved his hand over the limp Nate. "Come on. We need to hurry and get this done."

Yeah, they did. And did he really fucking care why the older brother hated the younger one? Fuck no. He wasn't Dr. fucking Phil.

"Grab the anchor." Magnum squatted down, grabbed the drugged Gallo under his arms, hauling him up and over to the edge of the boat. Drew lifted the anchor and, before Magnum was ready, tossed it over the side.

As the weight dropped quickly into the dark depths of the lake, he released the body and let it follow, causing a loud splash. When drops of cold water hit him, Magnum quickly stepped back to the center of the small boat. Tossing that dead weight over the side had made it rock more than he'd like. If he lost his balance and fell over the side, he'd be following the now drowning Gallo to the bottom of the lake.

But he wasn't done there. He stared at the Gallo who was still staring at the spot where his younger brother disappeared. Then the man turned his head and smiled at Magnum.

Fucking. Smiled.

Like this shit was all fun and games. *Asshole.*

"Ready to head back?"

Yeah, he was, but not with him. "Know it was you, fucker."

Gallo's eyes widened. "What?"

Magnum took a slow step toward him. If he moved carefully, the small boat wouldn't rock as much. "Know it was fuckin' you."

Gallo took a quick glance back to where Nate disappeared. "No, it was Nate."

"You took my woman and did that shit to her. *You.* Goddamn selfish bastard. Hurt a fuckin' woman to get your way like the spoiled motherfucker you are." He shook his head. "Not *a* woman, *my* woman."

His chest burned with a hatred he hadn't felt in a long fucking time. Not since he felt the same for the mother of his children the day he lost them because of her lies. The lies that not only tore him away from his kids but threw him in jail.

That hatred he had been forced to swallow. He wasn't swallowing the same shit tonight.

Magnum leaned in and got in his face. "You picked the wrong woman, asshole."

"I didn't pick anyone, Malcolm. You've got it all wrong."

"Too bad you got into an argument with your brother on this boat."

Drew's mouth gaped open. "What are you talking about?"

"The fight you got into. The tussle where you both fell over the side and drowned."

Gallo tried to rush past him to the helm. Magnum got there before he did by body blocking him, yanked the keys from the ignition and pitched them out into the darkness.

"What are you doing? We can't get back to shore without that!" Gallo frantically pulled his cell phone from his pocket.

Magnum ripped it from his fingers and whipped that as hard as he could in the opposite direction of the keys. A small splash could be heard in the distance.

"What are you doing?" Gallo screamed, sounding a whole shitload of panicked.

He should.

"Gettin' revenge for Caitie."

"We already did!"

"No, motherfucker, *I* didn't."

Magnum grabbed the man's hair at the back and with all his power behind it, he slammed the fucker's forehead into the metal steering wheel.

Gallo groaned then collapsed to his knees, out cold.

Magnum dragged the unconscious man over the side and tossed him in the same spot as his brother, doing his best not to tip the boat.

Because if he did, he was fucked.

Once the rocking stopped, he broke some of the fishing equipment, sent more over the side, then tossed some of the seat cushions into the water. Using his boot, he smashed a few things around the center of the boat. He did whatever he could to make it look like a struggle between the two brothers had occurred.

After he was done, he surveyed the damage to make sure it looked believable, then glanced back toward land.

Now he needed to find a way off the fucking boat and to shore.

Jesus fuck.

He tried to keep his shit together as he dug out whatever life vests he could find from under the seats.

He had to do this. He had no choice but to get into the water, even though his brain was screaming at him not to do it. But he needed to make his way to shore before the sun came up.

He needed to get back to the resort before anyone discovered the Gallos or the boat missing. He needed to get back to Cait and be in bed with her before anyone pounded on their door.

And as soon as the sun rose, they were hitting the road and heading home.

But he still needed to get to shore first.

And that wouldn't be a small feat.

He tried fitting into one of the life jackets but couldn't. He dug around more and found an orange vest that would fit around his neck and strap around his torso. It didn't fit well at all but it might keep his head above water. He strapped it as securely as he could.

When he dug out the rest of the vests and jackets, he also found a beach towel under one of the seats and wiped down every surface he had touched. He doubted the pigs would dust the boat looking for prints if it appeared as an accident due to a struggle, but it was better to be safe than a suspect.

After scattering a couple of the smaller life jackets into the water, the larger ones he stacked and buckled together, hoping he could use them to keep him afloat as he attempted to swim back to shore.

All he had to do was kick his legs, right?

Fucking simple.

Now, his brain just needed to believe it.

Even from where the boat was drifting, he could see the lights to the resort in the distance. He just needed to head toward them. And not fucking die along the way.

That last part might be the hardest.

He looked at the edge of the boat, then looked down at his boots. They would fill up with water and be just like that anchor. But he also couldn't leave them behind in the boat or near the bodies.

No evidence could be left behind proving he'd been on that boat. None.

Somehow, he needed to take his heavy boots with him.

He removed them, grabbed another vest, tied them together and then shucked his jeans, too, knotting them tightly around his boots. He needed to be as light as possible. He needed to be able to kick freely.

The goal was not to fucking drown.

"Fucking bullshit," he muttered as he took a deep breath, checked to make sure his balls were still attached, then moved toward the back of the boat, taking the towel along to wipe any remaining prints as he abandoned ship.

With his heart pounding a rapid beat, he slowly and carefully made his way onto the small rear platform next to the outboard, then sat on the edge with his lower legs in the water. He clutched the stacked vests to his chest tightly, hoped the one around his neck held fast and, with his boots in his other hand, he slipped into the lake.

For a second it felt like jumping out of the window of a ten-story burning building.

When the cold water surrounded him, his first instinct was to panic, but he fought it. He breathed. He floated in place with help from the vests. He tried to get his bearings.

Then once his panicked thoughts settled a bit, he kicked his feet enough to circle until he could find the resort's lights again. His beacon. Where Cait was.

Being solid and heavy, his own weight tried to pull him down. His own body wanting him to fail.

He blew out a shaky breath, the cold, dark water now

pulling at him as he used his foot to push away from the boat.

In the direction of the resort.

In the direction of Caitie.

She was waiting for him.

And he was sure she was freaking the fuck out.

Just like he was.

Chapter Fifteen

His heart was pounding in this throat. His lungs were struggling to fill. The muscles in his legs were screaming. A tight band squeezed his chest from the cold lake. His water-logged boots, dragging behind him, were slowing him down. But he was not letting them go. If he survived this, he wasn't going to fucking prison because of leaving something identifiable behind.

But he was beginning to wonder if he *would* survive.

He was swallowing more water than he should. And some had gone into his lungs, too, which made him cough and struggle for breath. It also made the panic rise.

He was going to fucking drown. Die right there in a fucking dark watery grave, all fucking alone.

Cait would never know how he felt about her.

He'd never touch her again. Hold her again.

He needed to keep going. Keep kicking.

But it was so fucking cold. His muscles and joints were beginning to lock; his brain was becoming sluggish.

He just needed to focus on two things: kicking and the shore.

No, that wasn't right. Kicking toward the shore and Cait.

Fuck him, both seemed so fucking far away.

———

Cait listened for a boat. Instead, she heard nothing.

Against his wishes, she had watched Magnum from their balcony, along with Drew and Nate Gallo, go down to the dock earlier and get into one.

Nate had to be assisted. One arm had been draped over Magnum's shoulders, the other over Drew's. And Nate's feet dragged behind them.

Was he dead?

Did she even care?

No, the only one she cared about was the big man who disappeared with the Gallo brothers a couple hours ago.

She had waited on that balcony, chewing her nails down to nothing, pacing restlessly, fretting for over an hour before she had run down to the dock. If he got pissed at her for leaving their room, he'd just have to get over it.

After a little while, she realized people might see her there because of the solar lights that were lit along the dock. She moved back to the shore and stuck to the shadows where she could wait undetected.

But she was not going back up to their room until Magnum returned.

Without knowing what Drew and Magnum had planned for Nate, she had no idea how long it would take.

Even so, she didn't care. She'd wait as long as it took.

He was afraid of the water, so she was shocked when he got on that small boat.

But he did. For her.

He faced his fears for her.

She covered her mouth with her hand to keep from

screaming out his name into the dark still night. To hope he answered. To locate him.

She stared out at the water, the moon reflecting off the smooth surface giving her a decent view of the area right off the shore.

But in truth, she'd hear the boat before she'd see it. It had left the dock dark, with no running lights at all, and she suspected it would return the same.

She strained her eyes and ears, searching for any sign.

Still nothing.

Her heart was in her throat and her pulse pounded in her ears as she kept surveying the flat lake. Only an occasional slow lap of a wave, most likely from a breeze, hit the shore by her feet.

At first, she thought she was imagining it. A splash, a grunt, labored breathing. Her gaze sliced again over the water and still *nothing*.

A few seconds later, she heard it clearly, an irregular splashing, not steady at all, as if someone was swimming. Or trying to.

Who the hell would be out in the water?

All the hairs on the back of her neck stood. Goosebumps exploded over her skin. Her heart that had been pounding, seized.

"Magnum," she called out softly, knowing her voice would carry over the water easily. "Magnum," she repeated, fear for him embracing her.

She swore she heard her name. She swore she heard his voice.

But that couldn't be. He couldn't swim.

What the fuck was going on?

More frantic splashing.

"Magnum!" she called out even louder, now not giving a fuck if anyone heard her.

Finally, she spotted movement. Maybe a hundred yards

out. Large, dark, moving awkwardly and with excruciating slowness toward shore.

It couldn't be.

Could it?

"Magnum!" she yelled, toeing off her sneakers. She rushed into the water, almost falling into it face first when her feet sank into the thick mud. She caught her balance and kept moving, fighting the suck of the sludge trying to slow her down. "Magnum!"

As soon as she was hip deep in water, she began to swim instead, doing a slow breast stroke so she could keep her head up and search the water line for him.

There!

Her chest compressed and her heart began to race as she swam faster toward him. He was coughing, almost choking, and it sounded wet as if he'd sucked too much water into his lungs. She kicked her legs more frantically and kept focus on the dark figure ahead, still trying to head in her direction. But he was slowing down even more. Almost to a standstill.

"Don't you give up!" she demanded, trying not to scream, as she put more power behind her strokes and legs. She put her head down and swam the hardest she'd ever swam.

And then she bumped into something in the water. She reached for it. It was cold, solid.

Magnum.

She ignored the sob that was ripped from her and grabbed a hold of him. "I'm pulling you to shore. Just do your best to float."

He said nothing. Just a wet cough bubbled up.

It didn't matter.

He was alive. He was breathing. And she had him.

She swam as hard as she could, holding onto him with all the strength she could muster, dragging him awkwardly through the water. And when she was close enough to shore, she put her feet down and found the mud again.

"Stand up," she ordered, still not letting him go. Making sure he was steady on his feet.

As his own feet hit the thick mud, he almost stumbled but caught himself. She grabbed his boots and the wet denim and yanked them free from his hands.

He threw the life jackets he had clung to during his swim farther out into the lake, then with painstaking slowness unstrapped and removed the life vest that had been hanging around his neck. He threw that away from him, too.

Then he turned to her, stood there and said nothing.

"We have to get you out of the water. Your skin is ice cold."

He didn't answer her, but he trembled from the loss of body heat.

She needed to get him warmed up and dried off as soon as possible. Cold water stole a person's body heat quickly. Even though the days were warm, the water was not, and he could easily go into hypothermia.

"Magnum," she said, shaking him, trying to get him to snap out of whatever daze he was in. His brain might be shutting down. "Please. We need to get back to the room." If he went unconscious, she'd never get him back. And she couldn't call anyone for help. She didn't want anyone to know he'd been in the lake or even near it.

By him admitting he couldn't swim to several of her co-workers, he'd be in the clear of anything that happened out there. She'd thought it unnecessary that he'd mentioned it to them, but now it made perfect sense.

But even so, she wanted to avoid any questions. He said she was his alibi, and that alibi would be they were in bed all night.

"Magnum," she said sharply.

"Cait." Her name was slurred, which was not a good sign.

She tugged on his arm and he followed her slowly as they fought their way through the muck, onto the grassy shore and once there, he stumbled to his knees. She swore he kissed the ground before, with agonizing slowness, pushing himself to his feet once more and shuffling alongside her back to their room.

It was a slow trek, but they made it. As soon as she had the door closed and locked behind them, she began to strip him of the soaked long-sleeved tee and boxer briefs he was wearing, dropping everything onto the tiled floor.

"Head to the shower," she ordered, stripping herself of her own wet clothes as she followed him.

As soon as she was naked, she pushed into the bathroom and past him, turned the water temp to warm and guided him in, following closely behind.

The shower was tight but they stood under the spray until he stopped shivering, his skin warmed up, his eyes became more focused and he wasn't so stiff.

"Baby," he finally murmured, once his teeth had stopped chattering.

That endearment never sounded so good.

She flung her arms around his middle, shoving her face into his chest and totally fucking lost it.

Just like the baby he called her.

Chapter Sixteen

HE REFUSED to talk about it. He wanted to keep her in the dark for her protection.

While she understood it, she didn't like it.

They had checked out before breakfast, before most of the people on the retreat began to stir.

Before anyone noticed the boat was missing, or Drew and Nate Gallo had skipped the last informal breakfast. Or even realized neither were in their cottages.

She and Magnum had spent the rest of their last night at the resort wrapped up together, their limbs tangled, not saying a word. Just sharing each other's heat and touch. A simple connection.

No sex. No conversation.

Just *being*.

They stopped just outside of Binghamton and grabbed a breakfast sandwich for her and two for him, along with some strong coffee before continuing on their long journey home.

Not much was said, though plenty needed to be.

Every time she tried, he'd only shake his head and squeeze her thigh or her hand. She wasn't sure if it was because he'd stared death in the face last night or because their week together was swiftly coming to an end.

Or both.

By the time they hit the New York/Pennsylvania border, her phone began to blow up.

Have you seen Drew?

Have you heard from Nate?

Did you talk to either of them last night? This morning?

Where are you two?

Are you okay?

She reassured the co-workers who texted her they were fine. That *Malcolm* had to return early this morning to deal with an issue at his business. She also asked them to keep her updated on Drew and Nate.

Then a text popped up from her mother: *I expect you and Malcolm for dinner tonight.*

Shit. That single text made her stomach churn more than the rest.

She quickly responded back: *It's been a long drive. It'll have to be another time.*

Her mother's answer? *Unacceptable.*

That was it. Just *unacceptable.*

She closed her eyes and cursed under her breath, catching Magnum's attention.

"What?"

"My mother wants us over for dinner tonight."

He was quiet for one heartbeat. Two. "Go. Tell her we fought last night and broke up. It's over."

It's over. Her head spun towards him. "What?"

"You heard me." He stared straight ahead through the windshield, holding the steering wheel in a death grip. "Did what needed to be done. It's over."

"It's not—"

"Cait," he said tersely.

"No—"

"Cait, don't make this fuckin' harder than it's gotta be."

She turned her head quickly to stare out the passenger-side window, to hide the hot tears that slipped down her cheeks. She did her best not to sniffle so he wouldn't hear it.

In her lap, her phone pinged again. She blinked several times to clear her vision enough to see the text. She read it out loud, her voice thick with her tears. *They found a resort boat drifting off shore. Signs of a struggle. No signs of Nate or Drew.* On the end of that was an emoji bawling its eyes out.

Fuck, what had they done?

Were she and Magnum no better than Nate or Drew?

Were they awful people?

Her fingers trembled when she texted back: *Oh no! I hope they're okay. Let me know as soon as you hear anything.*

Magnum had risked not only his life and his safety, but his freedom for her.

As she stared at the phone in her hand, another fat tear plopped onto the screen. "I love you," she whispered, unsure if he heard her, not caring if he did.

Because it was true. And he didn't want to hear it the other night but she needed to say it.

The only answer she got was him turning up the radio and filling the car with rock music that drowned out her muffled crying.

By the time Magnum drove around the back of Dirty Dick's, up to his house, and shoved the shifter into Park, divers were now searching Lake George near the resort and where the boat had been discovered drifting.

She knew she'd soon get the news about Drew and Nate's bodies being found. Then she'd have to nervously wait out the investigation, most likely answer a few questions from the police, and hope Magnum left no identifiable evidence behind. Hope to hell he'd made no mistakes to steer that investigation toward him.

She worried for him. But she kept that to herself.

They both got out of the Toyota, her eyes and nose red and swollen from trying to stem the quiet tears.

His nostrils flared and his lips pressed into a thin line when he glanced at her for a split second before grabbing his duffel bag out of the backseat.

He stood stiffly next to the car with his bag in his hand and his face unreadable as she went around the car and climbed into the driver's seat, adjusting it for her shorter height. When she was done, her bottom lip trembled as she stared up at him, waiting.

For something. Anything.

He gave her nothing but a soft, "Talk to your mom, tell her it's over." With that, he slammed the driver's door shut.

She started the car, put it in reverse, but kept her foot on the brake as she watched him disappear into his house.

She no longer had a reason to stifle the sob that filled the car as she drove away.

———

LESS THAN TWO WEEKS LATER, after speaking with the police in New York over the phone twice, she attended the double wake and both funerals, and stood amongst the crowd at the gravesites. She had shed real tears for Drew and Nate Gallo like the rest of her co-workers, their parents and their sister.

She had gone through a rollercoaster of emotions.

She also felt the loss deeply.

Not for Drew or Nate. But for Magnum.

Even so, the guilt of their death ate at her and she hadn't been able to sleep.

After a few nights in her apartment, she could no longer bear sleeping in her bed alone, so she'd gone home to the DAMC compound and decided to stay with her family for a little while.

Until the grief passed.

Until the hollow in her center filled.

The agency's offices were closed for those two weeks while everyone there not only grieved but reorganized since Hank was retiring immediately and Natalie was stepping into his shoes.

During that time, she contemplated whether she could even walk back through those doors and into her office.

Also during that time, she hardly left her bed in the spare room at Dawg and Emma's.

Emma would bring her food and her sisters would ask to come in, sit on her bed, and spend time with her.

They thought the Gallos' tragic death had hit her hard.

They were wrong.

While that still bothered her, it wasn't why she remained sad and empty.

A good reminder why she shouldn't care about what happened to Nate Gallo was the video. All she had to do was squeeze her eyes shut and it would play all over again in her mind.

She hoped one day she could forget it.

She hoped one day she could move on.

From all that had happened. That night in the motel after the celebration, that last night at the lake. And her time with Magnum in between.

She didn't think she could move on by continuing to work at the Gallo Marketing Agency. In fact, she knew she couldn't and needed to do something about that.

Her bedroom door being shoved open and bouncing off the doorstop with a loud *twang* made her startle and shoot upright in bed.

Her father stood in the doorway, his big hands on his denim-covered hips, his green eyes narrowed and holding a whole lot of pissed off. "Get the fuck outta bed now. Get the fuck downstairs an' sit at the goddamn table with your sisters. You're freakin' them the fuck out. There's no reason you should be this fucked up because of two rich mother-fuckers drownin'. None. What the fuck's goin' on with you?"

She swallowed, relieved he wasn't busting in demanding answers about her and Magnum. She had done a good job convincing Regan that things were over between them. And they were never seeing each other again.

So really, Regan had no reason to say a word to Dawg.

Her father was the epitome of a biker. He lived in his jeans, some sort of worn shirt that usually advertised Harley Davidson or some biker rally. He was full of tattoos, wore clunky silver rings on his fingers, heavy boots on his feet, a huge DAMC belt buckle at his waist and a thick, longish beard covered his lower face.

Being a big, burly biker, he could scare the shit out of anyone.

Well, except for Emma, her sisters and her.

He could be rough on the outside, but if you were in the small circle of people he loved, he was nothing but a kitten on the inside.

That kitten must have gotten drop kicked this morning.

"Get the fuck up," he barked, turning on the overhead light, then going to the windows and jerking back the curtains, letting in the morning sun to blind her.

"Dad."

"Don't you fuckin' 'Dad' me." He jabbed a finger toward her. "This is fuckin' bullshit. Never seen you like this. Need to go see Rissa?"

"What?" Rissa, Mercy's woman, was a sex therapist, but being a part of the club's sisterhood, she got roped into being everybody's shrink, if one was needed. "No!"

"Then get the fuck outta bed and act right," he growled.

Act right.

Just like that.

She took a deep inhale and pushed the covers off, dropping her feet to the floor next to the bed.

"Downstairs in five. You ain't down there, draggin' your ass down there. Put on a goddamn smile and talk to your sisters, since they're worried as fuck about you. They think you're fuckin' dyin' or some such shit."

She chewed on her thumbnail as her father turned on his boot heel and left the room, leaving her door wide open.

She normally loved her father, but right now, she wasn't even liking him a little bit.

A few seconds later, Emma's face peered around the edge of the door. She peeked inside, saying, "Looks like grumpy Papa Bear went downstairs." She stepped inside the room and closed the door quietly behind her. "You have him really worried, Cait. Scared, actually."

She frowned. "Sorry."

Emma settled on the bed next to her, wrapping an arm around her shoulders and squeezing them. "He loves you more than you know."

No, she knew. "Thank you."

Emma's eyebrows rose. "For what?"

"For being there for him. For giving him Lily and Lee-lee. For loving him as much as you do." She took a shuddered breath. "For being there for me these last ten years."

Emma gave her a soft smile. "Well, I love you, too. You're like my daughter. You *are* my daughter. You know that, right?"

Cait nodded and put her head on Emma's shoulder, curling an arm around her stepmother's waist.

"So talk to me," Emma whispered. "This seems a bit extreme for the loss of two co-workers, Cait, even if it was tragic. Were you in love with one of them?"

She pulled away from Emma with wide eyes. "What? No!" *Yikes.*

"It's like your heart's broken."

She stared at her stepmother. How did she know that? Maybe from when her daughter, Lily, was abducted by her biological father. That would be a valid reason to be heart-broken, not boo-hooing about a man telling a woman after a week it was "over." She needed to get over the whole thing. Maybe Emma could help. "You can't say anything to Dad."

Emma's lips parted for a moment. "Umm. I don't keep anything from him."

"I know. But if you want me to tell you, you need to keep this from him. Promise me. It's better for him... And for me." And definitely for Magnum.

The woman had the same shade of blonde hair as Cait and also the same complexion. The only difference between them was their height since Emma was shorter and the woman's eyes were blue versus Cait's green eyes which she had gotten from her father.

Most people thought they were sisters since Emma was only around fifteen years older than her. About a year or so younger than Magnum.

Cait grimaced.

Maybe it wasn't a good idea to tell Emma. Maybe it wasn't a good idea to tell anyone. But she needed to get out of this funk. And she was not going to Rissa. If she did, the fact she was seeing a therapist might spread through the sisterhood, causing concern.

She needed to protect Magnum no matter what. Because if the sisterhood found out she and Magnum had... She bit her bottom lip.

It would be bad. Disastrous, even.

Not that they would be upset with Magnum—they wouldn't, they'd probably be thrilled—but because none of them could keep shit from their ol' men and husbands. And as soon as one of the men found out...

Cait closed her eyes. "Emma, I need to speak to someone about this and there's no one I trust more than you." *Except Magnum and Dad*, she added silently.

Emma made a little noise of surprise. "I... Cait...

That's... Thank you for saying that. That means the world to me."

"So, you'll keep this to yourself?"

Emma's face became troubled. "As long as what you tell me isn't a danger to yourself or our family."

Just her heart. "It's not."

She nodded. "Okay."

"I'm in love with someone."

Emma's eyes flashed with excitement, then suddenly narrowed in concern. "I take it this is not something I should be happy about?"

It wasn't the *something* but the *someone* she might not be happy about. "I think he loves me, too, but..."

"But he doesn't want to admit it," Emma finished with an exasperated expression. "Sounds like one of the pigheaded bikers." Her eyebrows knitted together. "Oh my God. Is it Coop?"

"No!"

Emma dragged a hand over her forehead. "Phew. Your father would probably skin him alive if it was."

"Great," Cait muttered.

"I mean, any of the brothers would have to approach your father first and then Z..."

"Right." Those archaic Neanderthal rules of women being property. And there were steps a member had to take if they wanted that property.

"But it's not impossible. I mean, if you're in love..."

"It's not anyone in the DAMC."

"Oh. Who is it?"

"Here's the thing..."

"Oh God, Cait, you're scaring me. Your father's not going to like this at all, is he?"

"He may have a... *few* issues with this person. And... and none of that matters anyway. This person is afraid of becoming enemies with... or at least causing issues between..."

"Between?"

"Clubs."

Emma's spine snapped straight. "Clubs," she repeated. "Which clubs?"

Cait's heart thumped a rapid beat. "The DAMC and his."

"Who is he?" Emma whispered, her face now lined with worry. "We don't need another war, Cait. Please don't tell me he's from the Deadly Demons."

"No." Actually, Cait was surprised Emma would even think she'd get caught up with one of the bikers from the Demons. They were an outlaw MC down in West Virginia.

"Blood Fury?"

She really only knew Trip from the BFMC, and he had an ol' lady. "No."

"Will you just fucking tell me?"

Cait's head jerked back in shock when Emma cursed. She always made Dawg say *fudge* instead of *fuck* around his daughters and in the house. Though, he'd broken that rule just a few minutes earlier.

"It's someone in the Dark Knights."

"The Dark Knights," Emma repeated in a whisper, confused. Until she wasn't. Her eyes went wide, her mouth dropped open and she covered it quickly with her hand. "No."

Cait said nothing.

"No, Cait! He's as old as your father and he didn't approach."

Not *as* old but close. "I know."

"Oh my God." Emma jumped to her feet and began to pace. "I mean, I love Magnum. I do. He's almost like one of us. But... But... he's not." She groaned. "Oh fuck." She slapped a hand to her forehead as she walked the length of the spare bedroom. "Did you...? Did he...?"

Cait grimaced again.

"Oh shit," Emma whispered, staring at her with wide blue eyes. "This is not good. Not good at all."

"I'm not DAMC property," she said weakly.

Emma's eyes went even wider. "The hell you aren't. Try telling that to Dawson." She shook a finger toward the door. "You go down those steps and tell him that to his face."

"I'll pass."

"Right, because you know what he'll say."

"I'm an adult."

Emma laughed almost hysterically, her pace picking up as she moved from the wall on one side of the room to the other, like a caged tiger. "Sure you are." She stopped abruptly. "It's not just the fact he touched DAMC property without permission, Cait. It's his age."

"Do you think Dad will have a problem with that?"

She threw her hands in the air. "Hell yes! They're practically the same age."

"But that shouldn't matter."

"Oh, good luck with that. It *doesn't* matter, Cait, until it's his *daughter*. Then suddenly *everything* matters." She began pacing again, one hand on her hip. "Trust me on that." She suddenly spun on her and stopped. "Do you think Dawson hasn't noticed the interest Magnum has shown you over the years? The interest you've shown him? Do you not think he hasn't watched the two of you closely to make sure..." She blew out a breath. "He's mentioned it to me, Cait. He's mentioned..."

"What did he say?"

Emma's blonde eyebrows shot up her forehead. "I... Uh..."

"Great," Cait muttered. That was not good. But none of it mattered, anyway. "Doesn't matter, Em, he doesn't want anything to do with me."

"Oh, that's a crock of bullshit right there. Yes, he does.

Magnum's just being smart about it." Emma raised a palm and shook her head. "He knows the problems it would cause. He's the one being the adult, Cait. As he should be..."

"I can't help who I love."

Her blue eyes went wide again. "Better find a way. For your father. For Magnum. This could tear everything apart." Emma returned to pacing, slower this time. "I'm sorry. I'm so sorry, Cait. But... this is not good."

"He said it's over, anyway." Every time she said that the knife in her heart twisted another turn.

"I'm sorry for that, too. But it's for the best. You have your whole life ahead of you... You'll meet the right man."

"Emma," Cait whispered, a heavy weight crushing her chest. "I never expected that from you."

Emma's face crumbled. "I know... I..."

"He's not like a Shadow Warrior. He's *Magnum*."

"I know... I just... I'm sorry. *Shit*." Emma wiped a rogue tear off her cheek and sniffled. "I want to be supportive, I do. But this scares me, Cait. Things are so good right now. I don't want that to change."

"Do you really think this would cause a war?"

Emma paused her pacing. "Yes, it could. You know why?"

She didn't wait for Cait's answer.

"Because your father will freak out and go after Magnum before he's come to his senses. It'll be a knee-jerk reaction. Both could be hurt or killed, and then the bad blood between the clubs will begin. There's no way either club will sit back and take an attack like that without doing a counterattack. It's stupid, but it's the way it is. Diesel would never sit back and allow Magnum to do anything to your father, or even you, without some sort of price." She shook her head. "The fucking pride and stubbornness in these men... It can be dangerous sometimes. We all breathed easier when the last Warrior was gone. Now..." She clawed at the neckline of her shirt. "Suddenly, I can't breathe at all." She dropped to her knees in front of Cait. "I can't lose him, Cait. Your sisters can't, either. Magnum would not allow your father to make him pay that price and not fight back."

Cait rubbed at the deep ache in her chest. "I don't want either of them to be hurt... or worse. I don't want to be the cause of bad blood between the clubs. I know how important the Knights are as allies." She dropped her head and blew out a breath. She lifted it and whispered, "But I love him."

Emma closed her eyes but said nothing.

"He sacrificed himself *for me*, Emma. He could've died doing it. He risked his life *for me*. Dad needs to see that, but... I can't tell him any of that or why. I can't. It's the reason I didn't go to Dad or Diesel, or even Mercy, in the first place. I tried to protect them because I knew if I told them what I told Magnum, it would've caused a knee-jerk reaction, just like you said. A dangerous one."

Emma opened her eyes and stared at her for the longest moment. Finally, she said, "I don't know what he did for you and I probably don't want to. But men who love their women do that, Cait. Your father would die to protect me and you three girls."

And that had been one of her fears. That Dawg would go off the deep end, rush into the Gallo agency and kill Nate with his bare hands. "That's the thing, I'm not a girl any longer."

"You might be twenty-five, but you'll always be his little girl. Don't ever expect him to see you differently, even when you reach his age now."

"I don't know what to do about Magnum."

"You do nothing. You move on."

Her stomach churned as she whispered, "I don't know if I can."

Emma sighed, then gave her a sharp nod and squeezed Cait's hands. "Then it's time to get the sisterhood involved. That may be your only solution."

A solution that might work if Magnum went along with it.

He very well may not.

Chapter Seventeen

MAGNUM FOLLOWED his prez into the large building, the rest of his brothers on his heels as they moved single file through the door.

He was already on edge. He used to feel comfortable going to these things. Fundraisers, parties, pig roasts, anything with the Dirty Angels.

Today, he wasn't feeling any kind of safe.

Their club had been invited to a fundraiser being held by Ellie Walker for the Walker Foundation, her charity that funded prostheses for those in need and who couldn't afford it.

It was something his club always supported. Not only because it was a good cause, but because it had been started by Walker's woman. And Walker, one of Diesel's Shadows, was an amputee and a former Special Forces guy. Magnum and his brothers had the utmost respect for veterans.

Plus, D's crew were the main reason the outlaw MC, Shadow Warriors, were no longer a huge pain in all of their asses.

It also wasn't a hardship to attend a spaghetti dinner and bake sale where they could all stuff their faces. They'd been asked by the DAMC prez, Z, to bring their sleds to help their club provide motorcycle rides for the kids and ladies in exchange for donations.

While it was getting to be blue ball season, none of his brothers were pussies, so they'd all brought their sleds.

It had been over a month since he'd last seen Cait. He knew she was very active in helping Ellie fundraise for the foundation. *Hell*, all the DAMC women were.

Which was a good reminder of who Cait was and what she belonged to.

The Shadow Valley Community Center had a huge building that could be rented for large activities like these and it was packed.

Not just with bikers from the DAMC, but with some members of the Blue Avengers MC, a law enforcement club that Axel and Mitch Jamison both belonged to as well as Nash's husband/boyfriend/or whatever the fuck he was. Of course, Nash's other half, Cross, wasn't there, as he'd been banned from any DAMC activities until he retired his pig badge and dropped the word "oinker" from his resume.

When that whole thing between the two went down, it had caused a major cluster-fuck and Magnum understood why Nash had kept it secret for a while. It wasn't the fact that Nash was bi and Cross was gay, it was the fact that Cross was a pig and didn't belong in or around the DAMC.

Kind of like Magnum was feeling right now. Like the enemy walking among them.

Magnum's gaze sliced over the crowd not surprised to find it filled with a lot of current and former military, as well as folks from around the greater Pittsburgh area. The Walker Foundation was a good thing and most people came out to support it, not caring that it was backed by the local MC.

He jerked his chin up at Zak standing across the room

near his wife, Sophie, who was running the bake sale along with Bella and some of the other DAMC's ol' ladies.

He'd have to make sure to buy a dozen of her insanely addictive cupcakes before heading out.

But he was there to at least make an appearance. Support the charity with some scratch, fill his gut, satisfy his sweet tooth and then get the fuck out.

Hopefully, in one fucking piece.

He could do this. He could get through the next few hours and not let seeing Cait bother him.

But when he saw her through the crowd, her face pale, her green eyes pinned on him, he wasn't even sure he could get through the next few goddamn minutes.

He peeled off from his brothers, turned on his heels and walked right the fuck back out.

He couldn't do this.

Seeing her wasn't as painful as the day he walked out of family court reduced to being a sperm donor instead of a father, but it was damn well close.

How the fuck had she burrowed her way into his goddamn soul?

"Jesus fucking Christ," he growled, taking long strides back to his sled, which was sitting in line with the rest of the DKMC's at the other end of the parking lot. He quickly weaved his way through the vehicles that filled almost every paved spot. He kept his eyes focused on his escape vehicle, hoping that once he got on it and rode the fuck away, he'd be able to breathe again.

Who would've thought a woman like Cait could bring him to his goddamn knees?

She was too damn young.

She'd want kids, he didn't.

She was DAMC. He wasn't.

It wasn't like he hadn't laid awake at night wondering

how the fuck to make it work. He had. For too many goddamn restless nights.

Even if they kept their week in Lake George secret. Even if they kept what happened to Cait from everyone.

Even if he approached Dawg and Z...

Even if he was given permission to take what should be his...

If they allowed him to claim her... First at their table, then at his own club's...

Christ, even if all the fucking stars aligned, there was still one huge meteor that couldn't be ignored. One which could come crashing to Earth, destroying everything in its path.

Destroying him and Cait.

Would she eventually walk away from him when she realized how serious he had been about not having more kids?

And if he gave in to her and, for whatever reason, she ever walked away from him *with* their kids...

He might as well tie an anchor to his ankles and follow the Gallos to the bottom of the fucking lake.

As strong as he was, he wasn't strong enough to go through that ever again.

But he had thought about it. He had. It was fucking stupid and his brain kept telling him so. That one worn photo in his wallet, the one taken when Aaliyah was five and MJ was four kept reminding him of what he could lose.

In the end, it was one compromise he wasn't sure he could make.

And that right there would never be fair to Cait.

"Magnum!"

Fuck. He was only a few feet from escaping, he'd almost made it. "Not a good idea, Cait," he threw over his shoulder but kept moving.

He got to his sled and quickly straddled it. As he reached

for the starter button, she grabbed his hand. He stared at it for a moment then reluctantly lifted his gaze to her face.

Jesus fuck.

If his looked half as tortured as hers...

He turned his into a blank mask.

"Hey," she whispered, her brow drawn low, her mouth curved downward.

"Cait," he said. "Not a good time, not a good idea." He glanced back toward the building, trying to make his point.

She chewed on her bottom lip for a moment, then released his hand. Instead of reaching for the start button, he let it drop to his thigh.

He needed to leave.

But he couldn't.

He missed her. He wanted her. And he was goddamn fucked.

"I need to tell you something."

"Tell me what, baby?" *Fuck. Fuck. Fuck.* He didn't mean to call her that, but it unfortunately came naturally. He struggled to keep that blank mask in place, but it was threatening to slip.

All he wanted to do was hold her and tell her everything would work out. But *fuck him*, he wasn't going to lie to her. Or himself.

"What I wanted to tell you up at Lake George."

Fuck. What she whispered on the car ride home, what he pretended not to hear. "No."

She took a huge audible breath as her expression became hard and determined, her green eyes narrowed. "Well, guess what? I'm telling you anyway. So, you can close your fucking ears if you need to but I'm saying it whether you like it or not."

His chin jerked back and his fingers curled into fists. "If you think it's gonna change anything, Cait..."

"It changes everything."

Normally, she'd be right.

His jaw shifted and his expression became as hard as hers. "No, you're fuckin' wrong. Nothin' has changed. It's all the same, Cait. All of it. Except for those Gallo fuckers. That's what changed. That's it."

"No."

"Don't be so goddamn blind," he growled.

"I'm not being blind."

He dropped his head and shook it.

"Look at me," she whispered roughly.

"No."

"You're saying I'm blind but so are you. I need you to look at me."

"No, Cait." He lifted his head but stared past her, keeping his eyes toward the building's entrance. "This ain't gonna work. No matter how much you want it to." *No matter how much I fucking want it to.*

"You don't even want to give it a chance."

"Cait... You're killin' me here."

"You feel it, too."

He opened his mouth to deny it. He snapped it shut. "Don't matter what I feel, Cait."

"If I could convince my father... if the sisterhood could convince—"

"What the fuck? You told them?"

"Magnum..."

"Cait. It's not just 'cause of them. Tried to tell you that. Doin' what's best for you, can't you fuckin' see that?"

"You aren't."

"The fuck I'm not."

"But I love you."

Magnum closed his eyes and muttered, "Goddamn it."

"And you love me," she said softly.

His eyes flashed open. "Cait..."

"You do."

"Don't matter, Cait. Can't give you the life you want." He raised his hand. "Fuck that. The life you deserve."

"Because you're a biker?"

"'Cause I'm fuckin' sixteen years older than you!" he bellowed. "It's not just the age, Cait. Told you I'm not havin' any more kids. Don't fuckin' deny yourself that chance." He flung a hand toward the community center. "Don't deny that opportunity for Dawg. Or Emma. Or makin' your sisters aunts. In the end, you'll regret it. No... Don't say you fuckin' won't, 'cause that'll be a complete fuckin' lie." He reached over and grabbed her chin, forcing her to look at him. "Tell me you can live without havin' kids, Caitie. Say it. Wanna see your face when you lie to me."

He was right. She had ignored that fact, hoping if they could work things out between the clubs, he'd change his mind. That she'd convince him eventually.

It hit her now, he'd never be convinced.

Once again, she had been selfish and him selfless. He was denying his feelings for her *because of her*.

He was not taking what he wanted *because of her*.

To make sure she didn't make a mistake.

He was looking out for her. Sacrificing for her.

Once again.

But she got her stubborn streak from her father and she wasn't going to easily give up. It wasn't in her DNA.

"Look at Diesel. He didn't want to be a father. Now look at him. Those girls are his life. His everything."

"Malcolm and Aaliyah were my life, too, Cait. Bein' forced to walk away from them killed me. It kills me to this day they're now adults and could easily change that and they don't fuckin' want to. They may never want to. Can't do that again. Can't go through that again. Not ever. Loved my goddamn kids. Woulda given up everythin' I had to be with them, to spend time with them. Woulda sacrificed *every-thin'*, Cait."

The agony in his words sliced through her. "I would never do that to you," she whispered, unable to keep her bottom lip from trembling.

He turned his head and looked past her again, his face twisted, his eyes troubled. "An' I wanna believe you... Not sure I wanna be raisin' babies in my forties, Cait. No, I'm fuckin' sure. I don't. Find someone else." He stabbed the starter button and his bike roared to life. He heeled up the kickstand. "Made a mistake comin' here. Won't happen again."

He twisted the throttle and his Harley shot forward, making her step backward to keep from being clipped.

Her toes might have survived him leaving, but her heart might not.

HOUSE. Now.

Cait's pulse raced and her fingers trembled as she thought about that text from her father over and over again.

She parked her Toyota in the driveway at his house in the compound and sat there for a few minutes, staring at the closed front door.

Wondering what the hell might happen once she stepped through it.

When she had texted Dawg back asking him what was up, he only repeated his original text. *House. Now.*

Damn, she felt like a teenager all over again.

Her father had never been as strict with her as her mother had been, but he'd been overly protective.

She had sent Emma a text: *What's the matter?*

Emma had texted back: *I'm doing what I can. Just hurry.*

That made the knots in her stomach twist even tighter.

She pressed her forehead against the steering wheel and tried to get her breathing, her heart rate and her spinning thoughts under control.

She wasn't having any luck.

"Caitlin!" she heard bellowed from the house.

She lifted her head to see her father standing in the doorway. Fury coloring his face.

Oh fuck.

Fuck.

Fuck.

Fuck.

She glanced around quickly to see if anyone in the club-owned neighborhood was outside and had heard her father yelling.

She saw no one, so she quickly scrambled from the car before he kept bellowing his displeasure like a Grizzly bear with a thorn in his paw, and everyone came out to see what the problem was.

Once he saw her heading toward the front door, he disappeared inside.

She glanced at the flowers and shrubbery Emma had planted in front of the house, wondering if she should expel the contents of her stomach behind them before stepping inside. Especially since each step up to the porch felt like a step closer to her own funeral. It might save her stepmother's carpet.

"Better get the fuck in here right now before I go kill that motherfucker an' not give you a fuckin' second to explain."

Oh fuck.

She shut the front door behind her and moved into the family room where her father waited with one hand jammed on his hip, his phone in the other and his face already close to purple with anger. Emma hovered near him, trying not to look panicked but failing.

"Promised Em I'd give you a chance to explain. Givin' you one motherfuckin' minute."

He tossed his phone at Cait and she barely caught it. Was it the video? Had someone sent it to him?

Blood drained from her face as she lifted his phone, hit the power button to light it up and then almost dropped it with what she saw.

It wasn't the video.

It was the picture of her and Magnum sandwiched together on the steamboat dance floor. The one her mother had been sent.

How the fuck did Dawg get it?

Cait quickly scanned the texts that preceded the photo: *You've ruined her. I had such high hopes for her. That she would do better despite your half of her DNA. You HAD to get involved. You FORCED me to give you visitation when she was still impressionable. And now look, the bright future she could've had, is no longer that. This is your fault!*

Had she found out who Magnum really was? She wouldn't put it past her mother to have him investigated. Or was she pissed about her leaving the Gallo agency and taking the job Ellie offered her at the foundation? Was she blaming that on Magnum or Dawg?

Fucking hell!

Scrolling, she saw more texts—a lot more, because her mother *always* had plenty to say—but her father didn't give her time to read them before he jerked the phone from her fingers. "That up at that fuckin' retreat like Regan said?"

"Why would she send that to you?"

"Why was Magnum up at a goddamn work retreat with you? Know he wasn't workin' for the same company you were. Know he'd have no reason to go on vacation at Lake George an' this was just some fuckin' coincidence. Know it 'cause your fuckin' mother also happened to mention you two have been seein' each other for eight fuckin' years!" The sharp rise of his booming voice made her wince. "Now, I *know* that can't be fuckin' right. 'Specially when eight years ago you were *underage!*" His chest expanded and he continued, "Caught you two eyeballin' each other one too many fuckin' times. But figured Magnum would never step where he shouldn't. Figured that fuckin' man knew better. Guess I was fuckin' wrong an' was fuckin' my baby girl behind my goddamn back."

"No."

Dawg's eyebrows shot up his forehead and he roared, "*NO?*"

"Honey," Emma whispered, reaching for Dawg's arm.

He pulled it away and spun on his wife. "How much did you know?"

"I..." Emma started, blanching.

"Nothing!" Cait screamed at him. "Nothing. She didn't know shit, Dad. Jesus!" She planted a hand on her forehead. "The eight years was a lie."

"That fuckin' picture a lie?"

She was going to kill her mother. There had been no reason to stir up shit. None. She'd told her two months ago that her and Magnum were over. At the time, she thought it had satisfied Regan.

Apparently not.

She still needed to take cheap shots at Dawg whenever she could. She still needed to dig for dirt. She had to bitch about every decision Cait made on her own and blame him. It served no purpose.

The only problem was, every one of those dirty shots caused complications for Cait. But of course, just like the messy visitation fight, Regan didn't give a shit how it affected her daughter.

Not. One. Bit.

"Why did she send you that?"

"'Cause your mother's a goddamn bitch!" Dawg bellowed.

Cait blinked.

"Dawson!" Emma yelled at her ol' man.

Even though she had no doubt he hated Regan with every cell in his big body, he'd always kept his thoughts to himself.

"You're old enough I shouldn't gotta deal with her goddamn bullshit anymore. What you did..." He shook his head. "Your mother's the least of what I'm fuckin' pissed about."

"Dad," she tried to say evenly. He needed to calm down and see reason. "Dad... It's not what you think."

"No? He didn't fuck you?"

Cait's mouth dropped open. She never once talked to her father about who she'd had sex with and never planned on it. And while, in reality, it was none of his business, he was making it his business only because Magnum belonged to another MC.

She grimaced. "Dad, it's not what you think," she tried again.

"You fuckin' kiddin' me? Think I'm fuckin' stupid?"

She forced a, "No," up her closed throat.

"Dawson, you need to calm down."

Dawg spun on Emma, jabbing his finger in her direction. "That motherfucker touched DAMC property without permission. Went behind our backs an' stole what belongs to us. What belongs to me. He touched *my fuckin' daughter!*" he roared.

"Stop it," Emma said sharply, her face lined with worry. "*Please.*"

"He needs to pay."

Cait rushed up to her father and grabbed the edges of his open flannel shirt, yanking on them. "Dad! No. It's all my fault. I swear."

"Gonna kill that motherfucker."

"No, you're not!" Cait said sharply.

His green eyes dropped to her and he growled, "You don't get that say."

"The fuck I don't!" Her father had lost his fucking mind!

Dawg yanked free of her fingers and began moving quickly toward the interior garage door.

If he got on his bike and went to Zak or Diesel... or any of them... If he left that house, shit was going to go sideways fast and someone was going to get hurt.

Or dead.

And the easy and loose brotherhood between the clubs would be broken forever. Peace would turn into war.

She needed to stop him. She needed to fix this. Now.

Unsure what else to do to get him to listen and out of complete desperation, she screamed, "Dad! I was raped!"

Emma gasped and her father went completely solid, his back to her.

She never wanted him to know that. She had never wanted anyone to know. But she no longer had a choice.

Dawg spun on his boot heel and roared, "He raped you?"

Oh shit! She spoke fast. "No! It was someone else. I was drugged and raped. And I didn't know what to do. I... He helped me. I went to Magnum and asked for help and... and he helped me!" she yelled, her voice breaking. *God*, she hoped her sisters were nowhere in the house right now.

"What the fuck!" Dawg bellowed, his face twisting into more rage than she thought could be humanly possible.

Oh fuck. She lifted her palms out, still talking fast. "I didn't want anyone to know. I was trying to save my job... I was trying to save face... He risked everything for me!"

Dawg stared at her and whispered, "Who raped you?" The soft tone of his voice was deceiving. It was dangerous and deadly.

"It doesn't matter. Magnum handled it."

"An' forced you to fuck him in return?"

"No! No, Dad. He's not like that. You know him. He'd never be like that. Jesus Christ! You're not thinking straight."

He stepped closer to her and she didn't recognize the look on his face. "You're fuckin' right, I'm not. 'Cause not only did he..." His big body lurched. "But some motherfucker..."

She got scared when he lurched again.

Then he simply... crumbled. Right there. In front of her. Almost as if a baseball bat had struck him right in the middle. All air rushed from his lungs, his body bending over in half as he went down. Her big, tough, badass biker father fell to his knees only feet from her.

Him visibly shattering caused her to break inside, too. To see him affected like that ripped her apart.

This was another reason she never wanted him to know. To see her strong father falling apart made it so much worse.

For months, she had tried to remain strong about what happened to her, but seeing him like this made it impossible.

"Dad," she cried, tears burning a path down her cheeks as she rushed to him and slid to her knees, wrapping her arms around his big body as best as she could. "Dad," she said in a broken whisper. "I'm sorry."

She shoved her face into his neck, hiding her rush of tears in his thick beard.

"I'm sorry," she whispered again.

She heard Emma sobbing softly from somewhere behind them. Close but giving the two of them space.

Emma had to be hurting, too. However, right now Cait needed to hold onto her father and found it impossible to do anything else. She simply couldn't let go, nor did she want to.

He'd been her rock for the last ten years. Now, she needed to be his.

Chapter Eighteen

MAGNUM SAT at *his* table in *his* corner of Dirty Dick's. Nina had dropped off a bottle of Jack and a shot glass, and as she moved away—drawing her fingernails over the back of his fucking neck again—movement heading in his direction caught his attention.

Two large men were working their way toward him, not looking any kind of pleased to be there.

That meant they weren't there to shoot the shit. He wouldn't be surprised if they were there to shoot him. Probably right in the fucking nuts.

"Fuck," he muttered under his breath.

He hadn't been warned that they'd arrived since the prospects working the front door no longer stopped the Angels or even announced them. They were free to come and go in their bar just like the Knights were free to hang out and drink at The Iron Horse Roadhouse.

An unspoken courtesy between allies.

He had a feeling that was about to change.

Most likely, a whole shitload of things were about to change. And not for the better.

He didn't bother to stand and instead downed the shot Nina had poured him. "You packin'?"

Diesel only grunted and Dawg opened his cut, showing nothing tucked in his waistband.

That didn't mean Cait's father didn't have one hidden somewhere else.

His gaze slid past the two Angels to his own brothers who had all caught interest in what was going on in Magnum's corner.

He jerked his head slightly, an unspoken signal for them to relax. He wasn't sure if they did, since he returned his attention to the two men he considered friends.

He tipped his chin toward the chairs across from him. "Gonna take a weight off?"

He guessed not when Dawg said, "Respect should've been given by approachin' me first."

"And what would you have said?"

"Know what I woulda said."

"Yeah. That was the fuckin' problem. Why I never did."

"Problem for you, maybe, not for me. Forget she's my daughter. Touched club property without fuckin' permission."

"One thing I didn't forget, brother. Know she's your girl. Know she belongs to the DAMC."

"You were outta line."

"Made a mistake, and I fixed it."

"How's that?" Dawg asked, his hands on his hips, his boots planted solidly and spread apart on the concrete floor.

"Let 'er go," Magnum said simply. Although, there was nothing fucking simple about it.

"Problem is, *brother*, you didn't. Still got a hold on her."

He poured himself another shot and downed it in one swallow, his lip curling at the burn. He slammed the shot glass onto the wood table. "It was short. It was sweet. Now it's over. Told 'er that."

He expected Dawg to lash out, to grab a hold of him. To try to take him on. It would be stupid to do in Magnum's own bar, especially full of Knights, even with the DAMC enforcer at his side. Those two together were a powerhouse, but they were outnumbered.

However, Dawg was a father and Cait was his daughter. Fathers sometimes didn't think rationally when it came to protecting their kids.

He got that.

And he was surprised Dawg was keeping his shit together as much as he was. He tried to get a read off D, but it was impossible. But he figured D took Magnum touching Cait as a slight, too.

"Like 'em young?" Dawg asked sharply.

Magnum lifted his gaze and met the same green eyes as Cait's. "No. I don't. Like a smart woman who knows what the fuck she wants, doesn't play head games and's got a fuckin' spine."

Diesel grunted, but said nothing.

"She's barely a woman."

"That's where you're wrong, brother. You'll always see her as your little girl even when the rest of us don't."

"Old enough to be her father."

"Reason why I never approached," he told the man only a couple years older than him.

"But still got what you wanted. Back-doored us, thinkin' we wouldn't find out."

"Surprised she told you," Magnum muttered.

"She didn't."

Magnum lifted his head and stared at the man before him. "Fuck."

"Yeah. *Fuck*. Fuckin' cunt was a thorn in my goddamn side for years. Cait moved in, thought I'd be done with 'er. Gets off on fuckin' with me an' screwin' with my relationship with Cait. Bitter ol' bitch is still pissed she couldn't buy me off an' get me out of Cait's life. Cait don't know it, but Regan offered me five hundred K to walk away."

Fuck.

"To me, my daughter's worth way fuckin' more than a half mil. Got me?"

"Yeah," Magnum breathed.

"Got my blood runnin' through her goddamn veins. The only good that came outta me stickin' my dick in that selfish snatch."

Magnum's eyes slid from Dawg to Diesel and back. "Fucked up. Wanna make it right. Don't want issues for my club. Don't wanna fuck up our clubs' alliance. Will pay whatever price you think's fair for stealin' what was yours."

"Said *was.* Thinkin' you mean *is.* You touchin' her didn't change that. She still *is* DAMC property."

"Normally, that fuckin' price would be the ultimate one," D answered. "But she begged for your life." He yanked out a chair, flipped it around and settled his large bulk into it backwards. "Also don't wanna fuck up the alliance between the clubs. It's strong. It's needed. Between the Knights, the Angels and the Fury, we control the west." He glanced up at Dawg and ordered, "Sit down."

Dawg reluctantly pulled out the chair next to his club's Sergeant at Arms and straddled it, too. They were ready to deal but weren't going to relax while doing it.

Magnum's asshole was also tighter than he liked and would remain that way until they left or he stopped breathing. Because one or the other was going to happen. He just didn't know which.

"Told me what you did," Dawg said.

Jesus fuck. How many details did she give him?

"Asked you for help and you helped her."

Magnum breathed a touch easier.

"Shoulda come to me," Diesel grumbled. "My job to take care of all that shit. Pissed she didn't. Explained why.

Don't like it but get it. She was gonna go elsewhere, better she come to you. Still don't like you not comin' to me with it. Again, considerin' that a lack of fuckin' respect."

"And you know that ain't true."

D's dark eyebrows rose. "Yeah? Got Dawg's girl comin' to you instead of me an' you not comin' to me with it? Seein' that clearly as fuckin' disrespect. Then you fuckin' touch 'er? Huge lack of respect, brother. Wouldn't do that shit to you."

"Don't know 'til you're faced with it."

D leaned forward over the back of the chair. "Bullshit. Stepped on my toes," he jerked his head at Dawg. "Stepped on his. Hard to forgive, brother. Really fuckin' hard."

Dawg regarded Magnum as he said, "She came to you 'cause she trusts you. Came to you 'cause she thought you'd do the right thing. The right thing for her. Not our clubs. Made a sacrifice you didn't have to make. Made a decision that could've started a fuckin' war. In one way, gotta respect that. But gotta remember she's my fuckin' little girl. *Mine.* That's what's makin' this difficult. Wanna thank you an' kill you at the same fuckin' time. Goddamn lucky she loves you."

Magnum's heart squeezed at the last part. "Told you that?"

Dawg scowled. "So many fuckin' times never wanna hear it again. Gonna hear it in my goddamn sleep. Only reason you don't have a hole between your damn eyes right now. She'd never fuckin' forgive me an' not losin' her when I only got 'er a few years ago. She's mine. Nobody's takin' her from me. But willin' to give her to the right man."

Hold the fuck up. Were they there to negotiate with him and not neuter him?

Cait's father wasn't done yet. "Not sure that's you."

"It's not."

Dawg tipped his head back in surprise. "Was just a hole to dip your dick into?"

"No."

"Then what?"

"Love her enough to let 'er go."

"Fuck," D grunted, scrubbing a hand over his short dark hair.

"Wanna explain that?" Dawg growled.

He didn't. He was done talking about this whole fucking thing. "Like you said, almost old enough to be her father. She's young, needs to live her life and find happy elsewhere. Give you grandkids. That's not what I'm lookin' for."

Dawg stared at him and he stared back. Not one of the three of them moved a muscle. "She say she wanted babies?"

"Even if she said she didn't, know she'd eventually regret it if she didn't."

"Yeah," Dawg said softly. "Was always good with the girls. A natural. Don't want kids, gotta respect that. At my age, don't want any more myself. But," he rapped his knuckles on the table, "if Emma wanted another one, I'd give it to her. I'd give her anythin' she fuckin' wanted. Maybe that's the difference between you an' me, brother. So, maybe you don't love her like you think. Maybe it's good you ended it. 'Cause the man who gets her needs to fuckin' love her more than I do. That's gonna be hard to beat."

"Hard to fuckin' beat a father's love," D added, his eyes narrowed on Magnum, searching.

Magnum kept his face neutral. "Hard but not impossible."

"A good man will die takin' care of his woman, his kids. Not even think twice about it," Dawg said. "She said you could've died."

He pressed his lips together. Instead of answering, he poured himself another shot and downed it.

"That's sayin' somethin'," Diesel mumbled, watching Magnum's every move.

"Actually sayin' a lot," Dawg added. "Wouldn't say who drugged her and..." Dawg shook his head. "And did that shit to her. Didn't need her to. Put two an' two together. Just want to make sure whoever it was, who I'm thinkin' it was, was who you took care of. Otherwise, we're gonna make sure it's done."

"Those two motherfuckin' Gallos?" D asked him, his normally loud voice low so no one overheard them.

"Yeah," Magnum grunted.

"Both of 'em?"

"One was harrassin' her, the other did..." His gaze slid from D to Dawg. "What Cait told you."

"What 'bout the video?" D asked.

"Deleted what I found on the one's phone. Deleted it off her phone. Deleted it off mine. Not sure if there's more out there. Best guess is yeah, there is."

"Not likin' that," Dawg said.

Magnum tilted his head. "Did what I fuckin' could, brother."

D nodded.

So did Dawg. "Got that. Appreciate that. Disrespected us by not approachin', but gotta thank you for handlin' that shit how you did. Didn't have to, but you did. Figure that's worth a little leniency."

Magnum kept his eyes from rolling. *Well, thank fuck for that.*

"So, we're good?" he asked the two men.

"No, we ain't good," Dawg answered. "My girl loves you an' you got a thing for her. Somethin's gotta be done 'bout that."

Magnum's pulse thumped in his ears. "Like what?"

"You know what," D grumbled. "Got an exec meetin' next week. Gives you time to figure shit out. Gonna act like you didn't back-door us. You want 'er, you approach. We vote. If we all say 'aye?' Then you do whatcha gotta do at your own table. You figure it out."

Magnum cocked a brow at Dawg. "Really want me callin' you Dad?"

Diesel snorted. Dawg's mouth dropped open like a dead fish and he blinked a couple times before snapping it shut. Instead of answering, Dawg grabbed the bottle of Jack and drank directly from it.

"Thinkin' that's a no."

Dawg slammed the whiskey bottle on the table and wiped his mouth with the back of his hand, before pushing out a loud breath. "Know I wanna be called a granddaddy someday. Not wantin' to rush that but with a man like you, your age... "

"Like I said, she wants me, she gets me, nothin' else."

"Yeah. Not likin' that. Wanna claim my girl, you'll do what you gotta do to make her happy."

He didn't like being pushed like this. He didn't like it at fucking all. It was going to be his decision and no one else's. Not even Cait's. "Wouldn't give a fuck your grandbabies would be brown?" He needed to be sure about that before he made any fucking decision.

He needed to hear it. Because if there was any goddamn doubt...

Dawg surged to his feet and growled, "You're a stupid motherfucker if you think I would."

Diesel also pushed out of his chair with a grunt, but didn't say a word.

Dawg rapped his knuckles on the table again. "You know where we're at. Know whatcha gotta do. Now up to you to decide. She worth it or not? She is? You do it the right way. She's not? Then..." The man's nostrils flared, he tilted his head, then spun on his heels heading toward the bar's front door.

As Dawg disappeared, Magnum sat back, crossed his arms over his chest and lifted his gaze to Diesel's. "Don't want bad blood between us, brother. We gotta good thing here, don't want that fucked up."

"Yeah," D grunted. "Still goddamn torqued she didn't come to me to handle it."

Magnum jerked his chin toward the closed door. "He's why."

"Yeah, get that. Still ain't right." D tilted his head. "Didn't just step on his fuckin' toes, you fuckin' crushed 'em. He's lettin' you slide. Didn't hafta. Remember that."

With that, D turned and lumbered through the bar, his huge bulk disappearing out the door.

Magnum sat back and wiped his hands down his face. He wasn't sure if he should be relieved on how all that went or pissed that he was being pushed.

He didn't like being pressured. Not at fucking all.

———

HE'D SENT HER A TEXT. Gave her an address. Gave her a time.

She wanted to feel hopeful but was feeling sick instead. Her stomach churned, her mouth was bone dry, her pulse raced, and her knee bounced under the table at the diner he gave her the address for.

It wasn't in Shadow Valley and it wasn't in Knights' territory, either. It was out in the country where most likely an Angel or a Knight wouldn't accidentally show up.

But when he walked through the door, she spotted him immediately. Not only because he stood out due to being darker than everyone else in that diner. Not because he outsized all the occupants. Not because he wore a Knights cut over a snug cream colored long-sleeved thermal shirt that made her want to rip it off him and lick him from waist to throat.

No.

It was his larger than life presence as he moved his bulky body toward her sitting in one of the booths.

His expression was unreadable and that didn't help her nervousness.

He'd said a final goodbye that Saturday a couple months ago after the retreat.

He'd said a final goodbye again about a month ago in the parking lot at the fundraiser.

Would this third time be the last "final" time?

She hoped to hell not.

She knew something happened a few days ago between him, her father and Diesel, but she didn't know exactly what.

She only knew Dawg and Diesel came home in one piece, and when she demanded an answer from her father, he stated they'd settled some things.

Settled some things.

She had no idea what. She only knew right now the two clubs were still allies. Which was a huge relief.

Even so, she'd sent Magnum one single text after the day they talked to him.

One single word.

Sorry.

She didn't expect an answer but she'd gotten one a few minutes later: *Same.*

But that was all she got. Only enough to break her heart all over again.

Was both of them being sorry enough to change anything? No. But she had to respect the fact he was protecting her and also himself by letting her go. He knew she'd regret not having kids down the road.

He was right. She would.

She loved him but she also wanted children to love. She had thought long and hard over that single issue.

Yes, she loved him.

Yes, she wanted him.

Did she care his life revolved around being the Sergeant at Arms for the Dark Knights MC? No.

Did she care about their age difference? No.

Did she want to give up her choice to have children? Also no. And that was the problem.

Every time one of the ol' ladies in the DAMC sisterhood got pregnant and she got to finally hold that baby? Her heart melted and her motherly instinct pulled at her from deep inside.

Even being an aunt to Lily or Emmalee's children would eventually never be enough.

Her eyes didn't leave his face as he slid his big body into the seat across from her with a grunt. Before either of them could say a word, a waitress rushed up. "Coffee?"

With only a nod as his answer, she turned his coffee cup over and filled it. Magnum didn't thank her or even look at her, he only stared at Cait.

Cait gave the waitress a quick nod, a small smile and a soft thank you before she rushed away. Then she focused on the man across from her.

And her heart tore apart once again.

Because at that moment, seeing him, being so close to him, getting a whiff of the scent that was Magnum, she wanted to tell him she'd be fine with not having children. That he'd be enough for her. That their love for each other would be all she'd ever need.

She put her hand out on the center of the table and waited.

She closed her eyes when his large, warm hand enveloped hers. "I've missed you," she whispered.

His fingers squeezed hers. "Same."

That gave her the courage to say, "I love you."

She hoped he'd say, "Same," but he didn't. Instead he just grunted a, "Yeah."

Her eyes opened at his single word answer.

His dark brown eyes held something she didn't recognize. "Done a lot of thinkin'."

"Me, too," she said.

"Done a lot of soul searchin', too, Cait."

She stayed quiet.

"We're so goddamn different. So wrong for each other."

Was he here to break her heart even more than it already was?

"You're book smart, beautiful and young. I'm street smart, old and definitely not anything to look at. You've got your whole life ahead of you—"

"You've already told me that—"

"Just let me say what I gotta say, Cait."

She shut up.

"Need to get it all out on the table."

She nodded and said nothing, only squeezed his hand, encouraging him to continue.

"At twenty-five, got your whole life ahead of you. Done a lot of shit in my life you haven't done yet. Don't want you to miss out on a fuckin' minute of it."

"You can do it with me," she whispered.

He closed his eyes and pushed his broad back against the bench seat. "Cait."

She shut up again. But the waiting was hard.

He opened his eyes again and held hers. "Wanna do it with you."

She frowned. *What?*

"Wanna do it with you," he repeated more slowly. "Just need to be sure you know it ain't gonna be easy."

Her heart began to beat wildly.

What?

What was he saying?

"It ain't gonna be easy," he repeated.

Her eyebrows knitted together. "Are you making sure I understand that, or you?"

"Both. Being with you's gonna be easy for me. Givin' you what you deserve, won't. But will do whatever I can to make you happy."

"What are you saying?" she asked on a hitched breath.

"If I'm in, Caitie, I'm all fuckin' in."

"Wait. You're in?" What was he saying? He needed to be clear about what he was saying!

"No."

Her heart sank into her stomach. She tried to pull her hand away, but he held on tighter.

"I'm *all* fuckin' in, baby. All of it."

She stared at him for one slow breath, then another, wrapping her head around what he just stated. "Are you sure? You're old and shit, let's not forget that."

His chin jerked back, he blinked at her, and then he threw his head back and burst out laughing.

Holy shit, that was the best sound she'd ever heard. A smile pulled at her lips as she covered their clasped hands that they held at the center of the table with her other one.

"What changed your mind? Your blinding love for me?" She wiggled her eyebrows.

"Somethin' your fuckin' father said."

Her smile flattened. *Oh shit,* did Dawg threaten him? Is he doing this against his will? "What did he say?"

"He said at his age he's done havin' babies. Also said that if Emma wanted another one, he'd give her whatever the fuck she wanted. That's how much he loves her. Said that was the difference between him and me. Said maybe I didn't love you enough to do the same... Took a couple days to let those words sink in and when they did... realized I do."

He did. He loved her enough... But... "Stacy—"

"Stacy ain't you. Never was. Never will be, baby. Was a good woman, just not the right one. Made a lot of mistakes in my life, havin' babies with her would've been one."

Holy shit. "So, you want babies with me?" She wanted to launch herself across the table at him and squeal like a crazy woman. She forced herself to remain in her seat and take a calming breath instead.

"Wanna make you happy. Babies make you happy, then we'll negotiate how many and how soon."

"But again, you're old as hell, we can't wait that long. How are you going to throw a ball with our kid if you're using a walker?"

"Damn, woman," he mumbled. "Don't make me rethink this."

She shot him another smile.

"Need a promise, though, before I approach Dawg."

Again, that smile quickly disappeared. "You need to approach him?" *Unbelievable.* After all that happened? After all Magnum did for her?

"Still DAMC property, baby. Gotta do this from scratch if we're doin' this. Gotta do it right this time to keep the peace."

She opened her mouth and he lifted his free hand to stop her. "Don't even fuckin' say it."

That property crap always made her grind her teeth. "I was only going to ask what the promise was."

"Bullshit."

She rolled her eyes. "I'm assuming he'll say yes. Okay, so what's the promise?"

"You bear my babies, gotta promise me you'll never cut me off from them. Not ever, Cait. Even if you end up hatin' my guts for whatever reason."

"I'd never hate your guts."

"Yeah, lotta women say that 'til they do. You of all people should know what it's like bein' used as a pawn in that fucked-up game. Need you to remember that if shit ever goes sideways between us."

"Like I get tired of changing your adult diapers?"

"Fuckin' Cait," he muttered, but then smiled.

That smile was beautiful. And warmed her like the sun on a perfect summer day.

He was giving them a shot. He loved her and was willing to start a family with her when she was ready.

She never thought it would happen.

It was.

Holy shit!

And if the DAMC executive committee didn't vote unanimously on letting Magnum claim her, she was going in there and clubbing every single one of them.

Or she'd just sic the sisterhood on their ol' men. That threat might scare them more. Because none of them wanted their women pissed at them. Not a single one.

The power behind the sisterhood was insane. And she belonged to that sisterhood.

Soon she might belong to a second one. She had no idea how the Knights' women got along. But if they didn't, she'd work on building what the DAMC women had. Because there was strength in numbers, and they were all dealing with stubborn alpha male bikers who liked to remind them they were their *property*.

And they were oh so fucking wrong.

Out of the corner of her eye, she noticed two men stop at their table just out of arm's reach.

Magnum's gaze rose. So did hers and she frowned. Who the hell were they and why did they look pissed?

"What's a pretty white girl like you doing with a dirty n——"

"Hey!" she screamed too late to cut the man off, but at least she had drowned out his nasty slur. The blood rushed into her ears at what he'd called Magnum.

"No good man's gonna want you after having that between your legs," the other sneered. "White trash bitch breeding with a mon—"

Magnum only had to shift sharply in his seat and the men quickly moved on, almost stumbling over each other in their rush.

She shot to her feet and screeched, "You assholes—"

He reached across the table, grabbed her hand and yanked her back into her seat. "Sit down, Cait."

She glanced at him in surprise. "But—"

"Sit the fuck down," he said under his breath, since all eyes in the diner were now on them.

She flung her hand in the direction of the entrance where the two men disappeared. "You can't just let them... I can't just let—"

"That shit ain't nothin' new."

"But they called you a... a..." She couldn't even wrap her head around it. What decade were they in? Who said that kind of shit nowadays?

His nostrils flared and his jaw shifted. "Think that's the first time I've been called that?"

Cait closed her eyes, knowing now it wasn't. What the fuck was wrong with people? "How can you just sit there?" She expected more anger out of him than he was showing. Either he was hiding it well or he was used to it occurring. And if it was the latter...

"What do you want me to do? Punch them the fuck out right here in the diner? Wanna watch me get hauled off in front of you? Cuffed like an animal?"

"It doesn't bother you?"

"Babe, it's not the first time I've been called that. Not the second. Hell, can't even tell you how many times I've been called that. Ain't gonna be the last, either." He leaned forward, his knuckles planted on the table. "But, yeah, it bothers me. The day it don't is the day I'm dead. Best reaction to that is no reaction. Those fuckers were tryin' to get a rise outta me by insultin' me and insultin' you. Create a reason to call the pigs. Or a reason to draw me outside for them to jump me. By me still sittin' here with my 'pretty white girl' they fuckin' failed. And, baby, that's the best fuckin' revenge."

She reached across the table, grabbed his fisted hand and interlaced their fingers. The contrast between their hands was startling. His so huge. Hers so tiny.

He could have pounded those two men into oblivion.

She gave his fingers a squeeze. "You could've taken them both."

"Yeah. But by doin' that they aimed to take me away from you. You get that?"

"I'm sorry," she whispered.

"For what?"

She jerked her chin toward the door behind him. "For them. For anyone who thinks like that."

"Never apologize for someone else's ignorance. Told you we're different. You just got a taste of it. Gotta think long and hard over this, Caitie. We have kids, they're gonna be brown like me, they're gonna deal with that shit. Hopin' they won't, but know they will. Gonna be called all kinds of fuckin' names. Wish the world was a better place but it ain't."

Then it hit her. "Any kids we have will have the protection of two clubs." She held up two fingers. "Two."

"Two clubs can't protect them from ignorant comments. But, yeah. And you know if we have a baby girl, she's fucked. Gonna be a virgin her whole life. Any asshole who risks touchin' her may stop breathin'. Just a warnin'."

"You're still breathing and Dawg once said the same thing about me."

"Sure he said it a lot more than once. Wasn't for you

beggin' for my fuckin' life, I might not be breathin'. Should thank you for that."

"It was worth it."

"Was it?"

"Well, it will be. Can we go back to your place now or do you need to approach and get permission?" she teased.

He reached toward where he kept his phone in his pocket. "Lemme call Daddy Dawg and ask 'im."

Her eyes shot wide. "Don't you dare!"

He grinned.

Her mouth formed an *O* and her eyes went wide. She laughed. "Are you going to call him Dad?" A little snort escaped her as she laughed even harder. "Oh, please, you need to call him Dad."

"Seriously want me dead?"

She giggle-snorted again. "No, but..."

"Cait..."

She tried to stifle her laughter but she couldn't get what her father's reaction would be to Magnum calling Dawg "Dad" out of her head.

Magnum wedged himself out of the booth and held out his big hand. "C'mon, woman. Everyone's starin'."

She accepted it and rose to her feet. "They're just looking at my handsome ol' man."

"Least you didn't add the 'd' on the ol'," he said as he threw some cash on the table and helped her into her coat.

"Day's not over yet."

"D likes givin' Jewelee lessons. Might need to start givin' my woman some, too. Write up a lesson plan."

Those "lessons" gave D and Jewel three beautiful girls. "If school's in session, remember I still have my plaid uniforms."

"Know what you looked like as a teen. Know even better what you look like now. You ain't fittin' in those uniforms, baby, and that's a good thing."

"Is it?"

He slipped his hand from the small of her back to her ass and squeezed as he led her out of the diner. "Fuck yeah."

He escorted her back to her Toyota, noticing he'd parked his sled next to her car. She shivered at the thought of being a backpack on his Harley right now.

"Normal" people didn't ride their motorcycles in November. But true bikers rode until the weather made it impossible. Sometimes even then.

Her *soon-to-be* ol' man was a true biker.

They stopped at her driver-side door. "So, now what?" she asked, wondering what happened from there. She wanted to do nothing more than go home with him that minute.

He pulled a single key on a ring from his front pocket and held it up by one finger in front of her face.

Her heart skipped a beat. He didn't have to say what that was. She knew.

She fucking knew.

"Now you head to your apartment, grab some shit and head home."

Home!

She snatched that key out of his hand, causing him to grin. "And where are you going?" she tried to ask calmly, though her body was humming with excitement. She was impressed her words only had a slight tremor to them.

"Shadow Valley. Asked Z for a special meetin'."

She lost her breath.

"Gotta be there at eleven thirty."

She yanked her phone out of her coat pocket and glanced at the time. "It's eleven now!"

"Yeah."

"*Yeah?* It'll take longer than a half hour to get there!" she yelled in a panic. She tried shoving him toward his bike, but he didn't even budge. "You need to go now!"

His grin widened. "Baby, they'll wait."

"But I can't!"

His eyebrows shot up. "Then expect you naked and ready in my bed by noon."

"At this rate you won't be there by noon."

"Knowin' you're waitin' naked in my bed? The fuck I won't."

She leaned into him and fisted the thermal fabric at his chest, pulling him toward her.

His eyes became serious as his met hers. "You sure 'bout this?"

She didn't even hesitate when she whispered, "I've never been so sure about anything in my life."

His nostrils flared and he nodded slightly. "Yeah. Same."

Same.

Tears started to well, but they were happy ones this time. "I love you so much," she said on a shaky whisper.

"Same, baby."

She went up on her toes as his head dropped and his mouth crushed hers. She grabbed both sides of his face, holding him there as long as he allowed it.

Eventually, he pulled away and stepped back, giving them some space. "Gotta go."

"I'll be waiting," she said as he opened her door for her and she climbed in. He nodded as he shut it and then tapped the roof of the Camry.

She waited until he mounted his bike, started it and rode out of the parking lot.

She followed him out and then she drove *home*.

Chapter Nineteen

*H*OLY *SHIT, it was happening.*

It was happening!

The tall, black woman heading in her direction, pushing a stroller, was stunning. Same dark skin, same dark eyes.

It had to be her.

Cait squeezed her eyes shut for a second. It had to be.

Ever since Hunter gave her the information—every single day for the past couple of weeks—she'd come to this park a few houses down from where Magnum's daughter, Aaliyah, lived. Hoping, just hoping, to cross paths with her "by accident."

The woman who was headed toward the park bench Cait was sitting at could be a model. So stinking gorgeous.

She was surprised to find Magnum's daughter didn't live far from them, just north of Pittsburgh.

Now she just needed not to screw this up.

She nervously used her foot to roll the stroller in front of her back and forth.

They were simply two mothers with two babies finding companionship in the park.

Fuck.

Her stomach flipped and she was tempted to gnaw off every one of her fingernails as the woman got closer.

She could screw everything up. She could say one wrong word...

"Hi!" the woman greeted, her expression open and friendly.

Cait wanted to puke. "Hi," she forced out.

The woman tipped her head toward the other side of the bench. "Do you mind? It's gorgeous out today."

"No, please. Have a seat." Cait's pulse thumped in her throat.

The woman, who appeared the same age as Cait, settled on the bench and pulled her stroller to face her, just like Cait had done with Asia's.

"Do you like that brand of stroller?" the woman asked.

"I... I love it." *What's your name?* Cait's brain screamed. "I'm Cait, by the way."

"Aaliyah. But most people call me Liyah."

"Beautiful name."

Aaliyah leaned toward Asia, who was contently sucking on her own fist, and smiled. "She's beautiful. She's got the chubbiest cheeks. How old is she?"

"Four weeks."

"And those green eyes with that skin tone. Absolutely gorgeous. She could be a baby model."

Cait doubted her daddy would allow that, but she kept that to herself. Instead, she chuckled nervously because she was about to plant a seed. "Her skin tone has a lot to do with her daddy. Her eyes, though... I thought she'd get her father's dark brown eyes. She didn't. I was surprised when she got my father's, instead." Then she blurted out. "He's a biker."

Cait mentally groaned. That was fucking dumb.

Aaliyah's dark brows pinned together. "Oh."

Oh fuck. She was definitely going to screw this up.

"What's your baby's name?" she asked quickly.

"Devyn. He's eight weeks."

Her son wasn't as dark as her. But then Asia wasn't as dark as Magnum, either. It made her wonder about Devyn's father. "I'm sure your husband is thrilled to have a boy."

Gah. Dumb!

"It wouldn't have mattered to him."

It wouldn't have mattered to Magnum, either. But she thought Magnum freaked out a little more about having to protect a girl once they found out the sex of the baby. He wasn't as bad as Diesel was when Violet was born, but it was damn close. He insisted he knew where they were at all times. Even put a location app on her phone.

Just in case.

Cait pursed her lips at the past tense in the woman's statement, though. She could've sworn Hunter mentioned that Aaliyah was married. Had she misheard? She did have "baby brain."

She needed to push that aside for the moment and get back on track. She had no idea how long she'd have to talk to Magnum's daughter before the woman just up and walked away.

It was now or never.

She quickly said, "My ol' man is a biker, too. They always say you marry a man just like your father."

Smooth, Cait, jeez.

"What do you mean 'ol' man?'"

It made sense the woman knew nothing about bikers since she was never raised in the life. And she'd had no contact with Magnum since she was very little. Plus, he didn't join the Knights until after he was forbidden to see them by court order.

"My husband. In the MC world, it can mean the same thing, but not always."

Aaliyah seemed to accept that answer, but her face became troubled.

Cait pointed at a sleeping Devyn. He was so freaking cute! And it killed her that Magnum was missing out on seeing his only grandson. "What did his grandfather do?"

"His grandfather was a police officer. For the Pittsburgh PD. He's now retired."

What? Wrong grandfather.

"Oh... Was that your father?"

She shook her head. "No... I'm..." Her brow scrunched up. "No, I'm not sure... I don't remember much about my father."

"Oh, uh..."

"I was raised by my stepfather."

"Oh!" Cait chirped. "So was I. At least until I found out who my real father was."

Aaliyah's head twisted toward her. "You didn't know?"

Asia whimpered, becoming quickly unsatisfied with her fist meal. *Crap.* Just that little sound made Cait's breasts ache. She pulled the stroller closer to unbuckle the straps, picked up her daughter and took a quick look at her stepdaughter.

Yikes.

Her. Stepdaughter.

"Um, do you mind?"

"No, I might have to join you soon. If Devyn isn't sleeping, he wants my boob. Kind of like how his father was."

Again, past tense.

Cait forced out a laugh, unbuttoned her shirt enough to access her nursing bra, opening up one side and lifting Asia to her nipple. After a little encouragement, her daughter latched on. Hard.

Cait gritted her teeth for a second until her hungry little gremlin settled in, then she sat back with a sigh.

She needed to get back on topic and quick. "No, I didn't

know who my father was until I was almost fifteen. My mother never told him she was pregnant, so it wasn't his fault. In fact, she lied to me until she got caught. She didn't want me—or anyone, really—to know who my father was."

"Why?"

"Because he was a biker, and at the time, a strip club manager and she was embarrassed. While she came from a," Cait made air quotes with her free hand, "'good family.' Said being with him, even for a couple nights, was a huge mistake."

Aaliyah frowned. "That's harsh."

That gave Cait some hope that she might be open to meeting her father. "Yes, it is." Cait adjusted Asia in her arms as she continued to nurse. "Thing is though, he's awesome. Loves me, loves his granddaughter, loves my sisters and my stepmom. He's protective but a complete teddy bear with us. He's the best man I know, except for Magnum."

"Magnum," Aaliyah repeated softly.

Had she heard that name before? Did she even know her father was a biker? Had her mother ever mentioned it?

"Yes, that's my husband's road name since, again, he's a biker, too. His actual name is Malcolm."

Aaliyah shot to her feet.

Oh shit!

"Please... *Please* sit down," Cait asked, unwilling to move and disturb Asia. "*Please.*"

"Who are you?" she asked, grabbing the handles of Devyn's stroller.

"Please, just... give me a chance to explain."

"Who. Are. You?"

Asia made a little noise of complaint and Cait did her best to relax. "Please. Sit. Just give me a few minutes of your time."

"Why should I?"

"Because he loves you. It killed him to walk away. I think you've been fed lies like I was. It was unfair to him, as well as to you and MJ."

Her eyes widened at her brother's nickname.

Cait started speaking a lot faster. If Aaliyah walked away, this was over. And she would fail. She couldn't fail. Not for Magnum. "Your mother most likely lied to you like mine did to me. Her lies hurt our relationship a lot. She insists what she did, keeping me from my father, was best for me. It wasn't. There's nothing bad about having a father in your life who loves you one hundred percent. Even if love is all he can give you, it's priceless."

The woman blinked at her, dropped her gaze to her son and Cait watched her face twist in confusion.

"I'm sorry to drop all of this on you like this. But he's missing out on his grandbabies. Do you want to deny him that, too, just like he was denied being allowed to be your father?"

"How did you find me? Because everything you're saying proves this isn't just coincidence."

It certainly wasn't. It had taken time, patience and planning.

"Your father doesn't know I had someone look for you and MJ. He doesn't know I'm here. But I do know he loves you, even to this day. It killed him to walk away. He didn't want to, but he was given no choice. I don't know all the details and it really doesn't matter at this point. What matters is moving forward. Not missing any more time with a man like him. I missed out on over fourteen years with Dawg, my dad. Don't let Magnum miss out on any more time with you." She jerked her head toward her baby. "Or him."

Cait wanted to sigh in relief when Aaliyah released the stroller handles and sank back down on the bench, her body turned toward Cait. Her eyes once again falling to Asia as she nursed.

"As weird as this sounds... Asia might be Devyn's aunt, but they could grow up knowing each other. Being close. Being family. I don't want her missing out on that, either."

Aaliyah shook her head with a frown. "How old are you?"

Crap. "Is that going to be a problem?" Asia fell asleep and released her nipple.

"I don't know."

At least the woman was being honest.

Cait quickly tucked her boob away, grabbed a towel from the diaper bag and put Asia to her shoulder to burp her. "I'll be twenty-seven soon."

That frown deepened. "You're a step-grandmother at twenty-six."

A rush of breath escaped Cait's lips. "I guess so." Cait leaned toward her, dipping her head. "Do I have any gray hairs yet?"

Aaliyah's frown disappeared and she laughed. It sounded husky and it reminded her of Magnum's rich, deep laugh, but more feminine. "No. But you're only a year older than me."

"I know. That's a bit strange, right?"

"Yes, it is. But Devyn's father is ten years older than me. Or was."

She said "was" again. Past tense. "Was?"

"He was one of the officers shot and killed last year during that protest downtown."

Cait gasped. "In Pittsburgh?"

"Yes."

Holy shit. She remembered when all that went down in the news. Two officers were lost and three were critically injured during a march involving white supremacists. It was horrifying and made her scared at the thought of bringing *brown skinned*—as Magnum called them—children into such a hateful world. "I'm so sorry."

Aaliyah turned her dark eyes away from Cait to stare at something in the distance. "Me, too. He was a great guy. I was pregnant when he died and he never got to meet his son." She sniffed softly but no tears fell. "I loved him and," she turned her attention back to Cait, "I'd be a hypocrite if I said age mattered."

"I love your father. He loves me. He loves Asia. I know he misses you and MJ so much and he'd love to be there to help you and the baby. Be there to support you when you need it the most. We both would. We might be strangers but we're still family. Asia's your sister."

Cait noticed Aaliyah's throat undulate as she swallowed hard. Cait didn't know how she was keeping herself together after losing her husband. If something happened to Magnum... She would be destroyed. Even a year later. So she was sure Magnum's daughter was still struggling with that loss and finding herself a single mother.

Aaliyah cleared her throat roughly. "My mother said he physically abused her. That he abused us. She showed me pictures of bruises. On her, me and my brother. I can't imagine they were fake. But... Oh God, if they were fake, I have every right to be mad at her. If they weren't, I have every right to be mad at him." She groaned, a hand to her cheek, confusion in her dark eyes.

Cait's blood ran cold at the thought of Magnum hurting his own children. "Never," she whispered fiercely. "Never would he do that. I can't even imagine. He's more patient and gentle with Asia than... Than I expected, actually. I make way more mistakes than he does. And not once has he lost his temper with either of us. It would shock me if he did."

Aaliyah regarded her for a moment, hopefully taking Cait's words to heart.

"They were very young when they had us, I just figured trying to raise a family at that age became too much. Overwhelming. My mother said they were over their heads."

Two teenagers trying to raise two babies probably were.

"Maybe so. But that never meant he didn't want you and MJ. He fought for you. He *wanted* you more than anything. He would have given up everything to remain in your lives. If he'd abused you, he would have gone to jail."

"Mom said he did."

Cait's spine snapped straight. She took a sleeping Asia from her shoulder and cuddled her against her chest. She ran a fingertip over her daughter's dark cupid bow lips which were moving in a sucking motion as she slept. Had her father done time? He'd never mentioned it.

It didn't matter, it was in the past. Asia was his future. *They* were his future. Including his grandson if she could convince Aaliyah to give her father a chance. "If he did, it wasn't for that. I swear. Or it was because he was lied about."

"If she made up such egregious lies about him like that, I'm going to be very angry with her."

"That's not... I'm not here to make trouble between you and your mother. I just want to try to repair what's been broken. For all of us. We're now family. He was so destroyed by losing you two, he pushed me away because he knew I'd want kids and he couldn't bear to lose any more."

"Well, since your mother lied to you about your father and you dealt with the damage done because of it, I doubt you'd lie to your own children like that. At least, I'd hope not."

"I wouldn't. But he didn't want to risk that chance. He couldn't go through it again."

"How did you convince him?" She glanced down at Asia. "To have more at his age?"

"I didn't. My father did."

Aaliyah raised her brows.

"My father's MC and your father's are in an alliance. They know each other well. At first, my father had a huge problem with Magnum and me. It's a long story and not worth telling right now. But he knew what a good man your father is. And he came around."

"Does he have any more?"

"Any more?"

"Kids."

Cait shook her head. "No, this is our first."

"First," Aaliyah mumbled. "You want more?"

"Maybe. We're in negotiations now."

Magnum's daughter laughed. "Negotiations?"

"Yes. We're both stubborn as hell."

"Ah, that's where I get it from."

Cait smiled and nodded. "No doubt."

"He doesn't want any more?"

"Here's the thing... Now he does. Like right away. I keep reminding him it wasn't him pushing out Asia, who wasn't a small baby. I need time to forget the things this child did to me in places I thought were delicate."

Aaliyah laughed. "I'm laughing, but I hear you. Ugh. Devyn wasn't undersized, either. But, luckily, with him being the only 'man' in my life right now, I have no pressure to have any more any time soon."

"Well, your father is *old*," Cait teased. "But, like I said, he would love to be one man in your life."

Aaliyah's teeth caught her bottom lip as she stared at Devyn still asleep in his stroller. "Are you sure? You said he doesn't know you're here."

"He doesn't. I was hoping to run into you and also hoping you'd give me a chance. I didn't want to disappoint him if you didn't. I'm sure it would mean the world to him if you gave him a chance, too. Honestly, I was scared to do this. But he faced one of his greatest fears for me."

"Which is?"

"A story for another time. It's not important right now. What's important is, you'll say yes to giving him a shot. I'm so glad I gave my father one. I ignored the doubts and saw the truth. I just hope you can do the same with Magnum."

When Aaliyah didn't say anything, Cait began to panic. "Do you want to hold your sister?"

Dark brown eyes regarded Asia. A few seconds later, Aaliyah held out her arms and Cait placed her baby girl into them.

Aaliyah brushed a knuckle over a chubby cheek and swept her fingers over Asia's short curly black hair. "They have the same hair," she whispered.

Cait figured she meant Asia and Devyn. "I may need help with it. I have no idea what I'm doing," she admitted honestly.

Aaliyah's lips pressed together as she stared down at the baby in her arms. Cait could only guess her eyes were burning like her own.

Finally, Aaliyah raised her head and nodded. "I'd like that."

Oh, thank fuck.

"Can I give you my phone number and when you're ready we can meet here again? You don't have to give me yours. I'll leave everything up to you."

"You want to meet here?" She carefully handed Asia back to Cait. "With my father?"

"That'll be up to you. Only when you're ready. MJ, too. Whenever he's ready. No pressure."

"Okay."

Oh, thank fuck!

Cait rattled off her number as Magnum's daughter programmed it into her own cell phone.

Then Devyn was awake and they sat there in companionable silence as Aaliyah nursed Cait's step-grandson.

That thought made her a little dizzy.

It might make Magnum a little dizzy, too, when he found out his daughter and his grandson were only a month apart. In fact, Devyn was older than Asia.

She'd have to make him sit down when she told him. She didn't want him to lose his balance and break a hip.

Cait snorted. Busting on Magnum's age had become a regular thing and it made him laugh.

And hearing him laugh made her heart full.

Her phone dinged and she pulled it out of the diaper bag and glanced down at the text. *Y the fuck U near Fox Chapel?*

Oh shit, he was tracking her. She texted back: *2 meet a friend. B home soon.*

U good?

Perfect. Luv U.

Same.

Cait smiled at her phone, then at her daughter. Then she smiled at Aaliyah who was strapping Devyn back into his stroller.

Then she smiled all the way home and even sang a little bit with the radio, too.

Epilogue

Magnum twisted his head and watched his son, Malcolm Jr, scoop up his two-year-old daughter, Asia. His girl loved to laugh and did so loudly as MJ spun her in a circle.

He twisted his head again to find his ol' lady glaring at him across Dirty Dick's because she was about to pop with their son, Caleb. She'd been having Braxton-Hicks all fucking day and that did not make a happy wife.

But it made a happy Magnum since he'd soon get to hold his youngest son and his last child.

Because Caleb was it. No more after that. If he had to get his fucking balls snipped, he was doing it. Two babies in the house—though, Asia would argue *loudly* about how she was *not* a baby—was plenty. Add Devyn, another two-year-old terror and MJ's six-month-old and five-year-old baby girls and Magnum wanted to get on his sled, ride fast and far, never coming home.

He grunted. At least three of those hell-on-wheels would go home at the end of the evening.

He was getting way too old for this shit.

But... he had to fucking admit, he kind of liked his son

had tastes similar to his father. His wife, Valerie, was leggy, blonde and curvy as fuck.

Not that he'd noticed.

And, *thank fuck*, Aaliyah was still not ready to consider dating again.

Good. No man would ever be good enough. Not for her or for Asia.

And if she considered marrying a pig again...

Magnum shook his head.

Pig or not, he wasn't ready to lose his oldest daughter to another man yet. They were still only getting to know each other. Same with MJ.

Repairing those relationships had gone slowly and, for a long time, it was awkward. Conversation had been limited until everyone learned to relax, drop their guard, while looking toward the future and not the past.

Caitie had done what she could to make things go smoothly but she could only do so fucking much.

He loved the fuck out of her for it.

And he could never thank her enough for fixing things.

So, one way to thank her was to plant baby number two in her belly and now she was pissed.

He dropped his head and grinned at his boots.

She was the one who wanted kids, not him.

Though, somehow after Asia was born, he'd suddenly got on board with trying for a son.

The trying part was the best part.

The fucking puking and crying jags, not so much.

She hadn't been this sick with Asia, so he had a feeling his boy would be fucking trouble.

His grin widened.

A huff, a grunt and a groan approached him.

He lifted his head to see his woman waddling in his direction. By the looks of her stomach, Caleb was going to be a linebacker.

If so, his famous pro football son would be able to take care of his ol' man when he was... old.

Fuck. He made a mental note to buy his son a football as soon as he learned to walk.

"Hey, baby," he murmured as she finally got to him.

"What have you been grinning at?"

"The thought that I'm gonna knock you up again right away after Caleb's born."

Her eyes went wide, then narrowed dangerously. "We negotiated like you insisted!" she screeched. "That wasn't the deal."

"Yeah, and I'm fuckin' re-negotiatin'."

"The fuck you are. This is it. Your monster kid is going to destroy my—"

"Caitie," he stopped her. "Just fuckin' with you."

Her expression changed from a snarl to a wince and she rubbed at the small of her back. "I thought I was going to have to neuter you myself."

"I'm good."

"Be very glad because I wouldn't use sterile equipment when I did it."

It was his turn to wince. He placed a hand over her distended belly. "Soon?"

"I hope so. If he grows any bigger, I'm in trouble."

"Already in fuckin' trouble, baby. If you think Asia's a handful, wait 'til my boy hits the ground runnin'." He tucked a thumb under her chin and tipped her face up. "Mouth."

The corners of her lips twitched but she offered him her mouth and he didn't waste any time taking her up on that offer.

After a few seconds of exploring the mouth that was really his, he reluctantly released her. "Gonna get me some of that tonight."

Her eyebrows rose. "Maybe it'll induce labor."

"Hopefully he'll wait 'til I'm done."

She snorted.

He gave her another quick kiss. "Taste like sweet potato pie."

"Well, I had two pieces."

"Three."

She grimaced. "Okay, three."

She put her fingers over his on her belly and squeezed. He felt the press of her wedding ring against his hand, the one he had inscribed with: *One Knight ~ Every Night ~ Forever.* Not on the inside of the wide gold band, either. On the outside where everyone could see his claim. It was corny but he didn't give a fuck. She had smiled and hiccup-sobbed simultaneously when she read it.

"I can't help your kid loves to eat. And Liyah makes great freaking pie."

"That she does."

"I'll have to rope her into baking a bunch for the next Walker Foundation bake sale."

He grunted.

Thank fuck Caitie wasn't working for Gallo agency anymore. After everything went down in Lake George, she couldn't bear to return. As soon as Ellie found out, she snapped Cait up right away to be in charge of the marketing and advertising for the Walker Foundation, since they didn't have anyone to do it.

Her hours were more flexible, she could bring Asia with her to work when needed, and she loved her job. She was great at it according to Walker, who was relieved it was one less responsibility on Ellie's shoulders.

Even better, Magnum knew his wife was safe there and surrounded by people he trusted and who also loved Cait.

She moved until she stood in front of him and he automatically wrapped his arms around his ol' lady and pulled her into him, then planted his hands on her massive belly. He dipped his head and pressed his nose into her hair, inhaling.

It had been a great fucking day. This was the first real Thanksgiving he'd ever had. At least with all his family present.

For the last couple of years, they'd gone over to Dawg and Emma's, but this year since his family had grown, he decided to shut down Dirty Dick's for the day and use that space instead.

Even his sister, Maya, and her wife, Elena, had flown up from Florida with their twin college-aged boys to join them. He hadn't seen them in over ten years.

The women—Emma, Lily, Liyah, Val, Maya, Elena and even Lee-lee—had used the bar's commercial kitchen to make a huge spread. He and Daddy Dawg had pushed a bunch of the scratched tables together and covered the ugliness up with some sort of disposable table covers printed with godawful cartoon turkeys his woman had bought.

Thinking about Daddy Dawg must have conjured him up as he was heading their direction, his eyes focused on his daughter.

"Hey, Dad," Magnum greeted, keeping a straight face.

"Jesus fuck," Dawg answered like he always did when Magnum called him that.

"You mean *fudge*," Magnum corrected. "You got a grandbaby 'round here somewhere with big ears. Emma's gonna crack you upside the head if she starts screamin' *fuck*. And that girl of mine ain't afraid to use the healthy fuckin' set of lungs she was born with."

"Like you don't fuckin' curse 'round her."

Magnum grinned and shrugged. "My wife don't care."

Cait gasped. "I do, too."

"Since when?"

"Since she started talking and began to parrot everything her daddy says."

"Like you don't curse," Magnum reminded her.

"Only when necessary."

"Like in the labor room?" Dawg asked, jerking his chin toward her belly. "Soon?"

She rolled her eyes. "Yeah, Dad, Caleb put his arrival time on my Google calendar down to the hour and minute."

Dawg shot Magnum a frown. "Someone's cranky."

Magnum gave his father-in-law an answering grin. "Gonna take care of that later. Maybe try to get Caleb here sooner than later, too."

With a horrified expression, Cait slapped a hand over eyes. "Holy shit. You did not just tell my father that."

Magnum rubbed a hand over her belly where it was moving from his active linebacker son. "Think he knows how his grandkids were created."

"Doesn't mean we need to fuckin' discuss it," Dawg growled. "Now I need a goddamn drink."

"Standin' in a bar full of booze, Dad. It's on the house." Magnum smirked.

"Jesus fuck," Dawg muttered again, turning on his heels and heading behind the bar.

Another beautiful curvy blonde was suddenly in front of them.

"Are you two driving him to drink?" Emma asked, glancing over at her ol' man who was now downing a shot of something Magnum suspected was the strongest liquor he had on the shelf.

"Baby's comin' later, just tryin' to get him to relax."

Emma's face lit up. "He is?"

"Yeah, we're—"

Cait turned in his arms and slapped a hand over his mouth. "Stop it."

He grinned under her fingers.

Emma's face was bright red as she stared at them. "Oh. Uh... We used that technique to induce labor for Emmalee."

Cait's eyes went wide as she stared up at Magnum and her cheeks became just as red as Emma's.

"It work?" Magnum asked his mother-in-law, who, oddly enough, was younger than him. But then, there was nothing normal about their patch-work family.

"Uh... Sooooo..." Emma drew out. "Maybe we should watch Asia tonight, then?"

"That'd be good," Magnum said through Cait's fingers.

"I'm going to go crawl into a corner and die now," Cait muttered.

"I'll... uh... just go tell Dawson we're babysitting tonight," Emma said and hurried to where her husband was downing his third double shot.

Cait dropped her hand from his mouth. "You're going to turn my father into an alcoholic if you keep calling him Dad."

"He'll get used to it."

"Not thinking he will," she said, glancing over at the bar. Then her heavy belly began bouncing and she covered her face with her hands.

He frowned. "Baby, you laughin' or cryin'?" Because he never fucking knew. Being pregnant, she could be crying one minute and hysterically laughing the next.

It kind of scared the fuck out of him.

"Both," came muffled from under her hands.

He grabbed her hands and pulled them away so he could see her face. "You mad?"

She shook her head as tears slid down her cheek, but she was smiling.

Didn't make any fucking sense.

"No." She sighed, turned again and glanced around the

room. "This family is whacked. There's nothing normal about it."

"Yeah." It definitely wasn't normal.

He had a daughter who was almost as old as his wife. Another daughter who was younger than two of his grandkids. His mother-in-law was younger than him and he was almost the same age as his father-in-law. And, at almost forty-five, he had another kid on the way.

It was definitely fucked. Never in his fucking life had he thought any of this shit would happen.

But now he wouldn't have it any other way. And he knew she wouldn't, either.

He dropped his head and his eyes hit her green ones. "You happy?"

She gave him a soft smile. "Yes."

He asked her that a lot, luckily always got the same answer and always hoped he would.

"That's all that matters, baby."

He'd give her anything and everything he could to make her happy because she'd done so much to make him happy, too.

Everyone in that room was proof of it.

He'd done what he needed to do for her. And in return, she'd done the same for him.

Caitie wrapped a hand around the back of his bald head and pulled him down to her. She demanded, "Mouth," which made him smile.

He gave her his mouth.

When she was done with it, she whispered, "I love you."

And that smile became wider when he whispered against her lips, "Same."

———

CALEB DAWSON MOORE was born at 3:04 a.m. two days later.

———

**Turn the page to read the prologue for Blood &
Bones: Trip (Blood Fury MC, book 1)**

**Turn the page to read the prologue of
Blood & Bones: Trip
Blood Fury MC, book 1**

Blood & Bones: Trip (Blood Fury MC, bk 1)

*"Sometimes you have to burn yourself to the ground
before you can rise like a phoenix from the ashes." ~ Jens Lekman*

Prologue
Turn the key

TRIP STOOD in the middle of the deserted building, shaking
his head, wondering if it was worth the fucking hassle to
start the club back up. To reclaim its territory.

But what other fucking choice did he have?

He'd already had it set in his mind, not only to do it, but
to do it right this time.

He wouldn't let his father's club, which died a violent
death, just remain a memory. And a bad one at that.

But now that he had done his time in the Marines, done
his time in prison, he needed something.

Because he had nothing.

Except his granddaddy's run-down farm, a barn full of
farm equipment he had no clue how to use and didn't want
to, and the abandoned warehouse he was currently standing
in on the outskirts of town.

While he was in prison, his lawyer had shown up and read him his granddaddy's will.

Yeah. He got everything.

Sig got nothing.

Trip was sure his brother wasn't happy about that, if he even knew.

But most likely Granddaddy had made up the will when Trip was still doing time in the service and not doing it behind bars. Unlike Sig who had been in and out of county jail, or the state pen, off and on since he turned eighteen.

But now here he stood. In an empty building, feeling fucking overwhelmed. But still, it was something.

And something was better than nothing.

He also had new ink on his back and an old cut in his hand.

The leather was worn, the rockers and patches on it dirty. All except one.

One rectangular patch on the front had been torn off by his own fingers after using the point of his buck knife to loosen the threads. The patch that used to say "Buck" was now replaced with one that said "Trip." But above it, the patch that had deemed Buck as president remained. That now belonged to Trip.

He'd also used that same knife to remove the 1% diamond patch off the back. He wouldn't need that one anymore.

The club used to be outlaw. But Trip was determined to keep it above board. For the most part.

He'd spent many a night down in Shadow Valley talking with the members of the Dirty Angels MC, soaking up everything their prez named Z told him. Learning how to rebuild Blood Fury stronger than ever. How to keep the money flowing into the club's coffers.

One way to do that was to keep the members out of prison and, even better, keep them breathing.

Dead or incarcerated members weren't any good to a club.

And there had been too many of those in the Blood Fury MC in the past. It had been its downfall.

Trip didn't want that mistake to happen again.

So, they had to play the game. Keep shit on the up and up as best as they could. Become a powerful force, strong enough to withstand the occasional bump in the road.

He had no fucking clue how he was going to pull it off, but he would take the advice he was given and do his fucking best.

He scrubbed a hand through his long hair before tucking it up under his baseball cap, blowing out a loud breath and shrugging on his cut.

His cut.

It wasn't his father's any longer.

This club was no longer his father's, either.

This world, even as broken as it was, now belonged to Trip.

It was his and he wouldn't let anyone destroy it again.

The Fury was about to rise once more. This time stronger and smarter.

Get Trip and Stella's story here:
<u>mybook.to/BFMC-Trip</u>

If You Enjoyed This Book

Thank you for reading Magnum: A Dark Knights MC/Dirty Angels MC Crossover. If you enjoyed Magnum and Cait's story, please consider leaving a review at your favorite retailer and/or Goodreads to let other readers know. Reviews are always appreciated and just a few words can help an independent author like me tremendously!

Want to read a sample of my work? Download a sampler book here: BookHip.com/MTQQKK

Only Him *

Needing Him *

Loving Her *

Temping Him *

Down & Dirty: Dirty Angels MC Series™:

Down & Dirty: Zak *

Down & Dirty: Jag *

Down & Dirty: Hawk *

Down & Dirty: Diesel *

Down & Dirty: Axel *

Down & Dirty: Slade *

Down & Dirty: Dawg *

Down & Dirty: Dex *

Down & Dirty: Linc *

Down & Dirty: Crow *

Crossing the Line (A DAMC/Blue Avengers Crossover) *

Magnum: A Dark Knights MC/Dirty Angels MC Crossover

Guts & Glory Series

(In the Shadows Security)

Guts & Glory: Mercy *

Guts & Glory: Ryder *

Guts & Glory: Hunter *

Guts & Glory: Walker *

Guts & Glory: Steel

Guts & Glory: Brick

Blood & Bones: Blood Fury MC™

<u>Blood & Bones: Trip</u>

<u>Blood & Bones: Sig</u>

<u>Blood & Bones: Judge</u>

<u>COMING SOON!</u>

Blue Avengers MC™

Brothers in Blue: A Bryson Family Christmas

Everything About You (A Second Chance Gay Romance)

About the Author

JEANNE ST. JAMES is a USA Today bestselling romance author who loves an alpha male (or two). She was only thirteen when she started writing and her first paid published piece was an erotic story in Playgirl magazine. Her first erotic romance novel, Banged Up, was published in 2009. She is happily owned by farting French bulldogs. She writes M/F, M/M, and M/M/F ménages.

Want to read a sample of her work? Download a sampler book here: BookHip.com/MTQQKK

To keep up with her busy release schedule check her website at www.jeannestjames.com or sign up for her newsletter: http://www.jeannestjames.com/newslettersignup

www.jeannestjames.com
jeanne@jeannestjames.com

Blog: http://jeannestjames.blogspot.com
Newsletter: http://www.jeannestjames.com/newslettersignup
Jeanne's Down & Dirty Book Crew: https://www.facebook.com/groups/JeannesReviewCrew/

facebook.com/JeanneStJamesAuthor
twitter.com/JeanneStJames
amazon.com/author/jeannestjames
instagram.com/JeanneStJames
bookbub.com/authors/jeanne-st-james
goodreads.com/JeanneStJames
pinterest.com/JeanneStJames

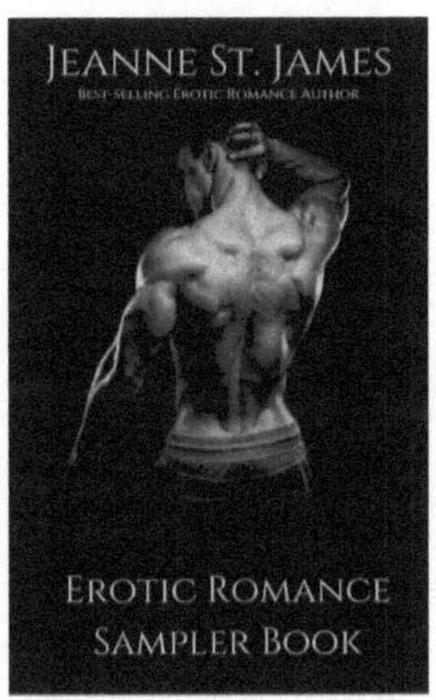

Get a FREE Romance Sampler Book

This book contains the first chapter of a variety of my books. This will give you a taste of the type of books I write and if you enjoy the first chapter, I hope you'll be interested in reading the rest of the book.

Each book I list in the sampler will include the description of the book, the genre, and the first chapter, along with links to find out more. I hope you find a book you will enjoy curling up with!

Get it here: BookHip.com/MTQQKK